AUTHOR'S NOTE

As you read *Love Lies Bleeding,* I hope you will be beguiled into believing that Pecan Springs, Texas, its inhabitants, and the surrounding Hill Country are real. This is not the case. The people and places in this book are entirely fictional, although the Hill Country is real and every bit as beautiful as I say it is. Any other resemblance to reality is a product of authorial sleight of hand.

One caution. To accurately describe the healing properties of herbs, I study the most up-to-date herbals, consult the latest research reports, and check with knowledgeable herbalists. But this information (particularly the historical herb lore and folk superstitions) is *not* intended to substitute for advice from a qualified healthcare practitioner. As a former lawyer, China Bayles would be the first to recommend that you do your own careful research and ask plenty of questions before you treat any condition with medicinal herbs.

Chapter One

A quiet life offers many joys, but none is as rewarding as the diligent study of herbs or the effort to gain some practical knowledge of nature. Get thyself a garden!

—Abbot Walafrid Strabo, 9th century

. . . and such gardens are not made
By singing:—"Oh, how beautiful!" and sitting in the shade.

Rudyard Kipling
The Glory of the Garden

I have taken the good abbot's counsel. I am getting a garden.

"But you've already got zillions of gardens," Brian objected on Thursday night at dinner, when I announced my intention. "What do you want *another* one for?" Brian is Mike McQuaid's twelve-year-old son. Brian, his father, and I have lived together since last May—eight months now.

"Not zillions," I said. I handed the boy a dish of steamed broccoli and watched him delicately extract the two smallest pieces and camouflage them with catsup. "There isn't enough space around the shop for *zillions* of gardens."

My name is China Bayles, and my shop—where I sell plants, herbs, gifts, and related sundries—is called Thyme and Seasons. It occupies one of the two shop spaces in a century-old stone building I bought after I bailed out of my career as a Houston criminal attorney and settled in Pecan Springs, Texas. When I made the move, I intended to split my time between growing herbs and minding my struggling new business—an effort I vastly underestimated. Basically, I wanted to get a life: enjoy my work, make a few friends, have some fun. Now, six years later, I have a great live-in relationship, a wonderful old Victorian house, friends I value, and satisfying work—mostly satisfying, that is.

But Thyme and Seasons isn't struggling anymore, and the behind-the-counter part of the business has mushroomed into a job and a half. Waiting on customers, maintaining the stock, and keeping the books doesn't leave me a lot of time for digging in the garden, a job I really enjoy, or for the tearoom, a big new project I've been wanting to get started. In fact, last winter, just before Christmas, the daily stuff became so overwhelming that I was ready to throw up my hands and say yes to Wanda Rathbottom's offer to buy the shop, which shows you how desperate I was. (Wanda Rathbottom owns Wanda's Wonderful Acres, a plant nursery on the outskirts of town. She is definitely not a person with whom I would choose to be marooned on a desert island, even if she did all the laundry.)

But after the holidays I closed the shop for a couple of weeks and went on retreat at St. Theresa's monastery for (as McQuaid put it) a realignment and balancing job. The first few days were a bit touch-and-go, because St. T's had its share of problems. But after the smoke cleared (literally, I'm afraid), there was plenty of time to rest, relax, and get my priorities straight.

I came back with a new attitude. I was determined to spend more time in the garden, write in my journal every day, do something for myself, like taking a pottery class or starting calligraphy, and make one or two changes in my relationship with McQuaid. One or two *major* changes, that is, like surprising him with a "yes" the next time he mentions marriage, which he does every so often.

Thinking about the past few years, about what McQuaid means to me and how lonely I would be without him, I've come to the conclusion that I'm ready to make a commitment. I still have plenty of reservations, mind you, and I haven't dealt with all the apprehensions that settle over my soul like a chilly fog when somebody brings up the M-word. I treasure my independence and autonomy, and I worry that marriage might compromise both. But I care for McQuaid a very great deal, and while I've been content with our live-in relationship, he wants more. And I do too, when you get right down to it—not security, exactly, but the sense of sustained intention that comes with a permanent relationship. Not to mention that I celebrated my forty-fifth birthday just before Christmas, and the gray streak in my hair keeps getting wider.

Planning for the shop is easier than making decisions about my personal life. To get more hours for garden work, I asked my part-time counter person, Laurel Wiley, to come in full time. Laurel has taken over most of the counter work, all of the ordering and stocking, and part of the bookkeeping. I gave her a raise to compensate for these extra headaches.

That leaves the tearoom, which is a project I've been wanting to get off the ground ever since I moved out of the back of the shop. I've already taken down a wall and put part of the space to work as sales area for the shop, but there's still plenty of floor space left, including an old kitchen. I'm no Martha Stewart, but even I can imagine how it would look—a rustic, French cottage decor blending with the existing stone walls and wide plank floor, with flowered chintz curtains, green plants, old furniture. I'm sure the tearoom will bring new business into the shop. The problem is that I don't want to run it myself, because I'm hoping to have time for the garden. So—bright idea number three—I contacted the local herb guild and offered to lease them the space if they would manage and staff the tearoom. The guild members were enthusiastic, and they immediately began wrangling over menus, debating decor, and discussing ways and means. Unfortunately, they haven't yet come up with a firm proposal for how they'll handle all this.

Meanwhile, I'm proceeding with the rest of my plan—new gardens all around the shop. An apothecary garden, a silver garden, a lemon garden, a fragrance garden, a tea garden, maybe even a small vegetable garden, which brings us back to broccoli, and to Thursday night's dinner table.

I gave Brian's arm a friendly pat. "There may not be space for zillions of gardens, Brian, but there's plenty of room for your favorite veggie. I'll grow enough so you can have it for dinner every night. We'll make broccoli sauce for your hamburgers. And there's broccoli dip and broccoli soup and broccoli muffins and broccoli ice cream—"

"Broccoli ice cream?" Brian gagged. "You're making that up!"

"You wish," McQuaid said. He heaped some more broccoli on Brian's plate and added another squirt of catsup.

''Eat up, kid,'' he growled, doing his imitation of the stern father, which somehow never comes off. ''It'll put hair on your chest. Make you grow muscles. Superman eats broccoli.''

''Grunge,'' Brian muttered, glaring at the broccoli.

''That's what I like about the younger generation,'' McQuaid said to me. ''They're so articulate.''

Brian changed the subject. ''Are you going to Waco with us on Saturday?'' His Scout troop was taking a two-day field trip to the Texas Ranger museum, the mecca of every true-hearted Texas boy and home to a couple of tons of antique guns, old Ranger photos, and Indian artifacts.

''Can't.'' McQuaid helped himself to mashed potatoes. ''Got to go to Austin to work on my research project.''

''That's all you do, work on that old project.'' Brian's tone became wheedling. ''Why don't you come with us, huh? You'd have more fun. Research is boring.''

''Research isn't boring. It's just another name for investigation.'' McQuaid is a criminology professor at the local university, Central Texas State, and a former Houston homicide cop. He was on leave for a semester, doing some sort of research for the Department of Public Safety. ''Rangers do research too,'' he added.

Brian frowned. ''You mean, they go poking around in old libraries and stuff, the way you do?''

''If that's where the information is. Crime scene work is only a small part of criminal investigation. You keep saying you want to be a Ranger when you grow up. Believe me, if that happens, you'll wind up doing plenty of research.''

Brian poked at his broccoli, not looking thrilled at the prospect.

"Just what are you researching, anyway?" I asked. McQuaid had never been very specific about the grant that was paying his salary this semester.

"Background stuff on the Rangers," he said vaguely.

I went back to tomorrow's plans. "You *are* going to be around tomorrow evening, aren't you?" I asked.

McQuaid looked up. "Tomorrow? Is it some sort of special day?"

Brian shot his father a glance of exaggerated disgust. "Don't be a jerk, Dad. Tomorrow's Valentine's Day."

McQuaid made a valiant recovery. "Of course it's Valentine's Day." He smiled at me. "I was thinking of taking you to Bean's for dinner." Bean's Bar & Grill may lack romance, but the food is first-rate and the owner is a friend. McQuaid glanced at Brian, who was leaning on his elbow, scowling down at his plate. "Just the two of us grown-ups," he added pointedly.

Brian roused himself to spear a bit of catsup-soaked broccoli, and spoke, monumentally pitying. "Well, I may be just a kid and not very articulate, but I sure as heck know what day it is."

That was Thursday night. On Friday morning, I wasn't thinking about Brian, or Valentine's Day, or even about dinner with McQuaid. It was a little after eight and I was sitting at the kitchen table with a steaming cup of orange spice tea and one of Lila Jennings' fabulously fattening jelly doughnuts, filled with blueberry jam and dusted with cinnamon sugar. The table in the kitchen at the back of the shop, that is, which is destined to become part of the new tearoom. Equipped with graph paper, pencils, and a ruler, and listening to Copland's *Appalachian Spring* on the radio—KMFA, in Austin, is one of the country's very few noncommercial classical music stations—I was happily sketching out my new garden.

I was joined in this pleasant enterprise by Khat, the seventeen-pound Siamese who lives at the shop. (I can't call him ''my'' cat, because he is very much his own creature.) Khat moved out of our house after eight months of fierce turf warfare with Howard Cosell, a crochety old basset with rheumatism who hates anything with whiskers. Khat seems quite happy here at the shop, where the customers stop for a pat and an admiring word, as if he were the handsomest cat in the world. Which, of course, he is. This morning, he was curled up on my feet, making small talk in a low, throaty purr, telling me how contented he is with his modest lot. No excitement, no chills, not even the thrill of the chase, now that Howard Cosell is out of his life. I entirely agree with Khat. I've lived in the madhouse of the world and been chased by hundreds of Howard Cosells. This is the way I like it—no chills, no thrills, no high drama.

There is something very satisfying about planning a garden—imagining the beds and paths, visualizing the herbs and flowers, conjuring up their colors and scents and textures. The particular design I was sketching tied dozens of different plants together in an attractive, pleasing, easy-to-maintain layout. It was a large rectangle, each corner of which would contain a different garden: a dyer's garden in one corner, a tea garden in another, a fragrance garden in the third, an apothecary garden in the fourth. In the middle was the fountain McQuaid built for me several years ago, and around that, mounds of low-growing thyme: garden thyme, lemon thyme, woolly thyme, gold-leafed thyme, French thyme, Corsican thyme. The rectangle was open on the side closest to the shop, with a cedar fence down the property line and knee-high boxwood hedges along each end.

It was already time to get the hardier perennials in the ground, so I had hired a couple of people to come over that morning and help me start building beds. Laurel's sister Willow was one of them, the other was Willow's friend Dolores Adcock. Both work part-time at Wanda's Wonderful Acres. When the beds were constructed, we would till compost into the soil, put in the hardier plants, and mulch (always an important step in central Texas, where the hot summer sun wicks all the moisture out of the soil). As soon as we could, we'd lay the brick paths—a job that probably ought to be done now, but there's only so much that three people can do.

I polished off the last of my doughnut, happily licked my fingers, and began thinking out loud as I jotted down plant possibilities for each of the four corner gardens. "Let's see," I muttered, applying my pencil. "In the apothecary garden I'll have aloe vera, horehound, garlic, comfrey, and peppermint. And sage, of course, and thyme. And I should probably add a couple of peppers and spearmint and throw in some licorice and—"

"Peppers? With horehound and peppermint and licorice? Good grief, China—what *are* you cooking up?" I looked up to see Ruby Wilcox.

When Ruby was a little girl, somebody told her that bright colors attract attention. She took the advice to heart. When Ruby is wearing her ordinary working clothes, you could stand on the fifty-yard line at Memorial Stadium and pick her out of the fans on the opposite side. Dressed as she was today, she could probably be seen from the Goodyear blimp at three thousand feet. She was wearing an ankle-length fuschia broomstick skirt, a lipstick-red T-shirt, and a jangle of neon-orange, yellow, and green hearts around her neck, the whole arrangement topped off by a fuschia ribbon tied in her extravagantly frizzed red hair. Ruby is six feet tall in her sandals, with gingery freckles and turquoise eyes (or green, depending on which tinted contacts she's wearing). Nobody who sees her *ever* forgets her.

"I'm not cooking up a dish, I'm cooking up a garden," I said. I eyed her outfit. "My funny Valentine," I said, with wry affection.

She wrinkled her nose. "Me, funny? What makes you say that?" But before I could answer, she had skipped to the next thought, like a stone skipping across a pond. Ruby never stays with anything for long. That's part of her charm. "What kind of garden?"

I looked down at my plan. "An apothecary garden," I said, glancing at the area I had just sketched out. She frowned, and I added, "A medicinal garden. Do you want a cup of tea?"

Ruby's face cleared. "Oh, a *healing* garden!" she exclaimed. She reached down to pet Khat, who arched his neck to permit her to scratch behind his ears. Her nails were lacquered red and studded with tiny gold glitter hearts. "When you get everything planted, we'll have a festival to welcome the devas and nature spirits and ask them to share their healing energies." She straightened up and snapped her fingers. "We'll have an atunement ceremony!"

''A whatsit?''

''An atunement ceremony,'' Ruby repeated patiently. ''We'll meditate with the plants. We'll open our chakras to their *chi* and bring our vitality levels in line with their energy vibrations. Get on their wavelength, in other words.'' She leaned over and sniffed my cup. ''Yum. Orange spice. Don't get up, I'll help myself.''

Ruby owns the Crystal Cave, Pecan Springs' only New Age shop. When I first met her, I was a bit put off by her weird talk, which includes frequent references to astrology, the tarot, fairies, and chakras. Not to be unkind, but I kept wondering when the people from the funny farm were going to invite her for a nice long rest.

But after Ruby became my tenant (the Crystal Cave occupies the shop space next to Thyme and Seasons), I began to get used to her bizarre vocabulary. For better or worse, I found that I could usually trust her intuitions—messages from her right brain, she calls them. Now, when she pulls out her tarot cards or her rune stones or even her Ouija board, I don't immediately burst into shouts of laughter.

I didn't laugh at the idea of devas and nature spirits, either. Instead, while Ruby lifted off the rooster tea cozy (a hand-knitted gift from McQuaid's mother) and poured herself a cup of tea, I said thoughtfully, ''Some sort of celebration might be fun.'' It would also attract paying customers. There are plenty of people who believe that plants have a spiritual life, and those who don't actually believe it are usually willing to entertain the possibility. Thinking of that, I added, with a little more enthusiasm, ''We could have some food and ask Laurel's cousin to play her harp. But it may be a month or so before everything is planted.'' I made a face. "And there's my other big project—getting the tea-room going. I have to find out whether the herb guild is going to lease the space, and what I have to do to get a permit from the Health Department."

Ruby drained the pot and set it down. "If you wait for the herb guild, you could wait all summer. Maybe two summers. That bunch can never decide on *anything*."

I was about to agree with her, when the patio door opened and we were interrupted by Sheila Dawson, elegant in a slim-fitting cherry-red suit, ash-blond hair drawn back into a sleek chignon, ankles trim in to-die-for red heels. But it isn't just Sheila's fine features and great figure that make her look like a million bucks. It's the way she carries herself, head up, back and shoulders straight. I've never seen her when she wasn't totally confident and unflappable.

"Hi, guys," Sheila said, and dropped her high-fashion handbag on the table with a thump. She sniffed. "Orange spice tea?"

"You'll have to put the kettle on." I pointed to the hot plate that has replaced my Home Comfort range, which I took with me when McQuaid and I moved in together. "It's after eight. How come you're not at work?"

Sheila filled the kettle at the sink, being careful not to splash water on her skirt. For the past year, she has been chief of security at Central Texas State University. If you didn't know she's a campus cop, though, you'd never guess it. You might think she's a Madison Avenue fashion executive or the CEO of an advertising company—until she unsnaps the specially designed side pocket of her red suede handbag and pulls out her snub-nosed .357. Sheila may look like a piece of Waterford crystal, but she's stronger than bullet-proof glass. Smart Cookie, Ruby and I call her. Tough Cookie, is more like it.

"I'm on my way to Austin for a meeting," Sheila said, sitting down. Khat stationed himself at her feet, where he could gaze up at her face. Cool, aloof, nonchalant male that he is, he absolutely adores Sheila. "I stopped in to see if the four of us could get together for dinner tonight. It's Valentine's Day."

The four of us, it went without saying, were Sheila and Blackie and McQuaid and me. Blackie Blackwell, the Adams County sheriff, is Sheila's current love interest and a long-time fishing and poker buddy of McQuaid's.

"Fine," I said, "if you don't mind going to Bean's. That's where we're having our big Valentine's date."

"Couldn't McQuaid pick a restaurant with a little less *romance*?" Ruby asked, straight-faced. "Fewer candles and roses, maybe? Not so many violins? Bean's is even less romantic than the Dairy Queen."

"Hey." I grinned. "Far be it from me to look a gift horse in the mouth on Valentine's Day."

Far be it. McQuaid hadn't brought up the M-word since Christmas, and Valentine's Day was the traditional occasion. While I did not imagine that there would be any romantic fanfare to McQuaid's proposal—just a simple "Don't you think it's time we got married?" and an equally simple "Yes," I was looking forward with special excitement to the evening. Sharing it with Sheila and Blackie would make it even nicer.

"Aha." Ruby eyed me. "Can it be that tonight is the night?"

"The night for what?" Sheila asked.

"For romance," Ruby said, clasping her hands dramatically. "For a proposal."

Sheila chuckled. "You know what China thinks about that. Show her a ring and she starts checking the exits."

"Oh, come on," I said. "I'm not *that* bad."

"Yes, you are," Sheila said. "You're worse. We'll meet you at Bean's. Is seven okay?"

I nodded. "No need to dress up," I said, although that's like telling Her Majesty to leave off looking majestic. Sheila can't help it. She's always dressed up, no matter what she's wearing.

There was a pause while Khat gently nuzzled Sheila's ankle. Ignoring him, Sheila gave Ruby a look that was obviously supposed to mean something. "Are you going to ask her, or am I?"

"Ask me what?" I said.

Ruby swung a sandaled foot. Her beautifully manicured toenails matched her fingernails. "You ask her," she said to Sheila. "She'll say no to me." She leaned over and snapped her fingers. "Come here, Khat. Let's see if we can find something for you to snack on." Khat looked around to see if Ruby was offering anything he coveted, decided she wasn't, and went back to nuzzling Sheila.

Sheila frowned. "I suppose that means you haven't told her, either."

"Told me *what*?" I asked crossly. "I wish you two would stop talking to each other over my head."

"Ruby got her concealed handgun permit," Sheila said.

My mouth dropped open. "You're kidding."

Ruby stopped trying to entice Khat, and sat up. "So

what's wrong with that? After what happened last week, I'd think you'd want me to protect myself!''

What happened last week was that Ruby's new red Toyota—her very first new car, bought with the down payment that had taken her months to save—had been stolen out of her driveway. Bubba Harris, Pecan Springs' cigar-chewing chief of police, had conducted the investigation himself (for whatever that's worth), but nothing had turned up so far. I wasn't hopeful. The Interstate from Dallas to Nuevo Laredo is like a long, narrow barge loaded with American autos bound for a new life in Mexico.

''Ruby,'' I said, ''it's too bad about your car, but a gun wouldn't have changed anything. You were asleep upstairs when it happened. Anyway, would you actually *kill* somebody just to keep a car—especially when it's insured?''

Ruby raised her chin, turquoise eyes flashing. ''The law says I can. During the night, anyway.''

Somebody—Sheila, probably—had been coaching her. Texas law is quirky on this point, allowing considerably more latitude in the use of deadly force than most states. It permits you, for instance, to use a gun to stop somebody from hot-wiring your car or even bashing in your car windows during the night—if a reasonable person would believe that this was the only way you could prevent the theft or the vandalism, or that anything less than deadly force would put you at risk of death or serious injury. Don't try shooting a hubcap thief in the back during the daytime, though. You might get off—juries in Texas are pretty independent. But then again, you might not.

''I didn't say you *couldn't* kill somebody,'' I replied. ''I asked whether you *would.*''

Every now and again, Ruby likes to pretend that she's Kinsey Milhone. I could see her learning to shoot and getting her permit. I could even see her buying a gun, especially if Sheila went along to make suggestions. Somehow, though, I couldn't see her blowing away a hopped-up kid who was trying to drive off with her car.

Sheila came to her rescue. "You don't have to think about that question just now, Ruby."

"If theft prevention is her reason for carrying, she'd *better* think about it," I said. "She needs to figure out in advance how far she's willing to go."

Sheila gave me a long look. "Lots of women own guns—more all the time. *You* own a gun. Why are you acting like Ruby's committing an unforgivable sin?"

"Yeah, I own a gun," I said darkly. I wouldn't have kept my Beretta if it hadn't been a gift from my father. The time we spent together on the range—precious little, actually—was my brightest memory of him. But the gun itself brings up only ugly memories. I used it once without thinking about the consequences, and somebody wound up dead. This is not something I think of without pain, and I think of it often.

"The kettle's whistling," Ruby said unnecessarily, and got up to turn off the burner.

With an effort, I lightened up a little. "Okay, if that's what you guys wanted to tell me, what was it you wanted to ask?"

"You're not in the mood." Ruby put loose tea into the strainer and poured hot water over it.

I turned to Sheila. "I'll bet I know," I said. "I'll bet you want me to sign up for one of your classes."

Smart Cookie is an excellent markswoman, good enough to win the handgun event at the Mother Shoot held by the Women's Shooting Sports Foundation last month in Houston. (It's called Mother Shoot not because they shoot mothers, but because it's the world's biggest women's shooting event—which also means it features the most Port-a-Potties, according to Sheila.) And good enough to teach regular handgun classes.

Sheila adjusted the pearls at her neck. "Well, how about it? You said you wanted to get away from the shop and do something different for a change. This is different."

"Right," Ruby agreed, setting the teapot in front of Sheila and plopping the cozy over it. "And you'd like the women who are signed up, China. They're your kind of women."

"What kind of woman is that?" I asked warily.

Ruby gave me her if-you-don't-know-I'm-not-going-to-tell-you look and went to the cupboard.

"Anyway," Sheila went on, stirring honey into her tea, "it's only a couple of evenings, plus a Saturday morning."

"Do you have any munchies?" Ruby asked, opening the cupboard doors. Khat abandoned Sheila and went to supervise Ruby's search of the shelves. "I haven't had breakfast yet."

I gave a resigned sigh. "Two of Lila's jelly doughnuts are in the bag on the second shelf. I was saving them."

"You were selfishly keeping them for yourself," Sheila remarked.

"You really ought to work on being more generous, China," Ruby added. She brought the bag to the table. "Do you want one, Sheila?"

"You bet," Sheila said, and took one. I eyed Ruby and Sheila enviously. My jelly doughnut would be on my hips forever unless I rode my bicycle for an hour this afternoon. Theirs would vanish without a trace.

Sheila returned my look. "So? How about that class, China?"

I hesitated. The Beretta isn't the problem, of course. Guns are neutral. The problem is inside me. Maybe shooting with Sheila would help to work off some of my attitude. And I *had* promised myself that I'd try to meet some new people, get involved in something different. "How much does it cost?"

Sheila wolfed the doughnut in three bites. "For you, half off," she said, her mouth full. "Comes to only fifty-five bucks."

"Hey," Ruby protested, "you're charging me sixty."

"I know." Sheila drank the rest of her tea and pushed her chair back. "I took off five for the doughnut."

Ruby's tone was injured. "For five dollars, Lila will sell you a dozen jelly doughnuts."

Sheila was picking up her purse when there was a light tap at the shop door, and Laurel—the reason I could sit around sipping tea and trading insults with my friends at eight-thirty on Friday morning—put her head through. "Hi, everybody," she said with her usual cheerfulness.

Laurel Walkingwater Wiley—brown-haired, brown-skinned, with wide, dark eyes—has a remarkable knowledge about herbs and plants of the Southwest, not to mention a passionate devotion to peppers. She is what some people irreverently call a chile-head. This morning, she was wearing her usual working clothes: jeans, a hand-woven Navajo vest, and a black T-shirt printed with fire-red peppers and the words "Lotza Hots!" Her hair was braided and tied with rawhide, emphasizing her high cheekbones. Laurel looks like what she is: half Cherokee.

"Sorry to interrupt," she went on, "but Willow and Dolores Adcock just came. They're ready to go to work whenever you are."

"Dolores Adcock?" Ruby asked with interest. "She's the woman Wanda sent over last week to help put in my new shrubs. I had her come back the next day and we cleaned up that big tangle of dead vines and stuff along the back fence."

"Oh, yeah?" I said. "What kind of a worker is she?"

"Very competent," Ruby replied. "She seems to know a lot about plants. She's a little shy, though. Doesn't say much."

"That won't be a problem," I said. "Willow talks enough for two people."

Sheila stood up and reached for her bag. "Gosh, look at the time. I need to be on the road."

"I'd better be going, too," Ruby said, with a goodbye stroke for Khat. "Say hello to Dolores for me, will you, China? Tell her the junipers are looking great." She glanced at my nails, which were still a bit grubby from the previous day's garden work. "Do you think McQuaid will give you a ring? If so, maybe I'd better give you a manicure first."

"I wish you guys would stop fussing about this," I said. "No, I am not getting a manicure. If McQuaid gives me a ring, he's going to have to put it on this grubby finger."

Sheila looked at me, incredulous. "Are you serious?

You'd actually say yes if McQuaid asked you to marry him?''

''She's going to say yes!'' Ruby shrieked.

''*If* he asks,'' I said. ''Maybe he won't ask. Maybe he's changed his mind.''

''I don't believe it,'' Sheila muttered. ''After all these years, you're finally saying yes.''

''Hey, wait, you guys. He hasn't asked.''

''But he will.'' Ruby was beaming. ''It's Valentine's Day, isn't it? The perfect time for a marriage proposal.'' She snapped her fingers. ''We'll have the wedding right here, China. In your new garden!''

''If you'll give me a chance to—'' I began.

Sheila nodded, approving. ''That's a very good idea, Ruby. You and I could do the wedding. Karen and I handled my sister's wedding, and it was a lot of fun. Karen did the food and I did the flowers.''

''Just a minute,'' I said. ''I really think—''

''Sure,'' Ruby agreed excitedly. ''I'd love to do the food. We can have the ceremony outside in the garden and food on the patio out there—or in here, if it rains.''

''And it could be a totally herbal wedding,'' Sheila said, getting into the spirit of the occasion. ''I'm sure China knows exactly how to do that. We could have—''

I whistled, shrill, between my teeth. That stopped them. ''You're going too far, you guys. You're way ahead of the game.''

Ruby shook her head. ''You're way behind, China. Four or five years, at least. Most of my friends have been married and divorced twice in the time you and McQuaid have been hanging out together.''

"Thank God I'm not most of your friends," I said.

Sheila leaned over and gave me a peck on the cheek. "See you tonight," she said in a conspiratorial tone. "I'll be looking for that ring."

As Ruby trailed Sheila out the door, she was happily humming "Here Comes the Bride" under her breath.

Chapter Two

Maria Sanchez's Hearty Mexican Garlic Soup

3 whole heads of garlic
3 tbsp oil
1 large onion, sliced thin
8 cups rich chicken stock
1–2 chipotle chiles, fresh, dried, or canned
1 tsp cumin or more to taste
¼ cup lime juice
sour cream or yogurt, sliced green onions, and minced fresh cilantro for garnish

Preheat oven to 400°. Separate the cloves of garlic. Arrange in a shallow pan, coat with 1 tbsp. oil, and bake about 45 minutes, until soft. Peel the cloves. Sauté the onion in 1 tbsp. oil, then purée in a blender with the garlic, adding ¼ cup chicken stock. Heat remaining oil in a large saucepan and add the puréed mixture. Cook until it begins to dry out and brown lightly. Add stock, chipotles, and cumin, and simmer 25–30 minutes. Add lime juice and pour into a serving bowl. Garnish with sour cream, green onions, and cilantro. Serves 6–8.

Bean's Bar & Grill may be short on romance, but it's long on Texas. It occupies a narrow metal-roofed stone building on Guadalupe between the railroad tracks and Purley's Tire Company. On a still night you can smell the mesquite smoke from the grill as far away as the Fina station.

Bean's is owned and operated by Bob Godwin, a Vietnam vet who lives with a golden retriever named Budweiser in a beat-up old trailer surrounded by goats, on the outskirts of town. Bob has thinning red hair, eyebrows like furry red caterpillars, a heart tattoo on his right forearm, and a serious paunch under his stained white apron. He looks at home in Bean's, where the pine tables go back far enough that second-generation customers can point out their daddies' and mamas' carved initials to the third generation, who haven't yet graduated to pocket knives.

When you want to go native in Pecan Springs, Bean's is the place, as long as you don't mind a little noise. The major action takes place in the back, where the pool tables, dart boards, and pinball machines are located. Eating and drinking and general merriment go on up front, where you can get a table with an unobstructed view of the 24-inch TV on a swivel arm over the bar, tuned full volume to the sports event of the evening. The chandelier over the bar is a genuine wagonwheel with red and green jalapeño pepper lights looped around it. A replica of John Wesley Hardin's famous gun and a photo of Bonnie and Clyde hang over a neon-lit Wurlitzer jukebox. The whole front half of a moth-eaten buffalo protrudes from one wall, with a wooden cigar-store Indian standing nearby. The Indian used to hold a sign asking people to refer to him as a Native American. Now he holds a dart board with a big ATF emblem pinned to it. (Waco is, after all, just up the road, and some people still hold a grudge.) If you're into cultural symbolism, you might find something instructive in this melange of Texas icons, but most folks are more interested in beer, nachos, and the action around the pool table.

McQuaid and I sat at our regular table by the window. Bob came over with a pitcher of Lone Star, two mugs, a red plastic basket of warm tortilla chips, and a chipped cup full of an incendiary salsa. A sniff will warm your cold heart. A mouthful will melt your fillings.

"Evenin', y'all," he said in his John Wayne twang, raising his voice above the lyrics of an old Bob Wills swing tune. His expression was gloomy, as usual. It is rumored that Bob hasn't smiled since somebody killed Leroy several years ago. Leroy was his favorite goat.

"Make that four mugs," McQuaid said, and picked up a menu. "Company's comin'."

"Sheila and Blackie," I told Bob, who knows everybody in town. "Happy Valentine's Day," I added, and he brightened.

"Same to ya," he said almost cheerfully. He gave me an admiring glance. "You shore look good t'night, China. Purty as five acres o' red hogs."

"Thank you," I said modestly. In honor of the occasion, I was wearing a wine-colored hand-knitted sweater, an ankle-length black skirt, suede boots the same color as the sweater, and McQuaid's Valentine present, a pair of gold hoop earrings, which had been wrapped up and sitting on the kitchen table when I got home. The topic of the day had not been raised, but the evening was young yet.

Bob turned to McQuaid. "When you goin' to make a honest woman outta this sweet li'l gal?"

"I asked her five minutes ago," McQuaid said, still buried in the menu.

"Hey," I protested. "You did not!"

"Whut did she say?" Bob asked.

McQuaid didn't look up, feigning indifference. "What does she always say? She said no."

"He's making that up," I said. "He has not asked me since Christmas."

Bob grunted. "Ya didn't ask her romantic enough is th' problem. Did'ja git down on yer knees?"

McQuaid lowered the menu. "No," he said. He regarded me quizzically. "Would you say yes if I got down on my knees?"

"I certainly would not," I said, indignant. "That's the last thing I'd—"

"You see?" McQuaid said with a twinkle to Bob. "Stubborn as a patch of Johnson grass."

Bob is an idealist with a strong sense of moral order. " 'Tain't nachur'l," he muttered. "Man like you, woman like her, y'ought'a be romantic. Perticularly on Valentine's Day." Recollecting what he was there for, he took his order book out of his back pocket. "Brisket's good tonight," he added. "An' Maria come over an' cooked up a king-size pot of garlic soup. Smells *real* garlicky back there." He raised his head and sniffed delicately. "Seems like that smell is workin' up this way, too."

Maria Sanchez runs the Taco Cocina in a little frame cottage on Zapata Street. She's best known for her breakfast tacos—chorizos and eggs and chile peppers, rolled up in her own homemade tortillas. But she is Bob's current girlfriend, and she's taken to dropping in now and then to stir up a pot of soup or a *guisada*—a thick stew flavored with ancho peppers, onions, and tomato, and slow-baked in the oven, so the meat is tender. All of Bob's patrons are hoping that the relationship lasts.

"Guess we'll start with a double order of nachos," McQuaid told Bob, predictably, and he went off.

"Happy Valentine's Day," McQuaid said to me, lifting his beer mug. He was wearing jeans and the black crew-necked sweater I gave him for his birthday, along with his Valentine's present: a long-sleeved silky white turtleneck under the sweater. Even with his rugged, lived-in face—the white scar running diagonally across his tanned fore-head, the twice-broken nose, relics of an action-packed ca-reer in law enforcement—the combination of black and white with his dark hair and tanned skin was glamorous and very sexy.

I smiled at him, thinking with pleasure of the long, quiet evening that stretched out before us: dinner and drinks with friends, a nightcap at home, and bed together—a special occasion, because it was Valentine's Day. The thought warmed me. The nice part of living with somebody who turns you on is knowing how the evening is going to turn out. "Same to you," I replied. "How did your research go today?"

"Okay," he said, with a noncommittal shrug, and swigged his Lone Star.

That was as far as I usually got when I asked him for

details about this particular project, so I didn't press him any further. Whatever he was up to, he must be pretty involved with it. He'd seemed unusually quiet and preoccupied lately. But it was his business, and I didn't pursue the matter. McQuaid and I give each other lots of space. In fact, personal space—room for friends, for interests outside the relationship, time alone—has always been a big issue for me. I want lots of space, and I'm more than willing to reciprocate.

"Pretty as a red hog, huh?" McQuaid set down his beer with a wry grin. "If I were you, I'd slug him."

"He meant it as a compliment."

"I'd still slug him." McQuaid fell silent for a minute, then added, "So how was *your* day?"

"Very nice," I answered happily. "Willow and Dolores Adcock and I worked in the new garden. We got a lot done—the whole thing staked and all the beds and paths laid out. We might have started tilling, but Dolores had to leave at lunchtime, and after that it was just Willow and me. All three of us are going to work tomorrow, though. If it doesn't rain, we should get the beds in. I've ordered another load of compost."

McQuaid regarded me, head tilted. "Dolores Adcock? She's working for you?" He sounded surprised, and maybe a bit wary.

"Yes. Why? Do you know her?"

"Not exactly." He hesitated. "Maybe it's not the same woman. Is she married to someone named Roy?"

"I think so," I replied. "I wasn't paying strict attention, but I think that's what she said. They're fairly new in town,

I understand. They came from somewhere in the Valley.''

''Laredo,'' he said reflectively. He leaned forward. ''What kind of person is she?''

''Dolores? Quiet, shy. Almost . . . oh, I don't know.'' I shrugged. ''Sort of nervous and jumpy, like she has a lot on her mind. She's appealing though—like a lost little kid, although she must be in her early forties. Anyway, she certainly knows plants. I'm thinking about hiring her full-time. She's only part-time at Wanda's—that's where Willow met her.'' I paused, curious. ''Why are you asking?''

''No reason. I met her husband once, that's all.'' He changed the subject. ''Did I tell you that your mother called?''

I made a face. My mother and I haven't been on the best of terms for thirty-something years, which is a longish time to be on the outs with your mother. There are reasons, however. Since I was old enough to tell time, I knew that four P.M. was Happy Hour and that Leatha would be soused by seven. A couple of years ago, she joined a twelve-step group and sobered up. Her transformation hasn't meant much to me, because the hurt goes too deep. I stay out of her life and aim to keep her as far out of mine as possible.

But getting straight changed Leatha. She found a decent guy, married him, and now lives on a ranch near Kerrville, where she is big-time into things like the Hospital Auxiliary and Friends of the Library. Like McQuaid's mother, Leatha is committed to seeing us married. I had made the mistake of casually mentioning, a few weeks ago, that I was considering the possibility. She was probably calling to ask if we'd set the wedding date. Knowing Leatha, she had already planned the big event, with white lace, red roses, and "Oh Promise Me." I just hoped that she hadn't congratulated the groom yet.

From Leatha's phone call, the conversation moved on to other cozily domestic matters—Brian's performance as King of Hearts in the Valentine's Day play on Tuesday night, McQuaid's parents' trip to Mexico City, my garden plans. From time to time we glanced at our watches and wondered out loud what could be keeping Blackie and Sheila. I was just about to go to the phone and call one or the other when the door opened and they both came in.

Sheila was slim and svelte in coffee-brown wool slacks and a matching tunic top, her shoulder-length blond hair combed smooth. Blackie Blackwell was more casual, in jeans, checked shirt, boots, and a white hat. You can tell how they feel by the countless little touches, and the soft way they look at one another. When they're together, they never stop smiling.

But there weren't any smiles this evening as they pulled out chairs and sat down. Sober-faced, Blackie reached for the pitcher and poured each of them a beer.

"What's up?" McQuaid frowned.

"We just came from a crime scene," Blackie said. "A shooting. I caught it on the radio just as we were leaving Sheila's to come here. That's why we're late."

"Anybody we know?" McQuaid frowned.

"Yeah." Blackie ran a hand over his crisp-cut sandy hair. "Roy Adcock. He's dead."

"Roy Adcock?" McQuaid's mouth dropped open. I added, startled, "Dolores Adcock's husband?"

''I told Blackie I thought she was the woman you mentioned this morning, China,'' Sheila said excitedly. ''The one who came over to work with you. Right?''

''That's right,'' I said. ''She worked until noon, and then left.'' I looked at Blackie. ''You said it was a crime scene. A shooting?''

Blackie nodded somberly. ''I knew Adcock when I was a kid. His father was a Ranger—worked with my dad from time to time.'' Blackie came from a line of sheriffs. ''That was back in the days when criminals were a lot less sophisticated. Cattle thieves and bank robbers were the worst of it, with a few arsonists and bootleggers thrown in for good measure. Now—'' He lifted his beer as if in salute. ''In his time, Roy Adcock was as good a Ranger as his dad. A real straight arrow. A helluva guy.''

''Dolores's husband was a Ranger?'' I asked, even more startled. Somehow, Dolores hadn't seemed like *that* kind of woman—although, if you pressed me, I probably couldn't tell you what kind of woman a Ranger's wife would be. Not somebody who worked part-time for Wanda Rathbottom, maybe. I looked at McQuaid. ''Did you know that? That Dolores' husband was a Ranger?''

''A former Ranger,'' Blackie corrected me. ''He resigned a year or two ago.''

McQuaid was leaning forward, tense. He hadn't answered my question. ''You said he was shot. How did it happen? When? Who did it?''

''Shot in the chest, point-blank range,'' Blackie replied. ''There were powder burns on his shirt. Wife found him when she got home about quarter after five.''

"It was *her* gun," Sheila put in, with a glance at me. "A mini-magnum, Taurus Custom 605."

I stared at her. "You're saying that Dolores Adcock shot her husband?" Remembering the slight, nervous woman who had worked with me that morning, I found it hard to believe that she'd left a morning's pleasant work with plants and gone home to shoot her husband. But stranger things have happened, I reminded myself. I had seen plenty of them when I was practicing law.

"The neighbor said they'd been having a lot of loud arguments lately," Sheila said. "It could have been domestic violence. Maybe Adcock was depressed at being retired. Maybe he took it out on her with his fists, and she shot him."

Blackie scowled at her. "Lawmen don't beat their wives."

"No kidding," Sheila said dryly. "Read the statistics, friend. It happens all the time."

"Maybe, but not *Rangers*," Blackie said.

"Rangers are better than anybody else?" Sheila asked, very quietly.

McQuaid's eyes were dark, his mouth taut. "Could Adcock have committed suicide?"

"Maybe," Blackie said. "But the outside door was open and there were muddy footprints on the rug."

"Mud on his shoes?" I asked.

"Bubba said no," Sheila put in.

Blackie turned the beer mug in his fingers. "Somebody could have come in through the door and shot him. Had to have been somebody he knew, though. There was no sign of a struggle."

"Most men don't shoot themselves in the chest," McQuaid said grimly. "Was there a note?"

"If there was, it hadn't turned up yet," Blackie said.

"Bubba's handling the investigation?" I thought of Dolores and wondered who she'd get to represent her, if she was charged with the crime. She needed a lawyer to step in at the very beginning and take charge. The quicker the defense starts building its case, the stronger that case is going to be. Maybe I ought to tell her about Charlie Lipton, who has an office down the block from Thyme and Seasons.

"Bubba's got it for now," Blackie said. "But the Rangers will probably step in and take over, since Adcock used to be one of theirs."

"Yeah." McQuaid's grin was crooked. "Whether Bubba likes it or not."

"He's not going to like it," Sheila said. "You know how he feels about interference. He won't like the Rangers messing in his territory."

To understand this complicated turf issue, you have to understand something about the Texas Rangers, who are totally unique in the United States. The Rangers, you see, came into existence before there was any local law enforcement. That was back in the days when Texas was wild and woolly, a bloody battleground where three very different armies—Plains Indian warriors, Mexican *vaqueros* and *caballeros*, and gringo settlers who called themselves Texans—struggled for the upper hand. Established during the Texas Revolution and armed with long rifles, horse pistols, and knives, the Rangers were charged with protecting the borders of the new republic from its enemies to the south, west, and north. They were up to the job, too. According to contemporary reports, every Ranger rode like a Mexican, trailed like an Indian, shot like a Tennessean, and fought like a dozen devils.

But time and civilization marched on, and after 1880, when the Indians were dead or relocated and the Mexican threat quelled, there weren't many enemies left. Led by independent and powerful captains, the Rangers roved the state, hunting down cattle rustlers and horse thieves, protecting the whites from the blacks and browns (and, on very rare occasions, the blacks and browns from the whites), and stepping in to help the local peace officer when a situation got out of hand. They were rough and tough and smart, and they were loners. The story goes that when a single Ranger showed up to help a sheriff handle a mob, the sheriff nervously inquired when the other Rangers would arrive. "You've only got one riot, haven't you?" the Ranger answered, sighting down the barrel of his gun.

"One riot, one Ranger." A good man standing firm against evil. The myth still persists, perpetuated by innumerable books, movies, and television dramas—and the Rangers themselves. "No man in the wrong can stand up against a fellow that's in the right and keeps on a'comin'," said an early Ranger captain.

But eventually the public began to disagree with the Rangers' version of what was right. Well-known Ranger commander William Sterling was tried in 1915 for shooting a South Texas rancher in the back, and Geronimo's captor, Tom Horn, was hanged for murder. Politicians had fallen into the unfortunate habit of paying their debts with Ranger commissions, and critics cried foul, claiming that the corps was honeycombed with hoodlums. In 1919, there was a general housecleaning and some of the bad actors were booted out. But it wasn't until 1935 that the Rangers lost their autonomy and were put on a par with the State Highway Patrol under the watchful eye of the Department of Public Safety.

That's where the situation stands today. The eighty-odd Rangers—eighty-five or so men and a couple of women—are organized into six districts, each headed up by a captain. But despite the increasing bureaucratization, improved supervision, and external control, Rangers are still notoriously independent. They develop their own caseload, set their own hours, cross jurisdictions pretty much at will, and report at their convenience. Some of their heavy-handed methods may be constrained by Miranda, the NAACP, the EEOC, and civilians' home video cameras, but they're still free spirits, the last best bastion of the good old boys. They're not always well liked by the local sheriffs and police chiefs, though. As I said, it's a turf issue.

"If the Rangers are taking over the investigation," Sheila remarked in an acid tone, "I hope they do a better job of it than they did in Waco or Corsicana or—"

"Watch your tongue, woman," Blackie said. His tone was joking, but his eyes weren't.

"Why?" Sheila demanded. "After that ridiculous investigation of those stolen high school transcripts in Odessa, nobody takes the Rangers seriously anymore. Margaret had a good look at the reports on that case, and she says—"

McQuaid reached for the empty pitcher. "Anybody want a refill?"

"Yeah," Blackie said. "Let's get another." He picked up the menu. "Your friend Margaret may be a Ranger," he added to Sheila, "but that doesn't give her the right to bad-mouth a bunch of good guys who are just trying to get a job done—a damn tough job, too." Having effectively closed the subject, he gave us all a pleasant smile. "Does anybody know whether Maria's in the kitchen tonight, or are we stuck with Bob's cooking?"

Maria's soup lived up to its garlicky fragrance, and Bob's mesquite-flavored brisket was quite acceptable. But it was Sheila and I who kept the conversation going. Blackie, clearly upset by the death of a comrade-in-arms, paid more attention to his plate and the pitcher of Lone Star than to the rest of us. McQuaid was withdrawn and preoccupied, his expression tense and troubled, and he said hardly a word.

In the restroom marked Heifers (the men's room is labeled Bulls), I pumped Sheila for more details about the shooting. She had spoken to the cop who answered Dolores' call, but she didn't have much else to tell me.

"Dolores said she came home from the grocery store and found him dead," she said, opening her purse and taking out her hairbrush. "When Blackie and I got there, the crime-scene team was already at work, so we didn't try to go into the room where the body was."

I leaned forward to look at myself in the mirror, which is so old that the silver is flaking off the back, showing patches of splintery board wall. Heifers is built like a barn, down to the rusty, cobweb-festooned tack that hangs on the wall. Not exactly feminine decor, but Bob had it handy, so he hung it up. "Did you talk to Dolores?"

"Briefly."

"How was she?"

I didn't know Dolores Adcock well, but she hadn't struck me as a particularly strong woman. It wasn't a question of muscles. She had pushed wheelbarrows and wrestled rocks and landscape timbers right along with Willow and me. But underneath, there was a certain fragility. She seemed to hold herself carefully, as if some part of her might break. Now that I thought about it, I realized that she reminded me of clients I'd had—one in particular, who had shot the husband who'd abused her.

"She was in shock, I suppose." Sheila glanced at me in the mirror. "But she was surprisingly together, under the circumstances. Pretty cool and collected. If it had been me, I'd have been screaming and crying."

That surprised me, too, given what I had guessed about the woman. "You said they argued?" I asked. Dolores had seemed too timid, too wary to be much of a fighter. It was hard to imagine her raising her voice. Maybe he had done all the yelling—and thrown a few punches, in the bargain.

"I didn't get the details. If you're interested, I suppose you could talk to the neighbor who mentioned it to the police." Sheila fished in her bag for her lipstick. "What's your take on this, China? Do you think she might have killed him?"

I frowned. "I wouldn't have said so. She's a good worker, pays attention, knows what she's doing. I liked her. But then, I spent maybe three hours with her—hardly enough to know her inside and out." I paused. "You said he was killed with her gun?"

Sheila nodded, making an O with her mouth, applying a sheer pink lipstick. "A nice one, too. Small as a .38 Special snubby, but with more punch. Ported, which reduces the recoil.''

''Doesn't sound like a gun for amateurs.''

''Hardly.'' Sheila smoothed her mouth with her little finger.

''How do you know it's hers?''

''I heard her tell the investigating officer.'' She paused. ''Actually, it was more like an admission. Like she didn't *want* to say so, but she thought she might get in trouble if she didn't tell the truth.''

''Well, I'll be curious to see what the investigation turns up.''

Sheila dropped her lipstick back in her purse and looked at me. ''So. What's Mike's interest in this case?''

''Oh, you noticed?'' I asked.

''How could I not? What's *with* him tonight, China? He hasn't said two words since the food came. Was he a friend of Adcock's?''

''I wondered that, too. He said they met once.''

''Seems kind of strange,'' Sheila said. She glanced down at the third finger of my left hand and raised one eyebrow. ''Well?''

I made a big show of adjusting my earring. ''See what McQuaid gave me for Valentine's Day?''

''Very pretty,'' she said, and waited, watching me with an expectant look.

I picked up my purse. ''Ready to join the guys?''

''Uh-uh.'' She leaned against the counter and folded her arms across her chest. ''Well?'' she repeated.

''Well, what?''

''Well, has he *asked* yet?''

"No, he hasn't," I said crossly. I tossed my head. "And if he does, maybe I'll just say no. Maybe I'm out of the stupid mood."

Sheila gave me a very serious look. "Don't be an idiot, China. Mike is one in a million. For pity's sake, marry the guy!"

I sighed. "I will," I said, totally contradicting myself. "When he asks."

"Well, if you feel that way, why wait?" Sheila gathered up her purse. "You're a liberated woman. If you feel like getting married, stop being coy and tell him so."

"Why didn't I think of that?" I said. "Thanks, Sheila. I think I *will* ask him. If I can get him to talk to me."

It wasn't easy. McQuaid's silence continued as we drove home through the chilly February night, the stars like chips of ice in the cold, black sky. We parked and hurried into the dark house. Brian was spending the night with a friend, so we had the place to ourselves. I shivered under my sweater, turned up the thermostat, then opened the liquor cabinet.

"What'll it be?" I asked, taking out a bottle with a seductive flourish. "Bourbon, brandy, or me? We can reverse the order, of course."

McQuaid was standing with his hands in his pockets, looking at the phone. He didn't answer right away. After a moment he glanced up. "What? What did you say?"

I grinned. "Brazen hussy that I am, I propositioned you." I went to him and put my arms around his neck, rubbing my cheek against his warm black-sweatered chest, enjoying the sweet redolence of Maria's soup.

I snuggled closer. "I was thinking we might indulge in a

smidgen of extramarital sin,'' I said. Or premarital foreplay. ''A bit of garlic-flavored Valentine vice,'' I added sexily. ''Where will it be? Your den, our bedroom, or—''

He pulled my arms from around his neck and stepped back. ''I'm pretty wound up tonight. You go on to bed, China.'' He wasn't looking at me.

I tried to swallow my disappointment, but it wouldn't quite go down. ''There's always tomorrow morning,'' I managed, trying to make it light.

''Sure. Tomorrow morning.'' He touched my cheek, his finger lingering, and his eyes met mine. But only briefly. He dropped his glance, dropped his hand, and went into the kitchen.

I stood for a moment. Over the years that McQuaid and I had been together there had been occasions when one or the other of us hadn't felt like making love. But there was something in his voice, in the expression on his face, that made tonight different. This rejection felt more like *rejection.* It had a certain finality about it, as if we might never make love again, or never again in the same way. It hurt, painfully, unexpectedly. And perhaps it hurt more because I had anticipated more. Tonight was to have been the night. The night.

I stood for a moment after he'd gone, wondering whether what had just happened had *really* happened, or whether I had exaggerated it. Then I went upstairs and turned on the bath water. I would feel better after a long soak. In fact, after a hot bath, I would probably decide that I was making much more out of this thing than it deserved. McQuaid was just tired and upset about Adcock. It would pass, and he would be back to his old self.

The bath had just started running when I decided to call Leatha. It was a good time, because I could always cut off the conversation with a hurried ''Ohmigosh, the bathtub is overflowing, gotta go, Leatha, goodbye.'' But when I picked up the phone, I realized that McQuaid was on the line, talking to someone. To a woman. A woman with a rich, throaty, *urgent* voice.

''I know you're upset, Mike,'' she said. ''That's why we need to talk this thing through. Can you get away tonight?''

My throat closed. My hand froze to the receiver like flesh to bare metal on a below-zero day. I wanted to put it down, but I couldn't.

''Not tonight.'' McQuaid's voice was ragged. ''You know how things are. China would ask too many questions. I haven't come clean with her. About us, I mean. If I didn't feel so guilty—''

The woman's chuckle was affectionately ironic. ''What did I tell you? You're too much of a boy scout.'' My heart was hammering so loudly, I knew they could both hear it. ''Well, tomorrow, then.''

Another pause. ''God, I hate this,'' he said. ''On top of everything else—'' There was a silence. ''Okay, tomorrow. where?''

''Come here. You say when, and I'll be waiting.''

''Is nine too early?''

''That's fine. Would you like some breakfast?''

''Yeah,'' he said. ''See you in the morning.''

I shivered violently and my hand came unfrozen. I replaced the receiver, feeling as if the wind-chill had suddenly dropped to 50° below.

Chapter Three

There grows no herb to heal a jealous heart.
Yiddish proverb

Ruby was excited. "Did you see the paper?" she cried, waving the Saturday *Enterprise*. "Dolores Adcock's husband shot himself!"

I looked up from the stake I had just pounded into the ground to mark the corner of one of the new beds—with all the violence I might have used if I'd been pounding it into that woman's heart. *That woman*, I was calling her in my mind, since McQuaid hadn't used her name. The Other Woman.

"I heard about it last night," I said, straightening up and rubbing the crick in my back, "from Sheila and Blackie. They were at the crime scene. So it's definitely suicide?"

"There is apparently some question, according to the newspaper. Dolores is quoted as saying that he *couldn't* have shot himself." Ruby brushed the leaves off the bench and sat down, the pale February sun spilling over her shoulder. Today's costume was more subdued than yesterday's, but just as striking: black-and-green jungle print leggings, a loose green tunic top, and a green print scarf caught up with a large plastic bullfrog. The eyes of the day were green.

"I met him," she said reflectively. "Roy Adcock, I mean. He came to pick Dolores up after she finished putting the shrubs in. Now that I think about it though, he didn't exactly seem like the type."

"The type to what? Beat up on her?"

"Oh, no. To kill himself. He seemed very calm, self-possessed. Although you know that old saying about still waters running deep." Ruby thrust the paper at me. "Here. You can read it for yourself."

I dropped my hammer, sat down next to Ruby, and scanned the story. Beyond the bare facts I already knew, I learned that Maude Porterfield, J.P., had not yet made a ruling as to the cause of death, but was reported to be leaning toward suicide. Maude Porterfield is seventy-four years old and has been a justice of the peace for forty-one years. She's seen everything. If she thought Adcock had killed himself, he probably had, even though she wouldn't make it official until the autopsy report came back.

It struck me as odd, though, that Adcock hadn't left a suicide note. People who kill themselves—especially those who are likely to be discovered by a family member—usually want to explain why they're doing it, or ask forgiveness, or say goodbye or I told you so. And there were those muddy footprints Blackie had noticed, which the article didn't mention.

"Interesting," I said, and gave Ruby back the paper. "Thanks for coming over to show it to me." I was more grateful than usual for her company—and even for the article about Adcock's suicide. Puzzling over what had happened would give my mind something to do, give me some relief from the telephone conversation playing over and over in my head, brutally, endlessly. The woman's voice, urgent: *Can you get away tonight*? McQuaid's voice, ragged: *I haven't yet come clean with her.* The voices of two lovers. And one of them was the man I lived with. And loved.

With an effort, I pulled myself back to the conversation. "Does it seem a little odd that the wife of a retired Texas Ranger is working part-time for Wanda?"

Ruby's eyes widened. "Dolores's husband used to be a *Ranger*? I wonder what happened to all their money. Baseball players make a mint."

"Not that kind of Ranger," I said. "A lawman." Come to think of it, the *Enterprise* hadn't mentioned that Adcock had been a Ranger. I wondered why.

"Oh." Ruby tilted her head curiously. Her hair was a gingery halo in the sun. "Well, I don't know. Maybe she was working because they needed the money." She frowned. "I wonder why Dolores didn't tell me he'd been a Ranger. She did say he'd retired early, though. I had the feeling that neither of them was very happy about it. I guess she didn't want to move to Pecan Springs. She liked it better where they used to live."

"Laredo," I said absently. Laredo is a border town, on the Rio Grande. "I wonder if he was sick or something." Maybe Adcock retired from the Rangers because he had a terminal illness. Maybe that was his motivation for killing himself.

Ruby lifted her green shoulders in a shrug. "Well, if he was, it didn't show. For his age, he was a good-looking man. Hardly any gray, a handsome mustache. Distinguished, in a rugged sort of way. Older than Dolores by maybe fifteen years, although you could certainly see the appeal. She acted like his little girl, and he was kind of like her daddy, taking care of her."

I was surprised, but I didn't doubt her take on the situation. Ruby sees a great deal, and her perceptions of people are usually accurate. "How old was he?" I asked. I thought back to the newspaper article and answered my own question. "Fifty-five? *That's* not old."

"I prefer younger men myself," Ruby said, stretching out her legs in front of her. "They don't give you as much grief about being independent, and they don't expect you to be there for them every minute." She grinned. "There are other benefits, of course. But you know all about that. McQuaid is five years younger than you, isn't he?"

"Nearly seven," I said looking away. *God, I hate this. I wish it could be out in the open.* But it wasn't out in the open. It was behind closed doors, in her apartment. He was with her right now, talking, touching, tasting. I closed my eyes. Something hot and sour rose in my throat.

"There you are," Ruby said happily. "Seven years is perfect." She looked down at my left hand. "Well? How did it go last night? Have you set the date yet?"

I shook my head. Seven years meant that McQuaid was still a couple of years away from forty. How old was the woman? Was she as beautiful and sexy as she sounded? I swallowed painfully. Jealousy had dogged me in the days when I was climbing the career ladder, and I remembered how it felt to want something that belonged to somebody else, or to fear losing what belonged to me. But this jealousy was worse. This was bitter as a green apple, raw as December, painful as a slashed palm.

Ruby frowned at me. ''What's the matter, China? You didn't say no, did you?''

''He didn't ask,'' I said with a shrug. ''I considered asking him, but last night didn't seem like the right time, all things considered.''

Ruby's ''Oh'' was disappointed. ''It's okay, isn't it?'' she added. ''You didn't have a fight or anything, did you?''

''Not . . . exactly,'' I said.

She leaned forward. ''Not exactly? What's that supposed to mean? Either you had a fight or you didn't. Which is it?''

I opened my mouth. ''Well, to tell the truth—''

Maybe I would have told her, maybe not. As it happened, I didn't have the chance, because we were hailed by a sturdy, broad-hipped woman trotting up the path. She was wearing a rumpled navy skirt, a red-and-yellow plaid jacket, and a yellow blouse, and she had a scuffed and bulging briefcase in one hand.

''For Pete's sake,'' I said. ''It's The Whiz!''

Back in the old days, when I was a law student, Justine Wyzinski had inspired me with passionate hatred—a hatred based on jealousy, I freely admitted. Justine, who had sat next to me in first-year criminial law, was better and faster than I was at almost everything. From torts to trusts, from civil procedure to criminal jurisprudence, she threatened to get the better of me every time. But jealousy spurred me on, driving me like a demon, making me feel I could never be as good as she was. Every class in every course we took together—and it seemed as if we took *everything* together—was like a ten-K run. I would pursue Justine, pass her, lose it, and fall back to get my second wind. This insanely competitive marathon earned her the nickname The Whiz, while people called me Hot Shot. The marathon went on until we got to Law Review, collapsed at adjoining desks, and decided it would be less exhausting to run relay, so we could both win, and even manage to be friends.

After law school, we went separate ways. I went to Houston and joined a prestigious criminal defense law firm. The Whiz, who had never given two hoots about money or prestige, joined the San Antonio D.A.'s office as an assistant prosecutor. A couple of years later, she left to open her own law practice, specializing in family law and domestic violence. That's where she is today, still functioning at the speed of light. When I think about her, I can't help feeling competitive. Occasionally I even feel outclassed. I wonder if the feeling will ever go away.

Justine rushed up, her brown hair flying around her ears. ''Good to see you, Hot Shot,'' she barked. She nodded at Ruby. ''And your assistant investigator. Glad I caught you both together. That way we won't waste any time. Are you two working on a case? Do you have a couple of hours this weekend you could spare for me?''

These questions require a bit of background. Last March, my friend Dottie Riddle got into an argument with her neighbor over her cats. When the neighbor unfortunately ended up dead, Dottie was the prime suspect. I called The Whiz to help get her out of jail. The Whiz insisted that Ruby and I do the investigative work that would help her build a defense, which we did, with surprising success. As a result, she's decided that Ruby and I have a natural talent for investigating. I've tried several times to disabuse her of this ridiculous notion, but when Justine gets an idea in her head, she's like a dog with a sore foot. She won't leave it alone.

To make matters worse, Ruby (who watches all the reruns of *Murder She Wrote* and even makes notes on the plots) is flattered by Justine's mistaken assumption. "We can always spare time for *you*, Justine," she said, dropping her voice until she sounded like Kathleen Turner playing V.I. Warshawski. "Got a problem?"

I could see where this was headed. "Don't encourage her, Ruby," I said.

"Very good," The Whiz said. "We'll get right to work." She sat down on the bench Ruby had vacated, opened her briefcase, and pulled out a yellow legal pad with illegible scribbles all over it, like hieroglyphics on a pharaoh's tomb. "I'm on my way to Austin to see a client and I can only spare five minutes. Let me fill you in on the case as I know it so far."

"Stop," I commanded. I stood up and spoke slowly. "We do not work on cases, Justine. I plant gardens, Ruby consults the spirits. We are not PIs. I repeat, *not* PIs. Got it?"

The Whiz has never heard a discouraging word—or if she hears one, she doesn't let on. "I got a phone call this morning," she continued, flipping the sheets in the yellow tablet, "from an old friend. This woman fears that she might have inadvertently discovered some facts which may eventually become pertinent to the investigation of a death. She's worried that she may become involved—or that certain persons may *think* she's involved. Same problem either way."

"What facts?" Ruby asked eagerly. "Who died?"

"Hush up, Ruby," I said, feeling cross. "Don't say anything that will give Justine even the remotest idea that we are interested in—"

"Sorry, Ruby," The Whiz said, biting off her words

crisply. "I can't tell you the facts. I can't reveal my friend's name, or her relationship to the deceased. But I *can* say that she is afraid. She believes she may be in danger if she divulges her information."

"I see," Ruby said. "Well, in that case—"

"However," Justine added, "I *can* tell you the name of the deceased."

"Forget it!" I said emphatically. "Once and for all, Justine, Ruby and I aren't interested in playing detective. We have things to do. I have gardens to plant, Ruby has spirits to—"

"Whose death?" Ruby asked.

"A citizen of Pecan Springs," Justine said curtly, "which is why I'm here, of course. The last time we worked together, I was impressed by the way you two are plugged into the local grapevine. It's like you have radar ears. I want to know what people are saying about the guy who died. I want to know what you hear. In short, I want you to snoop."

"Whose death?" I asked, suddenly suspicious.

"You're right, Hot Shot," Justine said. "We're wasting time. His name was Adcock."

"Adcock?" I asked.

"Adcock!" Ruby exclaimed.

"Aha." The Whiz arched an eyebrow, looking from one of us to the other. "Do I detect, perhaps, a prior acquaintance with the dead man?"

I made an impatient noise. "Come off it, Justine. There is no prior acquaintance. I've never laid eyes on Roy Adcock."

"I have," Ruby chirped. "He wasn't bad-looking, either, for his age. Did you know he used to be a Texas Ranger?"

''Mmm,'' The Whiz said, very thoughtful. ''No, I didn't know that. Thank you.''

''You're welcome,'' I snapped. ''We'll send you a bill on Monday.''

The Whiz turned to Ruby. ''What else do you know?''

Ruby shrugged. ''They haven't lived in Pecan Springs very long. They moved here from Laredo after he took early retirement.''

The Whiz gave her a speculative look. ''Retired early, huh? How come?''

''We don't have any idea,'' I said. ''What's going on here, Justine? Did Adcock kill himself, or didn't he?''

''The newspaper says he did.'' Ruby held it up.

''The newspaper?'' The Whiz snatched it and scanned the article. ''Interesting,'' she muttered. ''Very interesting.''

''Well?'' Ruby asked. ''*Did* he kill himself, or didn't he?''

''He may have pulled the trigger,'' The Whiz said judiciously, ''but something that happened just prior to his death may have led him to do it.'' She held up her hand as if to silence Ruby's questions. ''I know, I know, I'm being mysterious. But that's all I can say at the moment. In fact, I've probably said too much already.'' Her eye caught her watch and she began scrambling papers back into her briefcase. ''That's all the time I have, too.'' She snapped the lid and jumped up, with the air of General Patton ending a briefing session with his junior officers. ''I'll count on you two to put this case on the front burner and give it your full attention.''

''This is ridiculous,'' I said.

''You can count on us,'' Ruby avowed.

"That's the spirit," The Whiz said approvingly. She straightened her shoulders. "My friend is depending on you to turn over every rock, look under every bush, to dig up the facts." She looked at me. "I'm depending on you, Hot Shot, to figure out what it is we need to know." She clapped Ruby on the shoulder. "And on you, Ruby, to keep Hot Shot's nose to the grindstone. She's bright, but she's lazy."

Ruby grinned malevolently. "I'll keep her working, Justine."

"Right," The Whiz said, satisfied at last. She reached in her purse, pulled out a card, and gave it to Ruby. "Good luck, people. My cell phone number is on that card, or you can leave a message on my office voice mail. Don't sit on anything. Report it the minute you've got it."

"We will," Ruby said. "But don't we need a contract or something? I mean, if we're going to work for you—"

"A gentleman's agreement is good enough for me." Justine held out her hand. "Let's shake on it."

I folded my arms. "We're not gentlemen."

Justine gave me a look. "I'll send you a letter, then," she said. "Okay, gang, let's get on it." And with that, she set off down the path. Before she got out of earshot, I thought I heard the strains of "Whistle While You Work."

Ruby turned to me. "Well, shall we get started? I'll ask Laurel if she'll keep an eye on my shop today. I'm due a day off anyway. I've been working too hard lately, and—"

"Laurel has all she can handle with Thyme and Seasons," I said firmly.

"Well, then," Ruby retorted, "I'll call Holly Bright. She likes to work at the Cave because it gives her a chance to read all the books she can never afford."

"Ruby," I said, "you can't be serious."

Ruby put her hands on her hips and narrowed her eyes. "Of course I'm serious. Don't be lazy, China. We have a *client*!"

"Wrong," I said. "Did Justine say anything about paying us?"

Ruby frowned. "Well . . ."

"Of course she didn't. The Whiz expects us to do her a favor, that's all. She has a friend who says she's in trouble—and who may or may not be telling the truth."

"What do you mean?"

"Well, just for the sake of argument, suppose that Justine's friend was Adcock's girlfriend."

"His . . . girlfriend?"

"Sure. You said yourself that he was a good-looking man. And suppose she was with him just before he died, maybe having a little hanky-panky. There were muddy footprints by the patio door. Who's to say that they weren't hers?"

"Muddy footprints? How do you know?"

"That's what Blackie said. He and Sheila dropped in at the Adcocks' last night, when they heard the report on the police radio."

Ruby looked troubled. "You should have told Justine about the footprints."

I ignored her. "Suppose this friend of Justine's was there. Suppose she and Adcock had a fight and after she left, he shot himself. That might explain why there wasn't any note. He didn't want to confess that he was playing around."

Ruby grew thoughtful. "Or maybe he shot himself *while* she was there."

"Or maybe there was a struggle for the gun," I said, "and he somehow managed to shoot himself."

Ruby's green eyes widened. "Or maybe *she* shot *him*, and somehow managed to make it look like he shot himself!"

"There!" I said triumphantly. "Do you want to work for a murderer?"

"But you worked for lots of murderers," Ruby retorted. "You've said it yourself, over and over. Every accused deserves the best defense. Doesn't the same thing go for Justine's friend? Anyway, there's another explanation. Something you didn't think about."

"Oh, yeah?"

"Yeah. What if Adcock and this girlfriend of his were making out on the sofa and Dolores came home and found them. What do you think happened then?"

I frowned. "What happened? And how do you know?"

"I know what *could* have happened," Ruby amended. "She could have reached into a drawer, pulled out her husband's gun, and blasted away at point-blank range. And then she could have wiped off her fingerprints and pressed his hand around the gun. To make it look like he shot himself."

"You're talking about Dolores Adcock?" I asked skeptically, remembering the woman I had met—shy, thin, fragile—with a child's half-frightened, half-furtive look. "Somehow she doesn't strike me as the type who—"

"Of course she doesn't," Ruby said. "It's always the one you'd never suspect. Anyway, how well do you actually know Dolores Adcock? She could be anybody."

"Anybody?"

"Of course. Maybe she was in a mental institution. She

has that look, don't you think? Sort of paranoid, like somebody's out to get her. She looks like somebody who might have spent a some time in the state hospital.''

Sometimes Ruby's intuitions surprise me. ''Well, I have to confess that I wondered the same thing. But that's speculation. There's no evidence for—''

''If there's evidence, we'll find it.'' Ruby gestured dramatically. ''Dolores probably has a secret past that she doesn't want anybody to know about.''

''What about the girlfriend?'' I asked. While we were engaging in these absurd speculations, completely uncontaminated by facts, we might as well go a little further. ''If Dolores shot her husband in a jealous rage, wouldn't she have killed the other woman, too?'' I shook off the uncomfortable parallel, which wasn't a parallel at all. I wouldn't even pick up a gun, much less—

Ruby shook her head decidedly. ''If Dolores killed the other woman, everybody would know that her husband was cheating on her. No, she'd let the woman go, figuring she'd never open her mouth for fear of being implicated.''

I was silent for a moment. ''Anything's possible, I guess. You've got one thing wrong, though.''

''What's that?''

''It wasn't his gun that killed him. It was Dolores's.''

Ruby's green eyes widened. ''*Dolores's*?''

''Yes. Sheila overheard her telling the investigating officer. And according to Sheila, it's a shooter's gun—not your basic Saturday night special.'' I was showing off what I knew, and the minute Ruby reacted, I was sorry I had said so much.

''That cinches it, China,'' she said flatly. ''There is something *weird* going on here. Are you in on this investigation, or do I have to do it myself?''

I was feeling uncomfortable. ''Look, Ruby. This isn't a made-for-TV movie. It's the real thing. We don't have any business—''

She tossed her head. ''I guess that means you're out of it. I'll handle it myself, then.''

I looked at her. Ruby is my best friend, but she acts on impulse. I had no choice but to go along and try to keep her out of trouble. ''All right,'' I said, and added hastily, ''I'm not involved, mind you, and I'm not helping—I'm just along for damage control.''

''Wonderful,'' she said blithely. ''We'll begin with Dolores. I'll go call Holly, and meet you in five minutes.''

The whole thing was crazy, I thought, as I picked up my tools and started off after Ruby. A total waste of a pleasant Saturday morning, when I might be gardening and—

I paused. No, maybe not a total waste. Since Ruby and The Whiz had showed up, I hadn't thought once of McQuaid and that woman.

And then I stopped and stood still, thinking of them and feeling suddenly bereft.

Chapter Four

> Amaranth (the word means ''unfading'' or ''eternal'') is the generic name for a number of annual plants that have been used as agricultural crops, medicinal herbs, dyer's plants, and ornamentals. You may recognize the ornamental variety, love-lies-bleeding (*Amaranthus caudatus*). The handsome blood-red flowers look like dangling ropes of fuzzy chenille.
>
> China Bayles
> *China's Garden Newsletter*

> *Amaranthus* is under the dominion of Saturn, and is an excellent qualifier of the unruly actions and passions of Venus. . . .
>
> Nicholas Culpeper
> *Culpeper's Complete Herbal*, 1649

''What a terrible thing to have happened,'' Laurel said, when I went into the shop to tell her where I was going and why. ''Can you imagine coming home and finding your husband shot to death?''

''No,'' I said, with a little shudder. ''I can't imagine it.'' I looked around me. In this pleasant place, violence and death seemed remote, fictions dreamed up by TV scriptwriters. Of course, that was one of the reasons I had come here. To get away from the ugliness of the city, from the sleazy business of selling my time and energy to help people escape the consequences of what they had done—ninety-nine out of a hundred of them, anyway. Here, I didn't have to think about crime and crooks, or the iniquities and inequities of the law. Here, I could be at peace, happy with my work.

Standing in Thyme and Seasons, surrounded by a delightful variety of healthful, beautiful things, it's easy to feel this way. Three of the walls are built of exposed chunks of limestone, carefully fitted by the German craftsmen who constructed the century-old building. The floor is made of wide planks scarred by a hundred years of scuffling feet, and the wood ceiling is supported by heavy, hand-hewn cypress beams. Bundles of herbs and dried-pepper *ristras* and garlic braids and wreaths hang overhead and on the walls. The corners are filled with baskets of dried flowers—yarrow and tansy, love-lies-bleeding and prince's feather, sweet Annie and Silver King and larkspur and statice. There are racks of books and wooden shelves lined with jars and crocks of bulk herbs, bottles of vinegar, and packages of tea and other goodies. And in the area that used to be my living room, Laurel and I have arranged our Personal Care displays in old wood hutches and antique cupboards: soaps, shampoos, body oils, cosmetics, scents, bath herbs. One of the things I enjoy about the shop is putting all these lovely things on display for people to see and smell and touch and love—and buy, as I am reminded at the end of the week, when I run the cash register totals. So far, it's been a good year, although the first quarter isn't over yet. If business kept up like this, I'd be able to afford the tearoom remodeling in the second quarter.

"Tell Dolores that I'm sorry," Laurel said. "I don't know her very well, but I like her. Wanda says she's got a green thumb."

"That's how it looks," I said. "I was thinking maybe I'd hire her to help out in the garden this spring. Now, though, I don't know. She may not want to work, at least for a while."

Laurel perched on the stool behind the counter. "I'm hoping it will be slow here today. I've brought the notes for my research paper. I have to finish it by Monday."

"Another pepper paper?" Laurel is trained as an ethnobotanist. Her last couple of research projects had to do with the capsicums—hot peppers.

She shook her head. "This one is on amaranths. When I was in New Mexico last summer, I did some research on them. I plan to grow a few this summer. *Sangre de Castilla*, Blood of Noble Spain, is a great one. There's another one called Hopi Red Dye. You can use the bracts as a food coloring. Sure beats Red Dye number five."

"The only amaranth I've grown is the ornamental variety," I said. "There's some of it in that basket." I pointed to a bunch of love-lies-bleeding, with the oddly dangling blossoms that always remind me of ropes of dried blood.

"Did you know that it's also a medicinal?" Laurel asked. "In folk remedies, love-lies-bleeding was used to treat hemorrhage—nosebleeds, cuts, heavy menstrual periods too. It was also used as an anaphrodisiac, for killing the urge for sex. And in Sweden, it was a symbol of male chastity and purity. It was only supposed to be worn by virtuous knights—men who were incorruptible.''

''I wonder who they found to wear it,'' I said dryly, ''and what happened if a knight wore it and he *wasn't* pure? Was he struck by lightning or something?''

She laughed. ''One does wonder. By the sixteen hundreds, though love-lies-bleeding was being used to treat venereal disease. Which is your ultimate symbol of corruption.''

We would certainly have lingered on this fascinating topic, but Ruby came through the door between her shop and mine.

''We're all set,'' she announced. ''Holly will be here in a little bit to open up.'' She smiled at Laurel. ''Give her a hand if she has a problem, will you? This is her first time alone on the cash register.''

''Sure,'' Laurel said comfortably. ''We can trade off for lunch, too. What time will you be back?''

''I don't know,'' Ruby replied. ''However long it takes to dig up some answers.''

I gave it one last try. ''Let's think about this for a minute, Ruby. Dolores Adcock has just lost her husband. Is this the time to go barging in on her?''

''This is exactly the right time,'' Ruby said. ''When you're investigating, you want to question people before they have a chance to pull themselves together and put up a front.'' She frowned at me. ''You ought to know that.''

''Dolores? Put up a front?'' Laurel asked, startled. ''Why would she do that?''

''She might have something to hide,'' Ruby said. ''After

all, her husband was killed with *her* gun. Doesn't that seem a little odd to you?''

Laurel blinked. ''That is a little surprising, actually.''

''Even more surprising,'' Ruby said, ''because he's an ex-Texas Ranger. The cop kind,'' she added, before Laurel could open her mouth to ask what position he played. ''You'd think if the man was going to kill himself, he'd do it with his own gun.''

I came back to the main point. ''What are you going to say to her?''

Ruby gave me a lofty smile. ''Whatever comes into my head,'' she replied. ''I'll rely on my intuition.''

''I was afraid of that,'' I said. ''Listen, Ruby, I really don't think we ought to—''

''Excuse me,'' Laurel interrupted, ''but if you two are going to argue about this, would you mind going outside? Constance Letterman is coming up the walk, and I don't think you want her spreading gossip all over town.''

''We're not going to argue,'' Ruby said. ''We're going to *work*. Come on, China.''

I sighed. ''I guess I don't have any choice, do I?''

Sure I did. I could always go back to the garden, where I could pound more stakes, dig more dirt, and think about McQuaid and *that woman*.

By the time we got to the Adcocks' house, a few minutes after ten, the sun had been overtaken by clouds and the wind was almost chilly. The house, a gray ranch style badly in need of paint, was built on the side of a hill. It was still officially winter, but the frost-browned grass on the slope was already starting to turn spring-green, and one side of the yard was bordered by what had once been a rock garden. A few forlorn daffodils were in bloom, and I could see some straggling santolina. But the garden was smothered by last summer's weeds, and the whole place had an unkempt, uncared-for look. Dolores might have a green thumb, but she wasn't using it to the benefit of her own garden.

We took the cement walk to the top of the hill. There was a gray Oldsmobile parked in the carport, and behind it, a dark blue Chevy with Texas Exempt license plates—a state car, probably investigators.

"Are you going to knock or ring the doorbell?" Ruby asked in a whisper.

"Neither," I said. "This is your project." I gestured at the Chevy. "Are you sure you want to interrupt?"

In answer, Ruby punched the doorbell. In a moment, we heard the click of the latch and Dolores Adcock opened the door, the chain still in place.

"Who is it?" she asked. Her voice was thin and high-pitched, a little girl's voice, the words softened by a slight Hispanic accent.

"Ruby Wilcox," Ruby said. "And China Bayles." The door opened wider. The woman who looked out at us must have been in her early forties, but dressed as she was in faded jeans, loafers, and an old white T-shirt shirt hanging loose over small breasts and narrow hips, she had the look of an abandoned child. She was thin as a half-starved urchin, her face an exaggerated triangle, her deep-set dark eyes large, wide open, waiflike. The skin, creamy-brown, the gift of Spanish ancestry, was stretched taut across high cheekbones. The long, coarse black hair, parted in the middle, framed a wide forehead, dark brows. There was a kind of beauty in her, but it was a fragile, wary beauty with an edge of wildness, as if she were ready to turn and run.

"Hello, Dolores," Ruby said gently. "We were so sorry to hear about your husband, and wondered whether we could help." Ruby might be putting on an act, but it sounded genuine.

Dolores bit her underlip. "Thank you for coming, Ms. Wilcox," she said. She looked at me and her eyes brimmed with tears. "You too, Ms. Bayles. It's very nice of you to bother. But I don't . . . I don't think there's anything you can do."

"I know," I said. I suddenly felt like the worst kind of heel, intruding on the woman's private grief. "We won't come in, Dolores." I nodded at the Chevy in the drive. "We can see you've got . . . company. We just wanted you to know we were thinking about you. Call us if you need anything." I grabbed Ruby's elbow. "Come on," I said.

Ruby darted a look at me and pulled her elbow out of my grasp. "It might help to talk," she said to Dolores. "It does, sometimes. Things like this are pretty hard to deal with all alone." She peered over Dolores' shoulder. "If you're busy with the police, we can wait. Or we'd be glad to come back."

I felt like kicking Ruby, but Dolores didn't seem to notice her rudeness. She hesitated for a moment, then stepped back, opening the door wider. "Come in if you like. There's somebody from the Rangers here, but they're in Roy's office. And maybe it will be good to . . ." Her voice wavered. "To talk."

When the door closed behind us, the hall we stepped into was dark. I could make out a coat tree and a mirror over a small table, and a plastic ficus tree—the real thing couldn't have survived without light. Following Dolores toward the back of the house, we passed a door with a yellow tag on the knob. It had been taped shut with yellow crime-scene tape, but the tape was pulled loose, and the door was half open. I could hear movements inside, and the low murmur of men's voices. The investigators, I surmised.

Dolores stopped. "That's where I found him," she said. "That's his office. That's what we called it, anyway. It's really just another bedroom, with a door to the outside."

"You were out when it happened, I guess," Ruby said, and I gave her a dark glance. We had barely gotten inside the house, and she was already fishing for information. When Ruby gets involved with something, she gets *involved.*

"I was at the grocery store," Dolores said. "I'd just gotten home when I—"

The door was opened by a tall, broad-shouldered man in a dark jacket and gray slacks. "Oh, Mrs. Adcock," he said, with a slight smile. "I was just coming to tell you that we're finishing up. We're about to leave."

"Thank you, Mr. Dubois," Dolores said. She glanced at the tape. "Does that mean I can go in there if I need to?"

He nodded sympathetically. "We'll be taking the tape off when we leave. Captain Scott asked me to tell you that he'd like to speak at the memorial service. He's an old friend of your husband's. Do you have any objection?"

Dolores shook her head mutely.

"Then he'll come by this evening. Will that be all right?"

This time she managed a faint "Yes."

Dubois glanced at us, then turned back to Dolores. "One

more thing I need to ask, Mrs. Adcock. You told the investigating officer that the gun your husband used was your gun. Did you purchase it—personally, that is?''

Dolores flushed. ''No. Roy gave it to me. It was a . . . a birthday present.'' She cleared her throat. ''Is there some problem about the gun?''

''I don't know.'' Dubois gave her a shrewd, measuring look. ''If there is, I'll get back to you.'' He turned away. Dolores raised her hand and opened her mouth as if she were about to say something more, but he had gone.

We followed her into the living room, at the back of the house. It had a sliding glass door that opened out onto a small paved area, the rocky hillside rising steeply behind. There had been a garden against the hill once, but it was overgrown with weeds, and dry, brown grass had thrust itself through the cracks in the patio pavement.

I glanced around the room. I don't know what I expected to see, but I was surprised. It was decently furnished, yes—a new-looking green sofa, a couple of matching chairs at right angles to it, a square coffee table between the chairs, lamp tables at each end of the sofa, a television set in one corner. But there was no bric-a-brac or decorative pillows, no books or collectibles, no family photos on the piano, none of the personal touches that soften bare walls and give a room a welcoming, lived-in look.

I sat on the sofa. Ruby took one of the chairs, and Dolores took the other. ''We saw the article in the paper this morning,'' Ruby said. ''It must have been awful for you, finding him the way you did.''

''The paper has it wrong.'' Dolores reached for a pack of cigarettes that lay on the coffee table. ''He didn't kill himself.'' She put her hand down between the seat and the arm of her chair and fished out a lighter. Her hands shook as she lit the cigarette and drew on it, deeply. ''He was a good man, Ms. Wilcox. He had no *reason* to kill himself.''

I wanted to say that even good men sometimes found themselves faced with problems they couldn't solve, but Ruby spoke first.

''It was an accident, maybe. My uncle was cleaning his gun once, and shot himself in the leg.''

Dolores raised her shoulders and let them fall. ''I don't think he was cleaning it.'' She pushed herself out of the chair, went to the patio door and opened it, waving the smoke out. ''It was . . . well, you heard the officer. It was my gun. Roy gave it to me, and I kept it in the drawer on my side of the bed. I don't understand why it was in his office.'' She stood with her back against the doorjamb, half-turned from us, nervously smoking. Obviously, she was unable to deal with the fact of her husband's suicide, and talking to casual acquaintances like Ruby and me wasn't going to help her face the truth.

Ruby leaned forward. ''If it wasn't suicide and it wasn't an accident,'' she asked in an innocent, puzzled tone, ''how *did* your husband die?''

Dolores was still turned away, but I could see her struggling with an answer, starting to say something, rejecting it. ''I guess the police will have to decide that,'' she said finally. ''The Rangers, I mean. They're doing the investigation.'' Was I wrong, or was there a twist of bitterness in her words?

Ruby persisted. ''Could someone else have been here with him yesterday afternoon?''

Dolores's thin shoulders straightened and she raised one hand, as if to ward off a blow she had been expecting. "Of course not," she said quickly. Too quickly. "He was here all alone. I told the police that."

Ruby wasn't deterred. "How can you be sure of that? If you weren't here, I mean."

"He was here by himself." Dolores pulled savagely on her cigarette, tossed it to the pavement outside the door, and stamped on it. Turning, she lashed out, her voice rising out of control, becoming shrill. "He was alone, the way he always was in the afternoon. And if you're thinking that my husband was the type to mess around with—"

She clamped her mouth shut, her nostrils flaring, a painful flush staining her jaw. She ducked her head, closed the door behind her, and turned back toward us. "Why are you asking all these questions? Whatever happened, he's dead. Roy was a good man and he didn't do anything to be ashamed of. What does any of this matter to you?"

"I do apologize, Dolores," Ruby said, conciliatory. "I thought it might help to talk about what happened. But if we're upsetting you, we'll go."

Dolores sank back into her chair. "I . . . I'm sorry," she said. "I don't know what made me blow up like that." She rubbed her eyes with her fists, a child's gesture. "I didn't get much sleep last night. Roy always took care of everything. The finances, the insurance, all that stuff. I don't even know how much there is in the checking account. I guess I'll have to start digging through his papers, if I can bear to go into that room."

"The Ranger mentioned a memorial service," I said. "When will it be?"

"Somebody there, one of his friends or somebody, is making arrangements," she said. "Roy's first wife and son were killed in a car wreck ten years ago. His parents are dead. There was just us." Her voice broke. "Now there's just me. I'm all alone." If grief was tinged with self-pity, I couldn't blame her. She had been married to a man who had taken care of her, had made all the decisions. Losing him, she must feel frightened and adrift.

"If you'd like," Ruby offered, "I'd be glad to come over and stay with you."

"Thanks," Dolores said, "but I'm not very good company right now." She glanced at me and added, with an oddly abrupt emphasis, "Willow said you're a lawyer, Ms. Bayles."

"I used to be. I'm not in practice now."

"But she still keeps up her bar membership," Ruby said. "If I were in trouble, I wouldn't hesitate to ask her to help me."

Dolores' tongue came out and flicked her dry lips. "I'm not in trouble. I just want to ask—" She stopped. "Did I say something to make you think I'm in trouble?"

"Not at all," Ruby said quickly. "I just meant that China's an awfully good person to know if you need help." She stood. "And do call if you need anything." She reached for her purse, opened it, then shut it again. "I've left my business cards at the shop. China, do you have one you can give her?"

I fished in my purse, found a card, and handed it to Dolores. "If you have a question about your husband's will or his financial affairs, I can offer some general suggestions. But it would be better to talk to someone who can give you much more specific help. Charlie Lipton would be glad to help, I'm sure. His office is just down the street from my shop.''

''It's not about his will,'' she said, turning my card over in her fingers. There was an awkward silence.

''It's time we were going,'' Ruby said. She gave me a little push. ''You don't have to see us to the door, Dolores. We can find our way out.''

Dolores was still sitting in the chair, holding my card, when we left the room.

I have to give it to Ruby. She managed to get out the door, down the hill, and all the way to the street before she burst out excitedly, ''What do you want to bet that Justine's friend was here yesterday afternoon, and that Dolores saw them and—''

''Ssh,'' I said, and motioned with my head toward a dark-haired woman in a swirly orange skirt, purple sweater, red shawl, and sandals. She was walking along the curb on the other side of the street, with a bouncy golden retriever puppy on a long lead. She was watching us—oddly, I thought—and then she waved.

''Hello, Ruby,'' she called, and came across the street.

''Minerva!'' Ruby cried.

The two women traded hugs while the puppy circled them. After a moment they separated, unwound the leash from their ankles, and Ruby introduced the woman as Minerva West.

''Minerva is going to teach an astrology class at the Cave next month,'' she added, ''after the spring solstice.''

''Hi,'' I said, and held out my hand. Minerva's long, dark

hair hung loose over her shoulders and she was wearing a stylized stone goddess figure on a rawhide thong around her neck.

"Capricorn," she said.

"What?" I asked, startled. And then, realizing that she had guessed my Sun sign, "How did you know?"

"Minerva's psychic," Ruby said. "She could probably tell you your Moon, too."

Minerva studied me, her gaze direct and a little unnerving. "One of the fire signs, I'd say," she said. "Or first house, maybe."

"Bingo," Ruby said. "Aries, conjunct her north node." She turned to me, triumphant. "Isn't she amazing?"

Minerva, amused, shook her head. "I just pay attention, that's all." She smiled at me. "Earth and fire. Staying put, moving on. A difficult combination, but full of life, once you've mastered the contradictions."

I didn't understand a word of this astro-babble, but the part about staying put and moving on was a little too close for comfort. That had been my problem with McQuaid, wanting to be connected to him without being committed. Until very recently, anyway.

"Ask Minerva to give you a reading sometime," Ruby said. "She's good."

"Maybe that's not such a bad idea," I said. I instinctively liked Minerva, which I can't say for all of Ruby's flaky friends. The puppy started to pee on my sneaker, and I stepped back. "Do you live around here?"

"Mind your manners, Andromeda." Minerva tugged on the leash and the puppy forgot about peeing and started to sniff shoes, first mine, then Ruby's. "I live up there." She gestured toward the house next door to the Adcocks' on the south.

"Do you know Dolores Adcock?" Ruby asked. "China and I just dropped in to see her. Her husband—" She shook her head. "Well, you probably know as much as we do about what happened yesterday. Maybe more." The last sentence was almost a question.

"Actually, I was just thinking about Dolores." Minerva's dark eyes grew intent. "And wondering what I should do."

"You saw something, then?" Ruby asked. She paused and added, in a leading tone, "A woman, maybe?"

Minerva stared at her. "How did you know?"

"I'm psychic," Ruby said modestly.

"Dolores said something that made us think Mr. Adcock might have had company," I replied.

Minerva frowned. "I told the police that someone was there in the afternoon, but they didn't seem very interested. I thought maybe they knew something I didn't. Or that they might be protecting his reputation. He was an ex-policeman."

"Maybe we'd better start from the beginning," I said. "What exactly did you see?"

"Andromeda and I went down to the corner to put some letters into the mailbox. There was a car parked by the curb, just about where yours is now, Ruby."

"What kind of car?" Ruby asked.

Minerva shrugged. "Blue, sporty-looking. I'd seen it before, but I knew it didn't belong to any of the neighbors. Andromeda and I put our letters in the box, then stopped at the little grocery to get some veggies and salad stuff.

When we got back here, that's when I saw her, coming down the hill.''

''What did she look like?'' Ruby asked.

''Blond, very pretty, thirty-something, I'd guess. She was wearing slacks and a tweed jacket, and she was in a hurry. When she got to the street, she kind of ducked into her car. I got the definite impression that she didn't want anybody to see her.''

''What time was this?'' I asked.

''It was about three forty-five when we went to the mailbox,'' Minerva said, ''and just before four when I saw the woman. I paid attention because . . .'' She looked uncomfortable. ''Well, because the woman was acting suspicious, and because Roy is . . . was a very attractive man. With a very possessive wife.'' She pulled Andromeda back from the storm drain. ''Don't fool around there, Andromeda. I don't want to have to fish you out.''

''Do you think Dolores knew about the woman?'' Ruby asked.

''Actually, that's what has me bothered,'' Minerva replied. She bent over and picked up the squirming puppy, cradling her. ''Dolores works part-time at a nursery. She usually gets back about four-thirty or so, just about the time Andromeda and I go out to do a little yard work. So when I noticed her Oldsmobile parked at the corner and her in it, watching the woman drive away, it seemed . . . well, strange. It crossed my mind that she might be—'' Minerva stopped, and the puppy licked her nose.

''Might be what?'' I prompted.

Minerva made a wry face. ''Well, you know. Spying. To

tell the truth, I was a little amused. Roy always seemed so straight and nice, just a regular guy, not at all like a cop. I kind of felt sorry for him.''

''Felt sorry for him?'' Ruby asked.

''Well, Dolores has never liked living in that rented house. She didn't want to move to Pecan Springs in the first place. She yelled at him a lot. So when I saw the woman coming down the hill, looking sort of surreptitious, I figured that Roy was fooling around.'' She grinned. ''I thought, more power to him.''

The day before, I might have grinned back. Today, I didn't. ''How long have they lived there?''

''Only a few months,'' Minerva said. She paused, thinking. ''Since around Thanksgiving, probably. They were pretty quiet, except for the arguments. She's little, but she's feisty and hot-tempered. And shrill. He was the type to just sit there and let her yell until she calmed down.''

My impression of Dolores was obviously very different from Minerva's. But mine was based on only a couple of hours' acquaintance, while Minerva had lived next door for several months.

''What happened after the woman left?'' Ruby asked.

''I went home and did a little work in my studio. About five-fifteen, when I went into the living room to turn the television on to watch the news, I heard Dolores shrieking. I ran next door to see what had happened. Roy was dead. I was the one who called the police.''

''You didn't see her come home?'' Ruby asked. ''You didn't hear any gunshots?''

''No to both questions,'' Minerva said. ''My studio is on the other side of the house, and the windows were shut.

Anyway, I told the policeman about the woman I saw, and he wrote it all down.''

''Did he take a signed statement?'' I asked.

She shook her head. ''He told me that he'd get it typed up and that I should go down to the police station at nine this morning and sign it. But when I went, the woman at the desk said they didn't need a statement from me because it turns out that the Texas Rangers are handling the investigation. Plus, she said, they've just about decided that Roy killed himself, so anything I had to say doesn't really matter.'' Minerva frowned. ''Neither of which made a lot of sense to me. Roy didn't strike me as the kind of man who would kill himself unless he was sick or something. Then there was that strange woman, and Dolores waiting around the corner in her car. And how did the Rangers get into it?'' The puppy was wriggling, and Minerva put her down.

''The Rangers are involved because Adcock used to be one,'' Ruby said.

''No kidding.'' Minerva wrinkled her nose. ''I never heard of anybody who *used* to be a Ranger. What happened? Did he quit or get fired?''

''We don't know,'' Ruby said. She looked at me. ''Do you think maybe Minerva ought to talk to that Ranger we met at the Adcocks'? What was his name—Dubois, wasn't it?''

''It might be a good idea,'' I said, ''although he's probably read the investigating officer's report. But if you want to talk to him and make sure he knows what you saw, Minerva, you could call the Department of Public Safety in Austin and ask for him.''

''I'll think about it,'' Minerva said. ''I hate to get involved, but on the other hand . . .'' She looked at me. ''I just wish I knew what Dolores was up to, sitting in that car. That seems pretty weird.''

Ruby took a card out of her purse. ''If you think of anything else that you heard or saw yesterday—or any other day, for that matter, would you give me a call?''

Minerva frowned at the card. ''Excuse me, Ruby, but why are you involved in this? If Dolores is a friend of yours—'' Suddenly uneasy, she shifted her focus to me. ''I guess I shouldn't have been so quick to tell you all this stuff. I'd hate for it to get back to Dolores that I was bad-mouthing her.''

Ruby became reassuring. ''It won't get back to Dolores, Minerva. China and I have been asked to look into this matter by a certain lawyer, who—''

I coughed.

Ruby shifted gears. ''Anyway, we won't tell Dolores what you said. And we'd really appreciate a call if you think of something else.''

Minerva took the card and pocketed it. ''I just want to do what's right,'' she said. ''I know it could be embarrassing for Dolores if they start digging into Roy's sex life and discover that he had another woman. But it might be worse than embarrassing. Dolores and Roy did a lot of arguing, some of it pretty violent. If she suspected him of cheating on her—''

''Do you think she might have killed him?'' Ruby asked.

''Let's just say it crossed my mind,'' Minerva replied, and scooped up the puppy. ''Come on, Andromeda. Your mother has a big mouth.'' And with that, she went up the hill toward her house.

I turned to Ruby. "I thought you left your cards at the shop."

"I wanted Dolores to have your phone number," she said. "She seemed to be interested in getting some legal advice from you." She paused, musing. "Well. Minerva certainly was helpful, wasn't she? I mean, now we've got the facts. We've confirmed that Justine's friend was here, and that Dolores saw her, and—"

"Ruby," I said, "I hate to burst your bubble, but we don't have a single fact. All we know is what Minerva *says* she saw. Not to mention that the woman—if there was one—might not have been Justine's friend. She could have been the Avon lady, or an insurance person, or—"

Ruby turned to me, indignant. "What do you mean 'if there was one'? Are you suggesting that Minerva is lying?"

"You have to consider that possibility."

"But she's my friend! She wouldn't lie to me."

"Friends can lie as easily as enemies," I said. I thought of McQuaid and the Other Woman, and my heart twisted.

"But why would she?"

I said the first thing that came into my head. "Maybe she was involved with him, and she invented the woman in order to cover it up."

"Minerva?" Ruby made a disgusted noise. "My gosh, China, if I listened to you, I'd suspect everybody of hiding something!"

I shrugged. "Does Miss Marple believe everything she hears? If you're worth your salt as a detective, you won't accept Minerva's story until you've substantiated it."

"I don't see how I can do that. I doubt that Dolores will admit to spying on her husband. But maybe I could ask the neighbors on the other side. Maybe they saw the woman who visited Adcock—or saw Dolores's Oldsmobile.''

''There you go,'' I said. ''Ruby Wilcox, girl detective.''

Ruby became thoughtful. ''I wonder why Dolores wants to talk to a lawyer. I wonder what she's hiding.'' She looked at me. ''She *is* hiding something. You noticed that, didn't you?''

''Maybe it's grief,'' I said shortly. ''After all, she's just lost her husband. It hurts to lose someone you love.'' I should know.

''Well, if that's what it is, she's hiding it pretty well,'' Ruby said in a practical tone, as we headed for the car. ''I didn't see her crying.''

''Just because she didn't collapse in front of us doesn't mean she hasn't been crying,'' I said, coming to Dolores's defense. Obviously I felt more sympathetic to her than Ruby did.

''Then where was the Kleenex? And why are you taking Dolores's side? And come to think of it, where was Adcock's gun?'' We had reached the car and Ruby unlocked her door. Without giving me time to answer any of these questions, she added, ''There's something very odd going on here, China. If I were a Texas Ranger, I'd have a gun. In fact, I'd probably have more than one. And if I had a gun and wanted to kill myself, I'd use one of *my* guns, not one that I gave my wife for a birthday present.''

I stood still. ''You can't be trying to suggest that Dolores Adcock shot her husband.''

''Stranger things happen every day,'' Ruby said cheerfully, getting into the car. ''I wish I'd thought to ask her about his gun. And why he left the Rangers. That's bothering me, too.'' She slid across the seat and unlocked my door. ''But I'm sure about one thing, China. Dolores Adcock is holding back on us.''

I got into the car. ''Well, if I know you, Ruby, you won't rest until you've figured out what she's hiding.''

Ruby took my remark for a compliment and looked pleased. ''I think we ought to call Justine and tell her that we've turned up several significant developments. Then we can get started talking to the neighbors—''

''Correction,'' I said. ''*You* can get started talking to the neighbors. I've got other important things to do, like dig in my garden.''

Ruby put the key in the ignition. ''Well, then, you can call Justine.''

I folded my arms, feeling stubborn. And feeling a gloomy kinship for Dolores, whose husband might have been cheating on her. If Ruby wanted to dig up dirt, she could do it on her own.

''You're the hired gun,'' I said. ''You call.''

Chapter Five

> Love is not a potato. You don't get rid of it by tossing it out of the window.
>
> Russian Proverb

Ruby dropped me off at Thyme and Seasons and went off to call Justine. I had intended to spend the rest of the day in the garden, but it was starting to drizzle and the gray skies promised more. I couldn't be upset about the rain, which was coming at exactly the right time for the bluebonnets and Indian paintbrush. They bloom a lot better if February brings a couple of soaking rains—although in Texas these days, *any* rain is a good rain. We hadn't had a lot of it lately, and the news is full of dire reports about the drought, the worst in a century.

With the leaden skies and intermittent showers, the shop wasn't jammed with customers. I hung around for a while, chatting with Laurel and aimlessly straightening shelves. Then I went back to the old kitchen, politely removed Khat from his favorite chair, and sat down to look over the materials that the Health Department had sent me describing what I'd have to do to get a permit for the tearoom.

The application itself looked easy, but when I started reading a booklet called "Rules on Retail Food Stores Sanitation: Texas Department of Public Health,'' I began getting a bad case of heartburn. After a general introduction heavily laced with do's and don't's, there were eight pages of regulations on food storage and display, nine pages on equipment and utensils, four pages on sanitary facilities (half of it on garbage), and six pages on physical facilities. If the State of Texas had its way, I would install two new sinks (one for washing lettuce and radishes and one for rinsing mops), lay a new floor in the kitchen, refinish the ceiling beams, seal the stone walls, and build a laundry room and several storage areas. And under Section 437.0165, I was warned that the criminal penalty for operating an unapproved food service establishment was a Class A misdemeanor and a violation of Public Health District permit requirements, which was a Class C misdemeanor. Since each day's violation counted as a separate offense, the penalties could clean me out in a hurry.

I jotted down rough estimates, muttering curses on lawyers and bureaucrats and defenders of the public health. Renovation costs would be in the seven- to eight-thousand-dollar range, which meant getting a bank loan. Maybe the tearoom wasn't such a good idea after all. I added headache to heartburn, jammed everything back in the folder, and said goodbye to Khat, who announced with a disdainful sniff that he was glad to have his chair back and would I mind serving up a small snack before I left. Altogether, it had not been a good day.

But if working on the license application was difficult, not working on it was worse. Once I stopped reading regulations and calculating costs, my mind went automatically to McQuaid. Even before I put Khat's dish on the floor and headed out the door, I heard the echo of his voice on the phone, ragged and passionate. *God, I hate this. I wish it could be out in the open.*

There had been no companionable "good nights," no Valentine's kisses last night when he came to bed. I had pretended to be asleep, rigid and silent on my side, as far from the middle as I could get. He lay down quietly, careful not to disturb me, and slept on his side, facing the wall. It was a long night. I'd been eating a bowl of cereal and a banana when he came down shortly before eight this morning and announced that he was going to Austin to work on his research project.

"I don't know what time I'll be back," he said, and dropped a quick kiss on the top of my head. "So don't wait dinner."

I hadn't said anything, but I'd known where he was going. And it didn't have anything to do with research.

I put my head in the shop and said goodbye to Laurel, then got into my Datsun, which at the advanced age of twelve years and 150,000 miles needs new upholstery and a clutch. I sat for a few minutes, staring at the rain on the windshield, hearing last night's phone coversation playing over again and again, like a warped phonograph record with the needle stuck in a groove. Ruby would say I was obsessing, and she'd be right. I was tempted to drive over to her house and obsess out loud with her, but I rejected the idea. Ruby—girl detective—was obsessing too. She was probably interviewing the Adcocks' neighbors right this minute, trying to substantiate Minerva's story about Roy's mysterious blond visitor and see what she could find that would make Dolores look guilty.

I turned on the ignition, switching off the phonograph in my head, making myself think about something else. Dolores, for instance. I couldn't help feeling sympathy for her. Her grief for her husband might not be written all over her face, but it was bound to be hiding deep underneath. It would gnaw at her in the dark, at night, when she was alone. And if she believed that he had deceived her, that he'd had another woman, there would be anger mixed with the grief, or rage, or guilt. Over and over, until she couldn't stand the questions any longer, she would ask why he had needed somebody else, why *she* wasn't enough—pretty enough, interesting enough, sexy enough—to hold him. She would ask why he had killed himself and what she might have done to keep it from happening. She would . . .

I stopped. Yes, but. Ruby had been right. The fact was that Dolores didn't wear obvious signs of grief, and that she did not seem deeply saddened by her husband's death. She even insisted that he *hadn't* killed himself, although she couldn't suggest how else the shooting might have happened. Maybe it was a simple case of denial: she couldn't bear to see the truth because it hurt too much. Or maybe I was attributing too much of my own feelings to her, the grief and anger and yes, even the guilt *I* would have felt in her place. McQuaid and I had lived together for less than a year, and he wasn't my husband. But we had shared a great deal over the time we had known each other. And although it had always been hard for me to admit it, I loved him. I was ready for marriage, as ready as I'd ever be, anyway. Now, he'd found someone else. Now—

Damn. I'd come around again, full circle, back to Mc-

Quaid. McQuaid and that urgent, sexy voice on the phone. McQuaid and The Other Woman.

When I'm angry, I clean house. Scrubbing a floor or washing a window flexes the large muscles, gets the kinks out, lets me work off my resentment or indignation or outrage. When I'm worried, I cook. Cooking flexes the mental muscles, but it has a calming effect. In a culture with a fast-food fetish (ten-minute dishes, twenty-minute menus, thirty-minute gourmets), real cooking is a slow, sweet ritual that soothes and steadies. It's better than a tranquilizer.

So, into the kitchen. But first, I drove to the supermarket, where I bought a handsome salmon filet, a perky bundle of cress, a luscious avocado the size of California, and—imagination temporarily being supplanted by a desperate craving for a quick chocolate fix—a box of brownie mix, a bag of chocolate bits and another of walnuts, and a can of sour-cream frosting. On the way home, I stopped at Bart's Liquors and bought a bottle of champagne and one of the Texas zinfandels. This kind of worry called for *real* cooking.

Home is the large Victorian house that McQuaid and I leased last summer. It made sense to move in together. I wanted to use my living quarters behind the shop to expand Thyme and Seasons, and I loved the third-floor tower room at the top of the stairs, with the windows all around. McQuaid coveted the workshop for his gun collection. And Brian wanted more room for the multitude of frogs, snakes, lizards, and spiders that inhabit the terrariums, fishbowls, and screen-wire cages in his bedroom. (I don't clean in there anymore. Some of Brian's animal companions aren't all that bad. I've even gotten to like Einstein the iguana and Uhura, the hognose snake he found under the garden shed and named for one of his favorite *Star Trek* characters. But it's definitely unsettling to have a tarantula crawl up your dust mop.) In the nine months we've lived in the house, we've managed to fill up most of its odd little nooks and crannies. When it's time to move, God only knows what will happen to all this stuff.

But that's a different worry, and I had enough to chew on for now. I carried my groceries into the large, pleasant kitchen, turned on the lights against the late-afternoon twilight, and went about cooking.

For most of the years I practiced law, I lived in a Houston condo with a kitchen about the size of your average chicken coop. It was efficiently equipped with a posh refrigerator-range-microwave-dishwasher-sink arrangement, but the architects must have figured that any woman who could support a mortgage bigger than Dallas wouldn't have the time or the inclination to make pancakes from scratch or stuff a turkey for Thanksgiving. There was barely enough counter space to roll out an eight-inch pie crust. If you wanted to bone a chicken or knead bread or make a salad, forget it and call the deli.

My mini-kitchen phase has given me a great appreciation for the vast acres of counters and tabletops in the kitchen where I live now, and where also reside my old green-and-cream Home Comfort range and pine-topped worktable. I poured myself a sherry, stepped outside and picked a handful of the mint that grows behind the air conditioner, and whipped up the brownie mix, adding the extra chocolate bits (if I'm going to indulge in all those calories, I might as well do it right), some finely chopped mint, and a half-cup of walnuts.

When the brownies were in the oven, I went to the kitchen garden and picked a handful of fresh cilantro. Back inside, I went to work on the avocado, which proved (like some people) to be more beautiful on the outside than on the inside. But with a little fancying up, it would do. I halved it, then scooped out the meat, set the shells aside, diced it, and tossed it with a little balsamic vinegar, some Tabasco, and olive oil. I mixed this with diced tomato, chopped green onions, celery, cilantro, and a cup of the cress leaves, and piled everything back into the two half shells to marinate. In another ten minutes, I'd take the brownies out of the oven (I could smell the rich minty-chocolate odor already) and wrap the salmon for steaming. It was time for a break. I poured a second sherry, sat down in the wicker rocker in front of the window, and propped my feet on the windowsill, beginning to feel more at peace in my soul. But the door opened before I could take a sip, and McQuaid came in.

''Oh, hi,'' he said. ''You're home.''

''Yes,'' I remarked. ''I live here.'' I paused, then added, ''I thought you weren't coming home for dinner.''

''As I remember it,'' he replied in a diplomatic tone, ''all I said was that I didn't know what time I'd get here.'' He looked at my glass. ''What are you drinking? Sherry? I guess I'll have a beer.'' He headed for the refrigerator, opened it, and saw my salmon filet. ''Ah, salmon,'' he said.

''Excuse me,'' I said, ''but that's *my* salmon. Brian went to Waco, you went to Austin, and I bought myself a salmon filet. It's just big enough for one,'' I added pointedly.

He took out a Coors and turned around, spying the two filled avocado shells on the counter. ''Well, I see you've fixed enough avocado for two,'' he said, ''so maybe I'll just have that and a bologna sandwich. I'm not very hungry. I had lunch at Mother's.''

Mother's Cafe is a vegetarian restaurant on Duval, not far from where I used to live when I went to UT law school. The covered garden patio there is one of my favorite places to eat. When McQuaid and I are in Austin together, we often go there for dinner. It hurt to think of him sharing the place with someone else.

I tipped my glass, sliding the amber-colored sherry first to one side, then to the other, the questions sloshing around in my mind. After a minute I was startled to hear myself asking one of them. ''Who'd you have lunch with?''

McQuaid's broad back was turned to me. ''Oh, just somebody from DPS.'' He was carefully cool.

''DPS?''

''We were talking about the investi—'' He stopped. ''The project.'' He pulled one of the kitchen chairs over, sat down and took off his boots, then put his brown-stockinged feet on the windowsill next to mine. There was a hole in the heel.

''Which project is that?'' I asked.

''Hey, what is this? A cross-examination?''

''I was just asking.'' I looked out the window.

''Asking, schmasking,'' he said. ''You've got an attitude.'' He stretched, making a big show of relaxing. ''Anyway, it was just a lunch, that's all.''

I sat up straighter. ''I don't think so.'' However this came out, it was going to hurt. The sooner we got it over with, the better. ''I overheard your phone conversation last night, McQuaid. Part of it, anyway.''

His pale eyes darkened and his chin jutted out. "You were listening in on my private conversation?"

"I *overheard* it." I flexed my fingers, remembering how they had frozen to the phone. I couldn't have put it down if I had tried.

"You were deliberately listening," he said. His voice was hard. "Come on, China. You're a damn lawyer. You know the difference."

Two could play that game. "It's not my listening that's at issue here," I retorted sharply. "It's your *lying*."

He swung his feet to the floor. "My *what*?"

The phone rang. "Rats," I muttered.

"Don't answer," he said, flat and hard. "I want to get to the bottom of this."

So did I, but I am constitutionally unable to sit in the same room with a ringing phone. I picked up the cordless from the table next to my chair. It was Dolores. Her voice was thin and brittle.

"I want to talk to you," she said. "Can I . . . can I come over?"

"This isn't a good time, Dolores. I'm in the middle of . . . something."

McQuaid, surprised, waggled his fingers to get my attention. Dolores Adcock? he mouthed, and I nodded.

She was persistent. "I could come after dinner."

I felt sorry for the woman, who was obviously having trouble coping. I wanted to help, and under ordinary circumstances, I would have said yes immediately. But tonight was different. McQuaid and I had to talk this out, and when we were through I doubted that I would have the energy left to deal with anybody else's problems.

"I'm sorry, Dolores," I said. "I don't think tonight would be good, either. How about tomorrow, or Monday?"

McQuaid put his hand on my arm. "Tonight," he said.

"Just a minute," I told Dolores. I covered the mouthpiece. "What?" I asked, surprised.

"Find out what she wants," he said. "See her tonight."

"I already know what she wants. Ruby and I were over there this morning. She wants to talk to a lawyer."

"About Adcock's will? His insurance?"

"I don't think so."

"Talk to her," McQuaid said, very firm. When I hesitated, his fingers tightened and his voice grew rougher. "Damn it, China, for once in your life, do what I tell you. I have to go out tonight, but I want you to get her to tell you what she knows."

"Knows about what?" I stared at him. "Why? What's going on?"

"Do what I *say*, damn it!"

I shook off McQuaid's hand and uncovered the mouthpiece. "Sorry, Dolores. Tonight is fine. Do you know where I live?"

"I looked up your address in the phone book. On Limekiln Road, past the old quarry?"

"Take the first left," I said. "We're at the end of the lane. Is seven-thirty okay?"

"Yes." There was a brief silence. "One more thing," she said. "Please don't tell Ruby Wilcox that I'm coming over."

"Don't tell Ruby?" I was puzzled. "Why not?"

"Because she . . ." Her voice faltered. "Because she

doesn't believe me. She thinks I'm lying about the way Roy died. She's been talking to the neighbors.''

I hesitated. I don't normally keep things from my best friend, and The Whiz might think I was under some obligation to report everything I found out. But it was Ruby who had agreed to be Justine's Girl Friday, not me. I had made it very plain to both of them that I didn't want to be involved. Still, it bothered me.

Dolores took my hesitation for something else. ''Please, Ms. Bayles,'' she said, very low, imploring. ''I need to talk to somebody I can trust. I want you to be my lawyer.''

''I don't take clients,'' I said guardedly.

''I'll pay you,'' Dolores said. ''Just tell me how much.''

''I don't want any money, but I'll help if I can. Come over and we'll talk.''

Her relief was clear, even over the phone. ''Oh, *thank* you,'' she said.

McQuaid stared at me as I put down the phone. ''She wants to hire you? Why?''

I faced him. ''Were you listening just now, or did you overhear?''

''It wasn't the same thing as last night,'' he said intently. ''I was sitting right here, right beside you. I couldn't avoid—''

''Answer the question. Were you listening or did you overhear?''

''I couldn't help—'' he began.

I cut in. ''Neither could I.''

It was a Mexican standoff. We glared at one another for a long moment. Finally, he said, with an attempt at lightness,

"And what was all that bull feathers about my lying?"

"It's not bull feathers," I said, not letting him off the hook. "Who was it on the phone? Who did you have breakfast with? And lunch? Are you going to be with her tonight?"

He rubbed his jaw wearily, the steam gone out. "I've been wanting to tell you, but I—" He sighed. "It's a mess, China. A stupid, lousy, complicated mess. Peggy—" He stopped.

Ah. A name at last. "Is Peggy the woman you were talking to last night? The one with the sexy voice?"

He gave me a sidelong look. "Yeah, that was her."

I waited. Finally, I said, "Well?"

He sighed. "Yeah, okay. Well, Peggy and I, we—" He stopped and started again. "You see—"

And that's where we were when the phone rang again. "Let it ring," I said. "I want to hear about you and Peggy."

But he was already reaching for the cordless, glad for the interruption. The caller turned out to be Ruby. I shook my head, then thought better of it. Dolores had said that Ruby had been talking to her neighbors. I'd better find out what was going on.

"I just talked to Justine," Ruby announced without preamble. "I gave her our report."

"*Your* report," I said firmly. "This is your case, Ruby. I made it very clear that I'm not involved."

"Whatever," she said. "Do you want to waste time contradicting me, or would you rather cut to the chase?"

"What does that mean?"

Her voice was bubbling with barely suppressed eagerness.

"Would you like to hear what I found out when I questioned the Adcocks' neighbors?"

McQuaid got up and started to the fridge for another beer. I hesitated, wondering whether this was borderline unethical. But I hadn't yet talked to Dolores, and chances were good that what she wanted to discuss with me had no bearing on whatever case Ruby might be trying to make.

"Okay," I said. "What did you find out when you questioned the Adcocks' neighbors?"

McQuaid paused, his hand on the fridge door.

"Well, first I talked to the neighbor on the north. Mrs. Mosely, her name is."

"And what did she say?"

"She was talking to her mother on the phone and looked out and saw this woman—the blonde that Minerva told us about—going into the Adcocks' house through the back door. The door into Adcock's office, that is. She thought it was kind of interesting that he would have company while his wife was gone." Ruby's voice became slyly suggestive. "Female company. *Pretty* female company."

"Maybe this pretty female was selling insurance."

"At the back door? Mrs. Mosely didn't think she was selling anything. She thought something funny was going on."

"What time did she see this blond *femme fatale* at the back door?" I asked. McQuaid's head came around.

"Just after three."

"What time did she leave?"

"Mrs. Mosely didn't know. Her dog threw up on the carpet and she had to go clean it up, and then the UPS man delivered a new lamp she ordered and she forgot about the woman.''

''Did Mrs. Mosely substantiate what Minerva said about Dolores sitting in her car, watching?''

Beer in hand, McQuaid shut the refrigerator door with a thud. He was frowning.

''No,'' Ruby said, ''but Fannie Couch did.''

''Fannie?'' I asked, surprised. Seventy-something Fannie is a talk-show host on KPST-FM. Everybody in Pecan Springs listens to her morning radio show. She features old-fashioned chitchat, local events, and recipes, the sort of thing you never hear on big-city radio. ''Fannie lives in that neighborhood?''

''Right,'' Ruby said. ''Just across the street from where Dolores was parked. She knows Dolores, you see. They met when Fannie was collecting for the Cancer Fund. Anyway, she saw Dolores's car when she got home from the radio station a little before four. She waved, but Dolores acted like she didn't see her. Fannie said she thought it was a little weird that Dolores would be sitting out there, pretending like she was invisible or something.''

''You've told all this to Justine?''

''Word for word.'' Ruby was emphatic. ''She thinks we ought to sit down and talk it over. So I asked her for breakfast tomorrow. My house.'' Ruby lowered her voice conspiratorially. ''We were right, China. Justine's friend—her name is Elaine Emery, by the way—*is* the woman Minerva saw getting into that blue sports car.''

''How did you find that out?''

''Justine told me. She didn't want to, but I convinced her that we can do better work if we know exactly where we stand.'' She paused, triumphant. ''Well? Did I do good?''

''You did a great job, Ruby. I hope Justine pays you what you're worth.'' I was puzzled. Just this morning, Justine had wanted to keep her friend under wraps, as a possible material witness to a possible crime. Had Ruby so impressed Justine with her investigative talents that The Whiz had disclosed Emery's identity without a protest? Or did Justine have some ulterior motive for the disclosure?

''There's more,'' Ruby went on. ''This Elaine person is also coming for breakfast tomorrow.'' She paused, and added, a little more tentatively, ''I told Justine you'd be here too. You *will* come, won't you?''

I was trapped in an ethical dilemma. If Dolores was going to make me her confidante, it might not be right for me to attend that breakfast. On the other hand, I couldn't tell Ruby why I refused to go without violating my pledge to Dolores. To make things worse, I was now deeply curious about the mysterious Elaine Emery and the reason for her surreptitious visit to Dolores' husband. But I wasn't anybody's lawyer, and to hell with ethics, anyway.

''What time?''

''Eight,'' Ruby said. ''Would you mind stopping at the store for orange juice?''

''No problem. Anything else?''

''I don't think so. Have you heard from Dolores?''

''Dolores?'' I asked, all innocence.

Ruby was exasperated. ''I *told* you, China. The woman has something on her mind, and she wants to talk it over with a lawyer.''

''What do you think it is?'' I asked.

''It's staring you right in the face! Roy Adcock was

having an affair with Elaine Emery, and Dolores knew it. She had a *motive.*''

''A motive for what?'' I asked. ''We're not talking murder here, Ruby. From everything I hear, Roy Adcock committed suicide.''

Ruby made an impatient noise. ''Whose side are you on, anyway? You're being difficult again.''

''It's probably because I haven't had my dinner yet.''

Ruby was suddenly contrite. ''Gee, I'm sorry. You should have said so. What are you guys having?''

I looked toward the table. McQuaid was absently forking avocado from one of the two filled shells while he listened to my end of the phone conversation. ''Avocado and cress salad,'' I said, ''and salmon steamed in champagne.''

''Salmon in champagne!'' Ruby whistled between her teeth. ''What are you celebrating?'' She answered her own question. ''Your engagement! You're celebrating your engagement!''

''Hardly,'' I said. ''Our divorce, maybe.''

''You can't get divorced. You're not married yet.''

''Want to bet?'' I asked.

Ruby chuckled. ''Go eat your dinner. You'll feel better when you've got something in your stomach. And let me know the minute Dolores calls. See you in the morning, Sherlock.''

I went to the oven, took out the brownies, and turned the temperature up to 450°. Then I retrieved the salmon from the fridge and laid it on a piece of foil. It was pink and enticing, but I had lost my appetite.

McQuaid pushed away the empty avocado shell and gave me a hard look. ''Why is Ruby questioning the Adcocks' neighbors? Why was Dolores Adcock sitting in her car, watching? Who was she watching?'' His eyes narrowed. ''And what's this about some blonde at the Adcocks' back door?''

I began to chop cilantro and parsley. ''I want to hear about Peggy first,'' I said.

He gave me a long, steely look. While I been on the phone with Ruby, he had obviously reconsidered his position and had decided he wasn't ready to talk. ''There's nothing to tell,'' he said flatly.

I finished chopping, dumped the cilantro and parsley on top of the salmon, and poured a cup of champagne over it. ''I don't have anything to tell, either,'' I said. I folded the foil into a package, sealed the ends, and put it on a baking sheet.

McQuaid was implacable. ''I also want to know why you and Ruby are messing around in this thing. It's police business. How did you get involved?''

I put the salmon in the oven and set the timer for twelve minutes, not answering.

McQuaid scowled. ''Don't be childish, China. This is a very serious matter. I have an important reason for asking.''

''So do I.'' I faced him. ''Who is Peggy?''

''I thought we agreed to give one another a lot of personal space,'' he said defensively.

''Personal space is one thing,'' I said and added, calculating the effect, ''Infidelity is something else.''

''Infidelity!'' He slammed his hand on the table. ''How the hell can I be unfaithful to you when we're not even married? And how can we be married when you keep turning me down?''

I refused to let my voice tremble. "Is it true, then? You and Peggy have been having an affair? That's a real question," I added, in a level tone. "You can always say no."

He glared at me, the red flush creeping up his jaw. He didn't say no. What he said, finally, was, "Peggy isn't important. She doesn't matter. You know that. What matters is you and me."

It was true, then. He'd been sleeping with somebody else. With Peggy. The hurt sliced through my chest. My heart began to pound. "How long has this been going on? Weeks? Months?"

He shook his head. "Not months. Only the last few weeks."

"So it started while I was on retreat at St. T's?"

He sighed. "Yeah, I guess it did." He looked at me, his eyes dark. "Would you believe me if I told you that—"

The phone rang. McQuaid started to get up to answer it, but I put my hands on his shoulders and pushed him down.

"No," I said. "I want to know. Is it still going on? Is it over?"

"I told you, China," he said sharply, "it doesn't matter. Peggy doesn't mean anything to me." He jumped for the phone, grabbing it on the third ring. "Hello," he snapped. There was a brief pause. "Yeah. She's right here." He thrust the phone at me.

"I'm seeing you and Ruby first thing tomorrow," Justine said curtly.

"I heard," I said. I couldn't believe that McQuaid and I had just rehearsed those tired old clichés, like two characters on *All My Children*. But it wasn't a soap opera, it was real.

I sucked in my breath and clenched the receiver as if by holding onto it I could hold onto myself.

"Well?" Justine demanded.

"Well, what?" I asked. McQuaid picked up his beer and turned away.

"Ruby's just given me her report. What did *you* find out?"

"Ruby told you everything there is to tell."

"You let her do it all?" Justine was annoyed. "You didn't do any investigating on your own?"

McQuaid was turning the beer can in his fingers, looking out the window. "Justine," I said wearily, "I have reduced my hours at the shop in order to have some time for myself. Which does not, I repeat, does *not* include spending all day Saturday playing detective. Ruby went out and dug up some information for you. And if you ask me, she did a darned good job, under the circumstances. She hasn't been to PI school, you know."

There was a frosty silence. "You *are* coming to breakfast tomorrow?"

"Are you sure you want me to come? I'm not involved in this. It's just you and Ruby."

Her voice became slightly sour. "I've told my client about you. She wants to meet you."

"I thought you wanted to keep a lid on Elaine Emery because she's a material witness to something," I said. "What made you change your mind?"

"I didn't change my mind," Justine snapped. "Ruby's, at eight." And she hung up. I put the receiver down slowly. It sounded as if Elaine Emery had forced the meeting, against Justine's wishes. What did *that* mean?

McQuaid turned around again. ''Elaine Emery?'' He shook his head as if to clear it. ''And don't give me any more of this 'Who is Peggy?' stuff, either, China. I'll tell you about it when I think you can listen like a mature adult. So don't nag.''

''I am *not* nagging,'' I said stiffly. ''I *never* nag.''

''Good,'' he said. ''I'm glad we've got that straight.'' He tilted his chair back on two legs, and his voice became infuriatingly mild. ''Now, then. What does Elaine Emery have to do with the Adcocks? And what's this business about Dolores and the car? I am not asking out of curiosity,'' he added. ''You may consider these official questions.''

I stared at him for a moment. There was obviously much more to this than I knew. ''It sounds like you know this Emery woman. And just why are *you* asking official questions about Roy Adcock's death?''

''You answer my questions first. I'll answer yours when it's time. Come on, China. You might as well come clean with me. If you don't, I'll go over to Ruby's and ask her.''

Come clean? It was an unfortunate phrase. I glowered at him. But there wasn't any reason to withhold the facts, except for spite. And I didn't want to give him the satisfaction of knowing just how spiteful I felt.

''A woman named Elaine Emery paid a visit to Roy Adcock yesterday afternoon,'' I said, ''an hour or so before Dolores found him dead. Dolores knew about the visit, because she was parked around the corner in her car, watching, as Emery left. The neighbors on both sides suspect that Emery was Adcock's lover.''

McQuaid looked startled. ''His lover?''

''What is there about that idea that surprises you?''

He ignored me. "Okay. So how did you and Ruby get mixed up in this thing?"

"Justine Wyzinski came over this morning and asked us to see what we could find out. You know Ruby. She took it seriously."

"And how did *Justine* get involved?"

"Elaine Emery is her client."

McQuaid's mouth hooked down at one corner. "And I suppose this Emery woman is scared that she'll get mixed up in a suicide scandal. 'Rejected Lover Takes Life,' something like that."

"Maybe," I said. To tell the truth, that was the part that intrigued me. What was Elaine Emery's connection with Adcock? Was she his lover, as the neighbors thought, as Dolores might have suspected? But if Adcock had committed suicide, neither Emery's connection nor Dolores's suspicions were especially relevant, so why all the mystery? Unless, of course, Adcock *hadn't* killed himself, and Emery and Justine knew it. Maybe Ruby and I were having breakfast with a murderer.

McQuaid was frowning. "Emery sounds peripheral to me," he said, "but I need you to check her out and let me know."

"Peripheral to what?" I asked. "What is all this *about*?"

He became evasive. "It's a very nasty business, China. There's more to it than you know."

I did not snort my contempt for his statement of the obvious. "Did Adcock commit suicide, or did somebody take him out?"

He was guarded. "Travis County is doing the autopsy. You know how slow they are. The report won't be back for a couple of days. Until then, the assumption is that he killed himself.''

``Could he have been murdered?''

``Anything is possible.'' McQuaid looked at me, shaking his head. ``This is tough stuff, China. It could involve some very big, very bad guys. It could involve drugs, corruption, extortion, you name it. I don't want you and Ruby messing around. I want you *out*.''

``Okay,'' I said reasonably. I reached for the phone, calling his hand. ``I'll tell Dolores I can't see her tonight. And I'll tell Ruby to cancel breakfast. I'm sure she doesn't want to be harassed by any very big, very bad guys who have somehow gotten the wrong idea.''

``Not so fast.'' He put his hand on mine. He was stern, cop-serious. ``Number one, I want you to see Dolores and hear what's on her mind, although chances are it doesn't have anything to do with the case. Number two, I want you to go to Ruby's tomorrow morning and find out where Elaine Emery fits. Number three, I want you to tell me what you've learned.''

``Wait a minute,'' I said. ``Who am I working for? Justine, Dolores, or—''

``You're not working for anybody. You're just wearing my ears.''

``And who are *you* working for?''

He didn't answer, just went on talking as if I hadn't asked. ``And after tomorrow morning, you're finished. You tell me what you've found out, and you're out of it. Ruby, too. No more cops-and-robbers bullshit. Period. Do you hear?''

I gave a shrug he must have taken for agreement, because

his eyes seemed to lighten. ‘‘Good,’’ he said. ‘‘I’m glad we settled that.’’ He raised his head and sniffed. ‘‘Hey, is that the salmon I smell? Delish!’’

It was the salmon, sweet, flaky, a fragrant blend of fish, herbs, and fine wine. I wasn’t very hungry, but if you think I relented and let McQuaid have some of it, you’re wrong. I put a place mat and napkin on the kitchen table, garnished the salmon with fresh parsley and slid it onto a green Fiestaware plate, and ate the whole thing, right there in front of him.

I did let him have a glass of my zinfandel, though. He needed something to go with his bologna sandwich.

Chapter Six

One for the rook, one for the crow,
One to die, and one to grow.
Traditional seed-planting charm

Dolores had plenty on her mind, and she obviously wanted to talk, but she was having trouble putting it into words. After listening to her beat around the bush for several minutes, I shook my head.

"I can't help you unless you give me some specific information, Dolores. Not general stuff, details."

She moved forward to sit stiffly on the edge of the sofa. She was dressed in black slacks and a long-sleeved black pullover that covered her thin arms. Her long, thick hair was snugged back with a plastic barrette and her large eyes were bruised and dark-rimmed.

"I'm *trying* to tell you, Ms. Bayles," she said, low. "All I want to know is whether it's against the law for a person to take something from someplace where the police are investigating."

"I can't answer a question like that. I need specifics. Are you the person?"

Her lips quivered.

"What did you take? Was it relevant to the police investigation?"

She dropped her eyes, her jaw working.

"Did you take it from the room where your husband died?"

She sat silent.

"Well, then," I said, feeling that a dose of reality therapy might speed up the process, "how about this question, Dolores? Why were you sitting around the corner in your car, watching your house, when you told everybody you were at the grocery store?"

Her head came up, her eyes widening, her lips pressing together. "How did you—?" she whispered. She stopped. One hand clenched the other in her lap. "It was that nosy Ms. Wilcox, wasn't it?" she said bitterly. "Somebody saw me, and told her."

"Were you waiting to see how long your husband's visitor was going to stay?" I paused, and added, meaningfully, "His pretty blonde visitor, who used the back entrance to avoid being seen?"

Her mouth quivered, her eyes went from left to right. "Why are you saying things like that about him?" she whispered. "You have no right—Ms. Wilcox has no right—"

"Look, Dolores." I leaned forward. "I can imagine how you felt, seeing that other woman going up to your house, wondering what she was doing there. I know how *I* would feel if I were you. But don't you see what a terrible position you've put yourself in? Sitting in that car looks like spying. Spying makes it look as if you didn't trust your husband, as if you were jealous. A jealous woman might be angry enough to—"

"Stop it!" Her eyes blazed with a passionate fire. "Just *stop* it, do you hear? You can say all you want about me, but not about him. Roy didn't fool around. He was a good man, with a good heart. He took care of me. That was all he ever wanted, just to take care of me. He might have done bad things in his life, but he never—"

She stopped suddenly and just sat, the energy flickering out of her like the flame of a dying candle, leaving her drained and silent.

"Okay, so I'm wrong," I said quietly. "So straighten me out. Tell me the truth. I can't help you unless I know what happened."

There was a long silence. She sniffled, fished in her shoulder bag for an already-used tissue, and blew her nose. "All right," she said finally. "The woman who came to see him—she's a reporter. There was nothing between them, nothing romantic, I mean. He was *my* husband." The energy flared briefly, then died out again. "He loved me."

I raised my eyebrows. "A reporter?"

"An investigative journalist for some magazine in San Antonio. She was working on a story, and she thought Roy knew something that might help her."

"Did he?"

Her mouth said one thing, her eyes another. "No. He didn't know anything. Roy was a good man." I waited patiently for more, and in a minute she came up with it. "I mean, he didn't know what she thought he knew. And even if he did, he wouldn't tell *her*. A reporter?" She became sarcastic. "Give me a break."

"It all sounds very mysterious," I remarked. "What kind of story was this reporter working on?"

She chewed on her lip, deciding how much to tell me, and elected the minimum. "Drugs and stuff, I guess. The usual. Most people don't know it, but South Texas is a mean place. I told Roy he shouldn't have anything to do with her. He shouldn't even *see* her."

"Why?"

She lifted her thin shoulders in a shrug. "Because . . . because somebody might find out and think he was telling her stuff. I mean, people don't talk to a reporter unless they've got something to say. That's what I told him. I said, 'Don't you talk to her, Roy. Somebody's going to find out, and think you're telling secrets.' "

"Who might find out?"

Her eyes became dark. "Oh, I don't know," she said evasively. "Just . . . just people. There are lots of people who are afraid somebody's going to find out what they're doing."

"Did your husband have secrets?" I asked gently.

She looked trapped. "Maybe. Some, anyway. I mean, he used to be a Ranger, didn't he? Rangers know all kinds of stuff nobody else knows. And most of the time they just keep quiet, until they figure out a way to use what they know."

"If he had secrets, what would they be?"

Her fingers were trembling, and she laced them together in a gesture that was at once vulnerable and determined. "Well, he knew why he . . . why he left the Rangers."

"Why *did* he leave?"

"There was some kind of trouble. In Laredo, where we lived. That was his district, you see. His boss told him that he had to . . . to quit or get fired."

"He was involved with some sort of criminal activity?"

She sighed helplessly. "He wouldn't tell me *what* was going on. This happened just a year after we were married, you see. He always said that he didn't want me to get involved with his work because it was so sordid and ugly, not at all glamorous like they make it look on TV." She ran her tongue around her lips, moistening them. "Anyway, one day last summer, just out of the blue, he came home and said he'd quit. We put our stuff in storage and moved to Corpus Christi. We lived there for a couple of months, in a furnished apartment. He worked for a private investigator for a while. Then he . . . he—" She seemed to run out of steam.

"Then he what?" I prompted.

"Well, he said he was tired of cities and small-town life would be better, so we moved here. His dad used to be a Ranger, too. They lived here when he was a kid. He said we'd rent for a few months while we hunted for the right place to buy, a house with a few acres, maybe." She gave me an earnest glance. "He was always looking out for *me*, you see. He wanted me to have a place of my own. He was expecting an investment to pay off, and we were going to use that money to buy a place. Then we'd get our things out of storage and start all over."

"So you started looking for a house to buy?"

She gave me a tiny smile. "Well, not yet. We didn't really have enough money, because the investment hadn't paid off yet. And because Roy was . . . well, he was sort of sick, and he was going to the doctor a lot. In the meantime, I wanted something to do. I used to work in a pri—" She stopped abruptly, flushing. "A nursery I mean. I know something about plants, so I got a part-time job at Wanda's Acres."

I came back to the central question. "So why *did* he talk to the reporter, Dolores?"

She gave me a sad, lost look. "He didn't want to, but I guess he figured he had to. It was kind of like a confession, maybe. He'd been a Ranger all his life, you know. That's what he lived for, and it nearly killed him when he had to quit. After a long while, he seemed to get over it. Then he met her—the reporter, I mean—and it was like he was living through it all over again." She bit her lip. "It got so I couldn't talk to him. He was like a zombie, sitting around all day just staring, stewing inside himself. And he wasn't sleeping. He would get up in the middle of the night and sit at his desk. He was writing a lot of stuff on the computer. A book, he said." She twisted her hands in her lap and her eyes filled with tears. "I guess it finally got to be too much for him. That's why he shot himself."

I stared at her. "You know that for sure? That he shot himself?"

Twin rivulets of tears trickled down her cheeks. "He left a note," she whispered, the corners of her mouth quivering. "That's what I took out of the room, out of his office. Then I got to worrying that maybe I'd done something they could put me in jail for."

I should have guessed. "The note was addressed to you?"

She nodded, swiping at the tears with her sleeve. When she could speak again, she said, in a choked voice, "Whatever it was he did wrong back in Laredo, Ms. Bayles, he didn't hurt anybody. He couldn't have. He lived for his job. He loved being a Ranger. After he quit, it was like there wasn't anything alive inside him. And he was afraid. I didn't want to say so in front of Ms. Wilcox, but that was why he gave me the gun. He thought somebody might—'' She shook her head sadly. ''I don't know. Break into the house and murder us in our sleep, I guess.''

I reached for Dolores's hand. Her fingers were cold. ''I'd like to read his note.''

''You can't.'' She looked down. ''The note said I should burn it, so I . . . I did. I took it into the kitchen and burned it on the gas stove. All that's left are the ashes.''

I held her hand for a long minute, then let it go. ''Do you remember what he wrote?''

She glanced up at me quickly, and I caught a flash of something secret—bitterness? fear? When she spoke, I had the feeling that she wasn't telling me the whole truth.

''He said he didn't have any other choice. He said they were saying things about him that weren't true, but that he couldn't tell the truth without damaging good men, and he wouldn't do that.'' Her voice was ragged. ''He said he loved me and that if he was dead, I'd be safe. And that there was plenty of insurance.'' She began to sob, softly. ''I've been worried about that, too. Will the insurance be any good—since he killed himself, I mean?''

''When did he take it out?''

''When we got married.'' She gave a little hiccup. ''Two years ago.''

''Then it's probably good,'' I said. ''You can check with the insurance agent to be sure, but I suspect that the death will be covered.'' I paused. ''What did he mean about your being safe if he was dead?''

"I don't know," she said, sobbing harder. "I don't know what he meant."

I let her cry for a few more minutes before I asked, as gently as I could, "Why did he use your gun, Dolores?"

She looked up at me blindly, and shook her head. "I don't know that, either. He had a pistol in his office—his own gun, the one he always carried with him. And there are others." She stopped. "Why are you asking?"

"No special reason. Would you mind if I came over in the morning and looked over the office?"

"I wouldn't mind. In fact, I'd be glad if you would." She shivered. "But there's an awful lot of blood in there. On the desk, all over the carpet." Her voice grew faint. "I don't know how I'm going to get it cleaned up. I don't know if I can bear to do it myself."

"I'll be glad to take care of it," I offered, "as long as the police are finished with the room."

"Oh, *thank* you," she said, with an almost childish gratitude. "The Rangers finished up this morning, and Captain Scott came late this afternoon to go through Roy's personal papers. He and Roy were in cadet training together, years ago. He was looking for some of Roy's poetry for the memorial service." The sad lines of her face eased, and her lips curled into a smile. "Roy wrote poems, you know—good ones. Some of them were even published in the Ranger magazine. If he'd finished his book, it would have been a good one."

I nodded. "About the note, Dolores. It was addressed to you, so it is legally your property. Of course, you should have shown it to the police, to facilitate their investigation. But when your husband's death is officially ruled a suicide, there won't be any question about obstruction of justice. Just be quiet about the note, and you're not likely to get into any trouble.'' It was sloppy advice, but the best I could offer, under the circumstances. ''Do you have any other questions?''

''Well, yes,'' she said. She twisted her fingers together, her mouth curving down. ''It's about that woman, the reporter. I hate to see Roy's name dragged through the dirt. I want to stop her from writing about him.'' She looked up at me. ''Can I sue her for libel?''

I shook my head. ''The libel law doesn't apply here,'' I said. ''A dead man can't be slandered.''

There was a flicker of apprehension in Dolores's eyes. ''You mean, she can write anything she wants to about him?''

''I'm afraid that's the law,'' I said ruefully. ''You could try talking to her.''

''But I don't know her name, or which magazine she works for. Could you . . . do you think you could find her?''

''I can't promise,'' I said, ''but I'll get to work on it.''

I wouldn't have to work very hard. I was having breakfast with her in the morning.

The woman who climbed out of the blue sports car in front of Ruby's house was beautiful enough to gladden the heart and lighten the feet of the pot-bellied male jogger trotting heavily down the opposite side of the street. Her ash-blond hair was brushed smooth and pulled back from the delicate oval of her face, and her slim skirt and color-matched burgundy sweater showed off her figure in a tasteful, understated way.

Standing in the door beside me, watching Elaine Emery lock her car and start up the walk, Ruby said, *sotto voce*, "Wow, what a knockout. No wonder Dolores was jealous!"

"Aren't you jumping to conclusions?" I asked. "You don't know that Dolores was jealous. And this woman might have been visiting Adcock on business." I felt more than a little deceitful. I knew that Emery was a journalist and that Dolores *wasn't* jealous, but I couldn't share either piece of information.

"Jumping to conclusions?" Ruby retorted between her teeth. "Just *look* at the woman! If she spent the afternoon alone with McQuaid, wouldn't you be jealous?"

The remark, innocent as it was, stung more sharply than a hundred nettles. The night before, after Dolores left, I had taken a long, hot bath and gone to bed with one of my favorite mysteries, intending to wait up for McQuaid. I knew he'd be interested in hearing about the suicide note Dolores had destroyed, and about the Adcocks' hasty and unplanned departures from Laredo and Corpus Christi. I was curious, too. What had Adcock done to earn a dishonorable discharge from the Rangers? What secrets did he carry to his grave? What story was Elaine Emery working on? Maybe McQuaid would have some insights.

I had wakened a little after midnight. The book was on the floor, the light was still on, and McQuaid hadn't come home. It was after three when he slid into bed, very quietly, obviously not wanting to wake me. He smelled of cigarettes and whiskey, and his breathing was heavy. I lay very still, wanting him, but not wanting him to touch me. It was easy to guess where he had been and who he'd been with.

He was still asleep, or pretending to be, when I got up,

put on my clothes, and headed for Ruby's early in the morning. My feelings were churning like molten lava, and every time I tried to sort them out, all I could come up with were hard, hurtful questions. Did he love her? Even if he didn't, even if he wanted us to go on together, could I? I loved him, yes, but loving wasn't enough. I had to trust him too.

The blond woman had reached the porch. "Good morning," she said, holding out her hand. "I'm Elaine Emery." I noticed that her nose was generously peppered with freckles and that her front teeth were uneven. Irrationally, I felt better about her. But that might be partly due to knowing about Adcock's suicide note. Whatever else she was, Elaine Emery wasn't a murderer.

Ruby and I introduced ourselves. Ruby asked, "Where's Justine? We thought you were coming together."

"We were," Elaine said, and added ruefully, "Justine got a call at the last minute. One of her clients—somebody pretty important, I gathered—is in some sort of jam, and she rushed off to take care of things. I'm not really a client, anyway. And not even Justine can be in two places at once. She sends her apologies." She looked from one of us to the other with an engaging frankness. "I hope you don't mind that it's just me."

"No, not at all," Ruby said, opening the door wider. "Come in. Breakfast is almost ready."

Personally, I was relieved that Justine had another bonfire to put out. Mind and body, she travels at a constant warp-nine, which is tough to handle most of the time but very tough before I've had my second cup of coffee. And I was glad to hear that Elaine didn't consider herself Justine's client. It lessened my ethical predicament somewhat.

The three of us trooped down the long, high-ceilinged hall toward the kitchen, where Ruby had been making pancakes and sausage. Ruby's house, a tree-shaded Victorian with original shutters and gingerbread, once belonged to our friend Jo Gilbert, who died a couple of years ago. Ruby bought it and has been working like fury to fix it up. She painted the outside in shades of gray, green, fuschia and plum, like one of those Painted Ladies you see in San Francisco. Inside, she painted and papered the walls, stripped the woodwork and floors to the original light oak, and replaced the water-stained ceilings—not to restore the house to its original condition, which was probably sedate and boring, but as she put it, "to bring a little bounce into the old girl's life."

The old girl does bounce. A brightly striped Guatemalan rug runs down the length of the central hall. The hallway walls are painted the color of orange sherbet and hung with photos of Ruby's two daughters: Shannon, who is about to graduate from the University of Texas, and Amy, whom Ruby gave up for adoption twenty-something years ago and who recently resurfaced, to Ruby's delight and the general consternation of the rest of the family. From Amy's adoptive parents, Ruby managed to assemble a dozen photos of Amy's growing-up years, and these are hung on the wall, next to pictures of Shannon. Ruby's ex-husband, Wade, who divorced her several years ago to marry his twenty-year-old secretary, is not pictured.

The kitchen bounces too, with red-and-white striped wallpaper, white cabinets, red table with vintage cloth, green chairs, and a wainscot border of red and green watermelons. Ruby, dressed to match, wore green skinny pants, a green-

and-red striped tunic, and red flats, her frizzy red hair held back with a green-and-red striped band. She reminded me of Lucy, from the old *I Love Lucy* show. She bent over to take a heaping platter of sausages and pancakes out of the oven, where they'd been keeping warm.

"There's orange juice in the pitcher and coffee in the pot," she announced. "Here are the sausages and pancakes, and scrambled eggs are on the way. I hope you aren't on a low-fat diet. If you are, you're out of luck."

A few minutes later, breakfast was on the table and we sat down to it, making small talk about Ruby's shop and my business and Elaine's plan to move to the country when she could afford it, avoiding anything even remotely connected to the reason for this early morning gathering. When we got to the coffee, though, Elaine took a steno pad and pen out of her bag and put them on the table.

"Justine outlined for me what you two learned yesterday," she said, "but I'd like to hear it from you. I'll take notes, if you don't mind."

I cleared my throat. Now was the time to fess up. "Ruby is the one who actually dug up the information for you. In fact, I ought to say right now that I'm only a spectator, not a player. If you'd rather, I can leave, and you and Ruby can get to work."

"I understand," Elaine said. "But please stay, China. I may need your help." She turned to Ruby. "Okay, Ruby. Shoot."

Ruby was unusually succinct. She told the story as she had uncovered it, from our talks with Dolores and Minerva to her interview with Mrs. Mosely and Fanny Couch. She added a piece of information I hadn't heard, however. The night before, when she had made a last-minute dash to Cavette's Grocery for breakfast sausages, she had run into Maude Porterfield, the J.P. who had been called in to rule in Adcock's death. According to Maude, the prints on the gun were Adcock's, and only the absence of a suicide note had kept her from immediately ruling that he had shot himself. She was virtually certain that the autopsy report would confirm it. She added that the police had verified Dolores's story about being at the grocery store, from a time-and-date-stamped credit card slip she'd provided.

"So that clears Dolores," I said. Of course, I already knew that. The suicide note Adcock had written cancelled out the other options.

Then I caught myself. I hadn't actually *seen* the suicide note. If a wife had murdered her husband and wanted to make it look like suicide, she might forge a note. But if she was afraid that her forgery might be detected, she could claim that there had been a note, and that she had burned it. She might even produce the ashes to prove her claim.

And that, come to think of it, had been the scenario of a case which had been tried in Houston seven or eight years before. As I remembered it, a jury had refused to convict a widow of murder even though the prosecutor maintained that the victim had not intentionally chugalugged a fatal mix of alcohol and barbituates. The jury believed the grieving widow's story about a burned suicide note. The insurance company cried "foul," but in the end the woman made off with a six-figure sum to console her for the loss of her nearest and dearest. Less than a year later, her wedding to a man twenty years her junior made the Houston *Post*'s society pages.

"You're saying that Adcock's wife is under suspicion?" Elaine asked, surprised.

Ruby looked uncomfortable. "I thought she might have done it. She must have been pretty angry when she saw you. She probably suspected that you and her husband were up to something. Anyway, the wife is always a suspect, isn't she? And the thing about the gun still bothers me. Why would Adcock shoot himself with his wife's gun when he had guns of his own? Personally, I'm still not convinced. Maybe the killer did it with an entirely different gun and then took it away with him. Or her," she added with a meaningful look at Elaine.

The import of the glance was not lost on the other woman. Elaine leaned forward, her eyes intent, her voice hard. "I don't know anything about a gun, but we'd better get one thing straight right now. I was not romantically or sexually involved with Roy Adcock. And if his wife couldn't trust him to talk to another woman on business, that's *her* problem, not mine."

Ruby raised her shoulders and let them fall. "Well, then, I guess the only question we haven't talked about is why he did it." She poured herself a second cup of coffee. "Since it looks like you were the last person to see him alive, maybe you can answer that."

Elaine sat silent for a moment. Finally, she said, "I'm afraid I can't. Adcock was depressed and unhappy when I got there, and he seemed even more depressed when I left. But he didn't say anything that indicated he was thinking of killing himself."

"Why *were* you there?" Ruby persisted. "And why did you want us to dig up all that stuff from the neighbors?

When Justine talked to us yesterday morning, she said you had some information that might become pertinent to the investigation, but you were worried about getting involved. I don't remember whether she actually said it or not, but she certainly implied that you were afraid.'' She tilted her head curiously. ''So what's the deal?''

''It's kind of complicated,'' Elaine said. She opened her purse and took out a business card for each of us. ''I'm a freelance journalist. I specialize in crime reporting.''

Ruby blinked. ''*Crime* reporting?''

''Have you written anything we might have read?'' I asked, pocketing the card.

Elaine shook her head. ''Mostly, I write for the South Texas papers. San Antonio, Brownsville, Laredo. Local stuff, pretty small potatoes.'' Her eyes glittered. ''But I'm on the trail of something important right now. This isn't an article for the hometown newspaper. This is a book. A big one. The case has everything—drugs, money, sex, corruption, smuggling, you name it.''

''Is that why you were talking to Adcock?'' I asked. ''You were doing research?''

She nodded. ''He had information about a crime that happened a couple of years ago—at least, that's what I was led to believe.''

''Who told you?'' I asked.

She shook her head. ''Sorry. My sources are private, and I aim to keep them that way. Anyway, I talked to him, and found him—shall we say—reluctant to part with information I was pretty sure he had. I felt he wanted to tell me but something was holding him back.''

''Fear, maybe,'' I said, remembering Adcock's abrupt decision to leave Laredo, then Corpus, and the paranoia that had led him to buy a gun for his wife.

"Oh, he was afraid, all right," Elaine said, sipping her coffee. "When we met before, he tried to get me to tell him who had named him as a possible informant, just as you did. It was clear that he was scared to death. And while I was there yesterday, he got a phone call. All I could hear was his end of it, of course, and he was guarded. But whatever he heard from the person on the other end of the line seemed to stun him. He began to shake, and I thought he was going to cry. Before the call, our conversation had been going pretty well. He'd even seemed cooperative. But that call changed everything."

"Do you think someone knew you were there and was warning him to keep his mouth shut?" Ruby asked.

"It's possible," Elaine said.

"Did he mention any names?" I asked.

"Names?" She thought. "I don't think so. No, there was something—Dude, Duke, Dugan, something like that, maybe. I didn't quite catch it."

"What happened then?" Ruby asked.

"He asked me to leave. I figured I'd call him later and arrange another meeting. Of course, I couldn't know he'd be dead in a couple of hours."

"Did you see a gun?" I asked. "On the desk, maybe?"

Elaine shook her head. "If he had a weapon, it wasn't out where I could spot it."

Ruby scratched the tip of her nose. "Why did you send Justine to see us? You weren't *really* afraid you were mixed up in a crime, were you?"

"Well, yes and no," Elaine said. "Justine and I play

poker with a couple of other women on Friday nights, and we heard about the shooting on the ten o'clock TV newscast. The reporting was so vague that I couldn't tell whether Adcock had been murdered or shot accidentally, or what. Thinking about it, I realized that I might have been the last person to see him alive, and that the police might consider me a material witness. You can guess why I didn't want to talk to them. I needed to find out what was going on.''

''That's where we came in, I suppose,'' Ruby said.

Elaine nodded. ''Justine was driving to Austin the next morning and suggested that she stop and ask you two to fish around and see what you could find. It seemed like a good idea to me, since you know the territory. It's hard for a stranger to learn anything in a small town.'' She made a face. ''Believe me, I've tried.''

''Well, then, I guess you've got what you want,'' Ruby said. ''If Adcock committed suicide, you're off the hook.''

''As far as the suicide is concerned, that's probably true,'' Elaine said. She jiggled her pen in her fingers, looking thoughtful. ''But Adcock's death hasn't ended my interest in *him*. He had some information I need, some documentation too—if he was telling the truth, that is. It was in a green folder on his desk, mostly typed, some handwritten notes. I want to see what's in that folder. Can you help me?''

''Why don't you just telephone Adcock's widow and ask her for it?'' I suggested.

''Because she'll turn me down,'' Elaine replied. ''Adcock as much as told me she didn't want him to have anything to do with me.''

''Why?'' Ruby asked.

"Because she was afraid, too," Elaine said. "I'm telling you, Adcock was sitting on a big secret, and I do mean *big*. It could blow the lid off—" She stopped. "Dolores Adcock was afraid. She probably still is, for that matter, and with good reason." She frowned. "It's absolutely clear that Roy Adcock killed himself?"

"Maude Porterfield thinks so," Ruby said. She gave Elaine a searching look. "Are you thinking that somebody else might have done it—the person who phoned him, maybe?"

"Someone else could very likely have had the motivation," Elaine said grimly. "But if you're sure it was suicide—"

"I guess nobody will be sure until the coroner says so," Ruby said.

"About that folder," I put in. "I know Dolores. I could talk to her if you like."

"She seems to trust China," Ruby offered.

"More power to you, then," Elaine said, closing her notebook. "I'd rather be up front about this if I could." Her face hardened. "But I *do* want it, and I'll do whatever I have to to get it. If it's what I think it is, it's dynamite."

I studied her. There was no point asking her what she thought was in the folder—she wouldn't tell me. Better to see if I could find it and go through it for myself. And I might also be able to use the material as a way of helping Dolores get something *she* wanted.

"Is there anything in the folder that will incriminate Adcock?" I asked. "If so, it could be hard for his widow to hand it over. She wouldn't want to turn loose of anything that would make him look bad."

It took Elaine a moment to answer. ''There probably is some incriminating stuff,'' she said at last. ''But that's not what I'm after. Tell her I think I can write up the story in a way that will make her husband look like a hero. And if she's a little short of money—''

''I don't think money is an issue,'' I said, ''and I'm not even sure she wants to turn him into a hero. If you can promise to keep her husband's name out of your story altogether, you may be able to get what you want. Anyway, I'll float the idea past her, and see what she says.''

''I'll promise her the moon, if I can get that folder,'' Elaine said fervently.

''All I can do is try,'' I said with a little shrug. I had a pretty good idea I would succeed.

Chapter Seven

Of hemp, or *Cannabis sativa*: The emulsion or decoction of the seed . . . stays bleeding at the mouth, nose, or other places, some of the leaves being fried with the blood of them that bleed, and so given them to eat.

Nicholas Culpeper
Culpeper's Complete Herbal, 1649

Cocaine, the widely known anesthetic, is derived from the shrub [*Erythroxylum coca*]. Inca Indians regarded coca as a divinity. Coca is the only source of cocaine, which rapidly stimulates the higher levels of the brain, giving one a sense of boundless energy and freedom from fatigue.

James A. Duke
Handbook of Medicinal Herbs

The February sun was shining cheerily when I arrived at the Adcocks' a half hour later, and a few more daffodil blossoms had put in an appearance among the weeds in the rocky border. A tomato-red cardinal, decked out for early-spring courting, was perched in a nearby pecan tree, spilling his brilliant song into the clear, mild air. I rang the doorbell four or five times before Dolores appeared, somewhat harried.

''Sorry,'' she said breathlessly. ''I was in the closet, sorting Roy's clothes for the Good Will people. They're coming tomorrow.'' She shut the door behind me. ''Would you like some breakfast?''

''Maybe just some coffee,'' I said. There was a large open box by the door filled with shirts, pants, sweaters, shoes. Roy's things. Looking at them, I was suddenly struck by a deep, gut-twisting sympathy. ''Do you have to do that today?'' I asked. In Dolores's place I'd have closed the closet door and postponed sorting clothes until the pain was less new, less raw.

''It has to be done sooner or later,'' she said. ''I thought I might as well get it over with.'' I noticed that a night's sleep had helped. She seemed rested and less gaunt and her eyes had lost some of the sad, haunted look. But she still wore the furtive, half-fearful frown I had noticed before. She smiled tightly.

''I guess maybe you're thinking it's hard-hearted of me to get rid of his stuff so soon,'' she went on. ''But I couldn't stand the sight of his clothes hanging there in the closet, and him never coming back to wear them.'' She straightened her narrow shoulders. ''I'm going to do the drawers next. I'd like to be finished with all of the personal stuff before the memorial service tomorrow afternoon.'' She looked at me. ''You'll come, won't you? It will be at a chapel in Austin. Captain Scott is setting it up. I can get you the address.''

''Of course I'll come,'' I said. ''And my offer to clean the office still stands.'' With luck, I would find the green folder. Then I could talk to Dolores about giving a copy to

Elaine, in return for her promise not to drag Adcock's name into print.

"Maybe you'd better take a look first before you commit yourself," Dolores said sadly. "I peeked in there this morning, but it made me sick to my stomach. The thought of him, lying there, bleeding—" Tears came to her eyes, and her chin quivered. "Really, you don't have to help, Ms. Bayles. It's too much to ask." Her voice caught. "There's a lot of blood all over everything."

I felt like putting my arms around her the way you'd comfort a little girl who has lost her parents. But I only touched her shoulder reassuringly.

"No problem," I said. "Have you got plenty of cleaning supplies?" I was rewarded with a nod and a grateful smile. The phone rang just then, and she hurried off as I opened the door.

The room Roy Adcock had been using as an office was good-sized, fifteen by fifteen feet or so, with a sliding patio door that spilled sunshine onto the yellow carpet. It was almost as sparsely furnished as the living room, with a gray metal desk and chair that looked like U.S. Army surplus, a long folding table stacked with books and papers, a bookshelf, an overstuffed chair, a lamp. A laptop computer in a gray plastic case leaned against the desk. A large Rand McNally map of Texas was pinned to one bare wall, but there were no mementos or pictures anywhere in the room. There was no folder on the desk, and no gun cabinet, either, which I found puzzling. Dolores had said her husband had several guns. Where had he kept them?

What there was plenty of, however, was blood. A pool of it had dried like dark red tar into the carpet under the desk; there was a long, bloody smear on the desktop and a trail of bloody drips down the front, and a sinister splatter of dark red drops against the yellow wall. I studied the carpet for a moment, considering whether the large stain was something I ought to tackle, then went to the door. Dolores met me with a bucket of water, a sponge and a roll of paper towels, and a bottle of Pinesol.

"I can handle the desk and the wall," I said, "but I think you should call a carpet cleaner. It's a job for a professional with the right kind of equipment."

She sighed. "I was afraid of that," she said. "I would like to move at the end of the week, and I don't want to pay for a new carpet, on top of everything else. I guess I should call the landlady and let her know what happened. She might know somebody who cleans carpets."

It was obvious that Dolores was not wise in the ways of small towns. The landlady had no doubt read about Roy's suicide in the *Enterprise*, or heard about it at the beauty parlor. She was probably anxious about her carpet, but too polite to call and inquire.

"Do you have a lease?" I asked.

"I think so," she said hesitantly. "Do you think there'll be a problem?"

"If there is, maybe I can help," I said. I took the cleaning supplies and got a small smile in return.

"That phone call just now," Dolores said nervously. "It was from a . . . from somebody I used to know, a friend. He'll be over in a couple of hours. But I . . . I guess you'll be gone by then."

I could take a hint. "I don't think this will take too long," I told her, and turned to get started.

She lingered at the door. "I wish I knew what to do with Roy's papers and things," she said. "Do you think I should burn them?"

"It isn't a good idea to burn personal papers until you've made sure there are no legal documents tucked in them," I said. "There might be a will or title to a property—something like that. I'll glance through the papers if you like." It was a duplicitous offer, because I was really after the folder. But her permission would salve my conscience.

She considered the suggestion for a moment, uneasily, as if she were about to say no. Then she changed her mind. "I guess that would be okay. I suppose Roy might have had a piece of property somewhere that I don't know about. I've already located the checkbook and the insurance papers," she added. "I called the agent this morning to ask whether the policy was good. He said he'd have the adjuster contact me to start the paperwork." She gave me a sideways glance. "I hope you don't think I'm in a hurry to collect. I just . . . well, I'm going to need money, that's all. I felt I had to know."

"I understand," I said. "By the way, where did your husband keep his handgun?"

"In the bottom right-hand desk drawer." She managed a little smile. "I'm going to brew a fresh pot of coffee. When do you think you'll be finished?"

"Give me about half an hour," I said.

I went back into the office, closing the door behind me. Cleaning up the dried blood wasn't a pleasant chore, but it didn't take more than a few minutes. I spread paper towels over the carpet to keep from making a bad mess worse, and went to work on the desk and the wall with Pinesol and the sponge. When the grim job was done, I emptied the bloody water onto a stunted-looking yaupon holly outside the door and started through the desk drawers, working from the top down. I was looking for two things: the green folder, and Adcock's gun—although I was still wondering, as Ruby had, why the man had used his wife's weapon instead of his own. It was a perplexing question.

The green folder wasn't anywhere to be found, and the gun wasn't in the bottom drawer, as Dolores had said. It wasn't anywhere else in the room, either, I decided, after a thorough search.

I stood in the middle of the room, looking around, frowning. A couple of Rangers—Dubois and somebody else—had been there yesterday morning, investigating what they thought might be a crime scene. Maybe they had taken it. But why? Adcock's gun wasn't material to their inquiry. And if the Rangers had wanted to remove anything from the room, even a piece of paper, they were required to give Dolores a receipt. She would have known that they had taken it.

The fact of the missing gun had faded into the background, however, by the time I completed my search, which turned up several other fascinating items. The first was a key taped to the outside back of the bottom drawer. I wouldn't have found it if I hadn't pulled the drawer out completely. The flat brass key, clearly for a safe deposit box, was stamped with the number 128. I pocketed the key, meaning to ask Dolores about it. But it had been carefully concealed in a relatively inaccessible place, perhaps to keep it from her. It was my guess that she knew nothing about any safe deposit box. If I was right, Roy Adcock had locked up something important, away from his wife.

The second and third items piqued my interest, but since today was Sunday, there was no way of checking them out. One was a blank, undated receipt from Getzendaner's Gun Shop, with nothing on it but a serial number. The receipt probably meant nothing, but I'd check into it anyway. The other was a bill from Doc Clarkson for $210 for three office visits, from mid-December to late January. Attached to the bill was an appointment confirmation slip. Adcock was supposed to see the doctor tomorrow morning at ten-thirty.

Curiously, I turned the bill over in my fingers. Most men are uncomfortable around doctors. They don't visit them just for the heck of it, and they certainly don't schedule repeat visits unless they've got a good reason. Why had Roy Adcock seen Doc Clarkson not just once, but three times? Had he been suffering from a serious illness? Again, it was an item worth checking.

But it was item number four that captured my attention. I was doing a quick sort through a stack of books on the table—mostly true-crime paperbacks, with a smattering of law enforcement texts and Ranger procedural manuals—when I discovered an unsealed envelope tucked inside a copy of *Bad Blood*. In it was a batch of statements and deposit-withdrawal verification slips from the Bank of Cayman Island. With them was a Texas driver's license.

I stared at the statements for a moment, the skin prickling across my shoulder blades. Then I sat down in Adcock's chair and began scanning the documents, handling them by the edges. It appeared that the bank account had been opened about two years ago. The statements and deposit slips reflected an irregular pattern of deposits and withdrawals—irregular but definitely impressive.

I whistled under my breath. A total of a quarter of a million dollars or so had been funneled through the offshore bank. There wasn't anything like that amount in it now, though. The last balance was only a little over ten thousand dollars, the most recent withdrawal having occurred a little over a week ago. The account was listed under the name of John Wainwright. The address was a post office box in San Antonio.

I bent over the driver's license and studied it. The photo showed a good-looking dark-haired man with tinted glasses, a wry half-smile, and dark eyes. The name and address on the license matched the name and address on the bank account.

Well. It didn't require a law degree to figure out that Roy Adcock had been using the alias John Wainwright to shift sums greatly exceeding the salary of a Texas Ranger in and out of a foreign bank account. Several explanations for this kind of suspicious money-handling, none of them legal, went off like Roman candles in my head. Most involved drug trafficking, which is the largest and most profitable herbal trade in the world. Of course, most people who enjoy growing and using herbs don't like to think about this, but it's true, and it merits sustained reflection.

Until the middle seventies, most street drugs—marijuana (*Cannabis sativa*, or hemp), heroin (derived from *Papaver somniferum*, the opium poppy), and cocaine (a product of *Erythroxylum coca*, a shrub revered as a god by the Inca Indians)—moved into the United States through New York City. Then, prompted by Drug Enforcement Administration crackdowns in the Big Apple, the Colombian drug lords relocated their port of entry to Miami and began transshipping their herbal products through the Caribbean. DEA agents stepped up patrols along the Florida coast and began seizing boats carrying multi-ton cargoes of marijuana, cocaine, and heroin. But although the newspapers were full of accounts of successful interdictions and Washington's drug czar was trumpeting victory in the War Against Drugs, there was just as much stuff on the street as there had always been, if not more. How was it getting into the States?

You guessed it. Mexico—which shares with Texas a half-dozen busy border crossings, nearly nine hundred miles of river that's so shallow you can wade across it without getting in over your knees, and a venerable folk tradition of smuggling. A few years back, DEA agents busted a warehouse in Sylmar, California, and came up with twelve million dollars in loose change and almost seven *billion* dollars worth of cocaine. When they traced the route of this massive haul, it turned out that all twenty-one-plus tons of it had come across the Texas-Mexico border.

That got the feds' attention, to put it mildly. But even though the Government continues to throw more agents into the breach, the drugs keep on leaking across the border. Since the inception of NAFTA, commercial truck traffic over the international bridges has doubled or tripled. Tons of high-grade Colombian dope are driven through the checkpoints tucked into clay flowerpots, cheap toasters, and assembled-in-Mexico television sets. The *pasadores*, or border crossers, don't run much of a risk that their wares will be discovered. With millions of vehicles coming across every year, inspectors are lucky if they can search ten percent of them.

Of course, a system as large and well-organized as the drug import trade involves *mucho* players, from the impoverished South American peasants whose coca is their only cash crop, to warehouse owners in border towns like Nogales and Matamoros, to streetwise kids who market the stuff in Detroit or Chicago. It's no surprise, and no secret, that the skids are greased all along the way by corrupt law enforcement officials, who look the other direction when a shipment crosses their territory. The evidence I held in my hand suggested that former Texas Ranger Roy Adcock, alias John Wainwright, had been on somebody's payroll. And judging from Adcock's take, the services he rendered had not been inconsequential.

I sat back, thinking. The bank account cast a whole new light over Adcock's life—and death. The old adage "Those who live by the sword, die by the sword" does not lie. At first blush, Adcock's death might look like a suicide, but the autopsy surgeon had not yet recovered the fatal bullet and DPS Ballistics had not yet matched it to the suspected weapon. And even if all indications pointed to suicide, there would still be room (in my experience) for reasonable doubt. Drug lords are notorious for knocking off an associate when they have no more use for him, or when he knows too much and seems inclined to spill it. Their usual method is along the lines of the traditional assassination: the hapless victim's hands are tied or cuffed and a single bullet is pumped into the back of the head. But there's no tradition that can't be violated. If it was learned that Adcock was talking to a crime reporter, his name could have gone to the top of somebody's to-do list, and his murder made to look like a suicide. He might even have been forced to write a note to his wife, then made to shoot himself. And don't say that's not possible. Faced with unspeakable alternatives, you might choose to kill yourself rather than endure a slow, tortured death.

But whatever had happened to Roy Adcock, he was dead, and the manner of his dying was police business. Which left Dolores, and that was what was bothering me. Drug traffickers have been known to include their victim's wife and family among their targets, on the theory that the husband may have shared secrets with his dearly beloved. If Dolores could identify Adcock's colleagues in the drug business, she was in big trouble. And even if she couldn't, there was nothing to keep Adcock's partners in crime from *thinking* she could.

There was also the matter—and no small matter, either—of the IRS, which goes after widows without compunction. If Dolores's signature appeared with her husband's on a joint 1040, the IRS would assume that she had not only known about the money but had enjoyed the ill-gotten gains right along with her miscreant husband. Whether she knew about the account or not, Dolores was in a tough spot. If I were her attorney, I'd have to advise her that her best course of action was full and immediate disclosure. And all things considered, I might also suggest that she get the hell out of Dodge and lay low for a while.

I slipped a piece of blank paper under the driver's license, folded it over and taped it. Adcock's prints were probably all over the laminate, and it wouldn't do to destroy them. I picked up *Bad Blood*, tucked the envelope containing the bank records and driver's license into it, and stuck the book under my arm. The laptop computer I set on the floor just inside the office door, where I could pick it up on my way out. It was time to have a serious talk with Dolores.

I found her in the bedroom, emptying the contents of the bottom bureau drawer into a big box. She straightened up, pushing her dark hair out of her eyes. "Did the stains come off the wall?" she asked worriedly.

"Pretty well," I said.

"I don't know how to thank you," she said. She put the box on the bed. "The coffee is ready. Would you like a cup?"

I looked around. "Before we go into the kitchen, would you mind showing me your husband's guns?" Maybe the missing handgun was with the others. It was worth checking.

"I've been trying to decide what to do with them," Dolores said. She opened a closet, now empty of clothes, and pointed to the back wall. Lined up in military precision were a pump shotgun, a .22 rifle, a deer rifle with a scope, and an AR-15. It was an impressive arsenal. The shotgun, the .22, and the deer rifle were not atypical for Texas, where hunting ranks right up there with football as the favorite male sport between September (when white-wing dove season opens) and January (when deer season closes). But the AR-15 was something else again. A civilian version of the Vietnam-era M-16, it's designed to kill people, not game. It's the kind of gun you might have if you're in cahoots with drug traffickers. It fit the profile of Roy Adcock that was beginning to emerge in my mind.

I turned back to Dolores. "Your husband's pistol wasn't in his desk," I said. "Did the investigator take it?"

"Ranger Dubois?" Dolores looked surprised. "If he did, he didn't tell me. You're *sure* it wasn't there?"

"I'm sure," I said. "Can you describe it?"

"It's a silver-plated .45 automatic with lots of engraving. It was Roy's father's gun." She chewed her lip nervously. "Come to think of it, I haven't seen it for a while." She frowned at me. "Excuse me, Ms. Bayles, but why are you asking about Roy's guns? Is there . . . some sort of problem?"

"I'm not sure," I said. "Maybe we'd better talk. Okay?" I was about to turn away from the closet when something caught my eye. The closet floor was hardwood, like the bedroom, but a piece of beige carpet had been laid down under the guns. Beneath the edge of the carpet, I saw a sliver of green.

Bingo. The green folder. I bent over and pulled it out. Beside me, Dolores stirred apprehensively.

"What's that?" she asked.

"I think maybe it has to do with the reporter you asked about," I said. "Would you object to my going through it, Dolores? There might be something in it that would help me to locate her and convince her to lay off."

She glanced at the folder nervously. "I don't know," she said. The uncertain, half-fearful look was back. "Maybe I ought to . . . just burn it, or something."

"If you want me to help you locate that journalist and negotiate with her," I said firmly, "you're going to have to trust me."

"You're right, Ms. Bayles." She sighed, a little girl's long, sad sigh. "I really *do* want that business straightened out. Roy doesn't deserve to have his name dragged through the mud. He did a lot for me—it's something I have to do for him.''

''Then let me take his computer, too,'' I said, ''and see if there's anything on it that might help. Once I've located the woman, we can discuss the situation and you can decide what to do. You can probably make some sort of deal with her—you give her the information she wants, she promises not to compromise your husband.''

With a little hesitation, Dolores nodded.

''One other thing,'' I said. ''What was Dr. Clarkson treating your husband for?''

''I don't know,'' Dolores said, startled. ''He didn't tell me. How do you know?''

''There's a bill in his desk,'' I said. ''If he didn't tell you, it's probably nothing.''

She frowned. ''Maybe not. He didn't like to worry me about things. Like money, stuff like that. Lots of times, he didn't tell me what was going on. Except when he gave me the gun. Then he told me I should be careful, and look out.''

''Did he say what he was afraid of?''

Her glance slid away, and she didn't answer.

''Let's have that coffee,'' I said. When we were sitting at the kitchen table over steaming mugs of coffee, I took out the envelope and unfolded the paper to reveal the driver's license.

''Is this your husband?'' I asked.

She glanced at it and her face became still. ''Yeah, sure,'' she said. Then she caught the name. ''But that's not—'' She looked up at me and frowned. ''That's not his name. I don't understand, Ms. Bayles. Where did you get this?''

''It was hidden in a book, along with statements from an

offshore bank,'' I said, and told her what else I had found. As I talked, I watched the reactions that crossed her face. Surprise, shock, stunned bewilderment, anger. Then she half turned away, hiding her face.

''I don't believe it,'' she whispered. ''Roy knew what those drug people are like. He would never take money from them. He couldn't—'' She stopped, her eyes wide and full of hurt. ''It's not true! It *can't* be true!''

''Can you suggest another explanation?'' I asked gently.

Her mouth twisted and she closed her eyes for a moment. ''No,'' she whispered. Then she opened them and said, in a flat, dull voice, ''I can say it's a lie, but if that's the way it looks to other people, nobody will believe me.''

''A forged driver's license and bank statements are pretty strong proof,'' I said. ''As far as your husband is concerned, they speak for themselves. He's dead and nobody can touch him. But you're alive, and you have to deal with the problems you've inherited.''

She chewed on that for a while. ''What problems?'' she asked at last.

I could have started with my concern for her physical safety, but I decided to begin at the other end, which might be easier to handle. ''The first is the IRS,'' I said. ''If I were your lawyer, I would advise you to contact the district office, show them the documents, and let them do their own investigation. If your husband didn't declare the income—which seems pretty likely to me—your disclosure may help exonerate you from a tax evasion charge.''

''Tax evasion?'' she whispered. She twisted her hands together. Her complexion had turned a sallow, sickly color.

''I don't want to turn him in. I don't see how I can—'' She stopped, got control of herself, and went at it from a different direction. ''You said the IRS is the first problem. What's the second?''

''Let's take this one thing at a time,'' I said sympathetically. ''Why don't you think for a few minutes, and then we'll talk some more.'' I stood up and looked around. ''Which way is the bathroom?''

The bathroom, a white-tiled room whose only decoration was a pink plastic flamingo on the windowsill, was located at the end of the hall. I spent a few extra minutes studying the crooked tiles over the bathtub, giving Dolores time to reflect. I didn't want to push her into anything, but she had to face the truth, no matter how unpleasant it was. Denial wasn't going to get her anywhere—except maybe to tax court.

That was good advice for me, too, I reminded myself, as I turned to look at my reflection in the mirror over the sink. There was a vulnerable, trusting part of me that wanted to deny that anything bad was happening. That part wanted to go dig in the garden, make a batch of lavender potpourri, line the dresser drawers with scented paper, and hope that everything would turn out okay.

But there was another part of me, a different, harder China, with a more cold-blooded take on the situation. *McQuaid is cheating on you,* that China observed with brutal candor. *Are you going to let him get away with it? He's walking all over you, pushing you around, taking advantage of your trust. So what are you going to do about it, huh*?

I stared at my reflection. What am I going to do? The

answer to that question shouldn't be too hard. After all, I am a businesswoman with a couple of college degrees and fifteen years of a professional career behind me. I can sort things out and come up with a list of priorities and a plan of action. Can't I?

Can you? the woman in the mirror asked back, and then answered her own question. *Like hell you can*, she said. *Face it, China. It's a lot easier to tell Dolores what she should do than it is for you to figure out what* you *should do*.

There was enough truth in this exchange to make me feel distinctly uncomfortable, and I brought it to a quick end. I was heading back to the kitchen when I heard a short, hard knock at the kitchen door, and the scrape of Dolores's chair as she got up to answer it. Not wanting to intrude on her and her visitor, I hesitated in the hallway outside the kitchen door.

The person who came into the kitchen was a man, Hispanic, judging from the heavy accent. "*Hola*, Dolores," he said in a honeyed voice. "Are you glad to see me, *amor mio*? Ah, you are still very beautiful, just as I remembered."

I don't speak Spanish, but even I knew that he had just called her his love. There was a stifled gasp and a moment's silence, and I could imagine the embrace I couldn't see.

"Amado!" Dolores exclaimed breathlessly, after a moment. "I . . . did not expect you for several hours yet. You'll have to come back later. Right now I have compa—"

"Gallardo sent me," Amado interrupted brusquely. "He said to tell you that he wants to help. You are going back with me. Pack a suitcase. Anything else you want to take,

I'll send Manuel to get it.'' He chuckled under his breath. ''You remember Manuel, eh, from the old days? He remembers you, *muñequita*. We all remember you.'' He chuckled again. ''My beautiful little dolly.''

''But I *can't* go with you,'' Dolores protested, her voice suddenly high-pitched and frightened. ''The memorial service is tomorrow, and there are many loose ends to tie up, this house, other things. Please, *por favor*, Amado, try to understand. I can't just *leave*. It would not be right. And people would . . . would ask questions.''

I wished I could see her face. What was going on here? Why was Dolores afraid of this man? And who the hell *was* he?

A chair scraped across the floor—Amado must be sitting down. ''Loose ends?'' he demanded roughly. ''Bullshit, baby. You got nothing to hold you here. That man you married, that *gringo*, he's *muerto*. He's dead, finished. Forget this house, forget the people. You're free. I don't want no argument.'' His voice became soft, silky, but the threat was still there. ''Gallardo don't want no argument. He just wants to help.''

It was time to make my appearance. ''Hey, Dolores,'' I said loudly, ''I just thought of something I forgot to ask you—'' I stepped through the door, then stopped, pretending surprise. ''Oops,'' I said. ''I didn't know anybody was here.''

The man straddling the chair, arms along the back, was smoothly handsome and indisputably Latin. He was dressed in gray slacks and an expensive dove-gray silk shirt, open at the throat to reveal a chest hung with gold chains. His hair was dark and curly, and his mouth was arrogant. His head snapped up when he saw me, and his brown eyes turned hard, suspicious. He swiveled toward Dolores.

"Who the hell is she? You didn't tell me anyone was here."

"I tried." Dolores was making nervous little patting gestures, rearranging her hair, her blouse. I had been right. There had been an embrace, and the sexual tension still flashed between them, like cloud-to-cloud lightning. She glanced at him, and the attraction was layered with fear. She looked uneasily back at me, her pale cheeks mottled red.

"Uh, Ms. Bayles, this is Amado Du—"

"Acosta," the man said. "Amado Acosta."

The red in her cheeks flared. "Amado is the . . . the friend I mentioned."

Suddenly wary, the man stood up and pushed the chair away. He was loose-knit and powerfully muscled, his lean face darkly brooding, his lips full and sensual, a south-of-the-border Sylvester Stallone. "I didn't get your name," he said.

"China Bayles." I did not hold out my hand. "I'm a friend of Dolores's."

"Oh?" He put a proprietary arm around Dolores's thin shoulders. "Any friend of Dolores is a friend of mine."

Dolores pulled away from him, trying to smile. "I've been working for Ms. Bayles, Amado." Her voice was phony, placating. "She's a . . . she used to be a lawyer. She's helping me take care of a few things."

Acosta's mouth tightened. "Such as?"

Dolores stirred nervously. "Oh, little things." She made

a hasty, deprecatory gesture. "The lease on this house, Roy's insurance. Nothing worth bothering Gallardo about, Amado. I'm sure that he has more important business on his mind."

"Yeah," Acosta said, only partly mollified. "But if you need any more legal help, you let me know. I'll see it gets done."

"Oh, I will," she said, with a quivering smile. She reached out to touch him, then drew her hand back. "I . . . I'm so glad you've come, Amado. It's good to have friends at a time like this." Her eyes slid to me, then back to him. The emphasis on *friends* was suggestive and false at the same time. "Roy would have been glad, too. You were his . . . friend. He would like it that you came."

Amado's full lips tightened perceptibly as he caught on. "Yeah, sure," he said heavily. "*Amigos* are good when there's a death." His voice became lugubriously mournful. "Roy took real good care of you, Dolores. You're gonna miss him, that's for sure. Anything your old *amigo* Amado can do, you just let him know what it is." He thought of something, reached into his pants pocket, and pulled out a wad of hundred-dollar bills. He peeled off a couple and handed them to me. "Will this cover your time, Ms. Bayles?"

"Thanks," I said, trying to keep my voice from going hard. "But this isn't fee work. I'm just helping out."

Dolores' mouth had twisted when she saw the bills. "I don't want your money, Amado. I'm not a little girl anymore. I pay my own debts."

"Is that right?" He replaced the bills on the wad and the

wad in his pocket, giving her a slow, lazy, cruel smile. "I understood that Roy covered a big, bad debt for you, Dolores. Whadya give him to get you outta there?"

In a flash, her hand went out to strike him. Just as fast, he grabbed her wrist and held it. She yelped, a wounded cry. I stepped forward. He took a step back.

"Don't be a fool, Dolores," he said between clenched teeth. "You fight me, you lose. You know that, *muñequita*." With a hard push, he released her. She fell back against the table, grabbing her wrist, holding it to her chest.

I planted myself front of her, not looking at him. "So what do you think about coming to stay with me, Dolores?" I asked, as casually as if I were asking her about going to the grocery store. "As I was saying, a few days, a week—you're welcome for as long as you need to get your bearings and decide what you want to do."

Still holding her wrist, face mottled, eyes on the floor, she shook her head. Her coarse dark hair had fallen forward, hiding her face.

"Hey, come on," I said, more gently. "You saw that big house. McQuaid and Brian and I just rattle around in it. You could have your own room, plenty of privacy. You wouldn't have to see anybody if you didn't want to."

Amado had stiffened. It wasn't hard to figure out that I was offering her an alternative, a safe haven, a refuge from him. The idea that she might be inaccessible probably offended the hell out of him.

She looked up. Her eyes went to him and lingered for a moment, with a look I couldn't read. She hesitated, looked back at me, half-pleading, and then took a sidelong step toward him.

"I'm staying here," she said. Her chin came up, her voice became stronger, she took another step. "I'll be all right, Ms. Bayles. Honest, I will."

"That's my little *muchacha*," Amado said, pleased. His arm went around her, pulling her into the curve of his body. "You see," he said to me, boastful. "Dolores, she ain't alone. She's got friends."

"Yeah," I agreed. "She certainly ain't alone." I picked up the green folder and the envelope from the kitchen table. "You have my phone number," I told her. "Call if you change your mind, or if you want to talk about any of the matters we discussed—particularly the tax situation. In my opinion, that's urgent. And I'll be glad to give you a ride to the memorial service tomorrow afternoon."

"Thanks," Acosta said, cordial enough, now that Dolores wasn't going anywhere—was, in fact, leaning her slender child's body against him as if she had no strength, her face hidden in his shoulder, her dark hair rippling sensuously over his arm. "But there's need for you to bother about any of that stuff. I'll see that Dolores gets to the service. From now on, I'm taking care of her." He looked down at her and raised his hand to her cheek. "Right, *muchacha*?" he asked tenderly.

Dolores made a sighing sound and turned her back on me, her arm going slowly around Amado's neck, almost as if it were moving against her will. He held her tighter, his face triumphant.

I let myself out without any more goodbyes. When I headed down the walk toward my car, the computer in one hand and the folder under my arm, I saw that there was a late-model black Ford parked in the drive. It wore Texas tags, which I jotted down, and a Mexican *turista* decal. The car was unremarkable—exactly the vehicle you might expect to belong to a man who didn't want to be noticed as he drove back and forth across the border.

I glanced at my watch. I had been in the Adcock house for just a little over an hour. In that space of time, the plot of this mystery had suddenly gotten much thicker.

Chapter Eight

Menthe, a beautiful and innocent maiden, fell in love with Pluto, but her infatuation with the unruly god of the underworld was sadly unwise. Pluto's sympathetic wife, Persephone (a human whom the lustful god had kidnapped and carried to the underworld), vowed to save Menthe from being betrayed to the terrible fate that had seized her. She transformed the girl into the small, nondescript green plant we call mint. To this day, its haunting fragrance reminds us of the strength of purity over passion.

Adapted from a Greek myth told in
Tales From the Plant Kingdom,
by Candace R. Miller

I drove home, looking forward to sharing my discoveries with McQuaid, who had asked me to hear what Dolores had to say and to figure out how Elaine fit into the situation. He might be interested to learn that the man whom Blackie considered a ''straight arrow'' hadn't been totally straight, after all. (Given that McQuaid himself had a reputation as a straight arrow, and given that his course over the past few weeks had been decidedly shifty, this made for a rather interesting parallel, I thought.) He might also be interested to learn that Adcock had an *amigo* with south-of-the-border connections.

But McQuaid's old blue truck was gone from its usual spot in the drive, and the house was empty. I pushed down my disappointment, checked the clock, and decided that I had time for a quick bite of lunch before I went to the shop. On Sundays, we open at one—or rather, *I* do. The new schedule puts Laurel in the shop on Tuesdays through Saturdays, I work one to five on Sundays, and we're closed on Mondays. A nice arrangement, which is supposed to give me more free time. And of course it does, although it doesn't include the hours I put into gardening, bookkeeping, crafting, and taking Thyme and Seasons to herb fairs and craft shows. Sometimes I envy McQuaid's teaching schedule—classes twice a week, a few committee meetings, and plenty of time for research. Not a bad deal.

I fixed myself a grilled cheese sandwich with a side of cottage cheese and another of applesauce, and brewed a pot of peppermint-and-rosemary tea. I craved something clean and healthy to get the taste of the morning out of my mouth. I needed a lift, too. Rosemary is good for that, and the mint gives a gentle boost. The combination doesn't have the kick of coffee, but it doesn't have the caffeine, either.

When the tea was ready, I put lunch on a tray and took it to the windowed breakfast nook, which looks out over the large, open back yard. Last summer, I painted the window frame and the wooden table green, covered the seat cushions with a green plaid, and put a pot of red geraniums on the window sill. Today, feeling the need to be soothed by creature comforts, I put a matching green plaid place mat on the table and drank my fragrant tea out of a green mug. As I ate the first half of my sandwich and drank my tea, I thought.

The morning had given me plenty to think about. The evidence suggested that Adcock had been reaping handsome rewards for doing something illegal, almost certainly involving drugs, and that he had dumped his profits into the Cayman Island bank. Knowing how stubbornly closed-mouthed and protective the offshore banks can be about their clients, I doubted that anything could be learned about Adcock's activities from that source.

But the key to the safe deposit box was another thing altogether. If I were Roy, I'd keep a stash locally, where I could get to it in a hurry. Tomorrow morning, I'd drop by the Pecan Springs Bank. While I was at it, I'd drop in at the gun shop and bother Frank Getzendaner about the receipt I had found. And Doc Clarkson's office was only a few doors down from the gun shop—I'd pay a visit there, too. His receptionist is a woman named Nellie Williams, who just happens to be Laurel and Willow's aunt. The fact that Pecan Springs is a small town can sometimes be truly irritating. Right now, though, I was grateful.

I finished my cottage cheese and began on the second half of my sandwich. Something else was bothering me. If the discovery of the offshore stash had radically changed my ideas about ex-Ranger Roy Adcock, the events of the morning had also given me a new slant on his widow. Amado Acosta might be a friend, but their relationship was certainly more complex and intimate than that. A former or current lover, perhaps? The business about his being a friend of Roy Adcock's had struck me as totally phony, and Acosta himself seemed a very shady character. Did the man pose a threat to Dolores? Very likely, and in more ways than one—but there wasn't much I could do about it. I had made it very clear that she could come here if she wanted to leave. And she had made it equally clear that she intended to stay with him. Her last gesture, her arm coming up around his neck, had spoken for her.

But Acosta's appearance on the scene wasn't the only thing that troubled me about Dolores, now that I had the time to think about it. Her husband had been dead for barely forty-eight hours, and she was already getting rid of his personal effects, making plans to collect his insurance, and packing to move—hardly the doings of a distressed widow. Toss in a Latin Lothario with plenty of sex appeal, and I couldn't be blamed for feeling that Dolores Adcock might have deliberately set out to misrepresent herself and mislead me.

I frowned. What *was* her hurry? In the light of the evidence I had turned up this morning, and in the continuing absence of a coroner's confirmation of Adcock's suicide, I might revisit Ruby's original theory that Dolores's husband had been murdered. And if I were of a cynical turn of mind, I might even think that Dolores had killed him, or that she had been part of an assassination plot.

Thinking back, trying to be objective, I had to admit that Ruby's suspicions of Dolores might have some foundation in fact. Dolores only claimed that there was a suicide note—she hadn't actually produced it. And while she had responded to the offshore bank account as if it were a total surprise, she could have been putting on an act. It was entirely possible that she knew everything: knew about Adcock's phony identity, his Cayman Island account, his dealings with the drug ring. The bank account had been opened just two years ago, about the same time that they'd been married. Maybe Roy had shared everything with his new bride. Maybe he had even brought her into the scheme.

But thinking of Amado Acosta and wondering exactly what his Mexican connections were and how he figured in this developing scenario, I was suddenly struck by a new and even more intriguing possibility. Maybe it had been the other way around. Maybe it was *Dolores* who had brought her husband into the ring. A renegade lawman was a valuable asset to a smuggling operation. Had she charmed him, turned him, then married him to ensure his continuing cooperation? Granted, shy, innocent-looking Dolores didn't exactly seem the type, but what did that mean? She could have been used by somebody else, especially if she was in love with that somebody, or if he had some sort of dark power over her. Maybe that was where Acosta came in, with his underworld good looks.

But I was jumping to conclusions—interesting, maybe, but conjecture. I finished my applesauce and pulled the green folder toward me. It was time to stop speculating and look for some hard answers.

But the green folder didn't yield anything that seemed connected to the current situation. When I opened it, I found a jumble of press clippings, copies of reports, notes of interviews, and hand-written chronologies, all apparently related to a crime that took place a couple of years ago: the kidnapping and murder of a young man named Frank Harris, Jr.—a memorable crime, in more ways than one.

Frank Harris was the son of a wealthy family which had been active in South Texas politics for generations. After an undistinguished undergraduate career at the University of Texas Business School, the boy had joined the San Antonio-based family firm, the largest trucking concern in Texas, which kept a fleet of Peterbilt tractors and trailers sailing the Interstates from one corner of the state to another, and beyond. As the only child, Frank Junior was due to inherit the whole kit and caboodle.

But young Frank didn't live long enough to enjoy the fruits of the family labor. He fell in with evil companions and wound up both using and pushing. One night he didn't return to the family mansion, and the next day his daddy got a call demanding two million dollars in return for the release of the wayward son, the unmarked bills to be dropped into a certain trash can on the Riverwalk. Frank Senior made the required deposit, but Frank Junior didn't show up.

As the weeks went by, the expanding investigation involved the local police, the sheriffs of three counties, and the Texas Rangers, who ultimately took charge. At one point, the Rangers announced that they were confident of making several arrests, and they scheduled a news conference for the next day, presumably to declare the case solved. But the news conference was canceled, and that was the last anybody heard about arrests. Several months later, a couple of Kerrville kids out hunting for Indian artifacts found Harris' decomposing body in a shallow grave. The trail was stone cold, the kidnappers and the ransom money were long gone, and the case was never solved.

In the end, of course, the Rangers took the biggest hickey, in part because they had been so publically confident of success. The deeply aggrieved father, who knew which strings to pull and whose cages to rattle, took his complaints about the mishandling of his son's case to the State Capitol. His criticisms did not fall on deaf ears. They resulted in the resignation of the director of the Department of Public Safety and the appointment, about six months ago, of a new one.

I riffled through the newspaper clippings, scanned the reports, and looked over the interview notes, signed by Roy Adcock, who had apparently been a member of the investigating team. None of the names rang a bell, and since I didn't have more than a sketchy knowledge of the crime, Adcock's notes weren't very instructive. The investigators seemed to have started with a fairly substantial list of suspects, but hadn't had a lot of luck in paring it down. I wondered how many taxpayer dollars had been spent on the investigation, and whether anybody thought it had been worth it.

So much for the folder. I closed it, feeling frustrated. So Adcock had investigated Frank Harris's death, and run into a stone wall. So what? If the old murder case was related to Adcock's death, the connection wasn't obvious. Still, maybe I shouldn't dismiss it so easily.

I poured the last of the tea, added a spoonful of honey, and thought for a moment about Elaine Emery. Having seen the folder she was so anxious to get her hands on, I could make an informed guess about the project she was working on. It was the Harris case. She had wanted to interview Adcock because she thought he knew something that nobody else knew.

Sipping my tea, I reflected on her account of their conversation and remembered something else: the phone call that had interrupted it. Elaine had said that the discussion had been going pretty well until somebody phoned, and that when Adcock hung up, visibly upset, he had terminated their interview. Shortly thereafter, he was dead.

I put down my cup and leaned on my elbows, frowning. So? The man had gotten an upsetting phone call, and he had decided, after all, not to talk to a journalist about an old case. To assert a cause-effect connection between the two events was to commit a *post hoc* fallacy—a brand of illogical reasoning that lawyers regularly foist on unsuspecting juries. But the phone call bothered me. Who had phoned? Why had Adcock responded so emotionally? Was there any connection between Elaine Emery's visit and the call? Was there any link between the call and his death?

Suddenly I was curious—no, I was more than curious. I really wanted to know how Roy Adcock had died, and why, and how Elaine Emery was involved. And maybe I was just feeling churlish about Dolores, but I also wanted to know what *her* role was in all of this.

But there was more, of course. I glanced at the clock. It was now twelve-thirty, and I hadn't obsessed about McQuaid and Peggy for more than two or three consecutive minutes all morning. With any luck, I could go on being curious about Adcock's death and angry about Dolores's perfidy (if that's what it was) for several more days. I seriously doubted it, but the possibility did exist, and I have learned that it is important to be optimistic in life.

So there it was: a handful of good reasons to go on poking my nose into something that essentially didn't concern me. But the minutes were fleeting. I rinsed my dishes, changed into slacks and a sweater, and drove to the shop, the Adcock matter still on my mind. After I unlocked the doors, retrieved the cash drawer from its hiding place under the dust rags, pushed the wooden plant rack out front, and waited on two early-bird customers, I dug out Elaine's number and telephoned her. I wanted to let her know that the folder had surfaced and ask her some questions about it. But I got nowhere with that plan, because what I heard when I dialed the number was Elaine's recorded voice crisply instructing me to leave a message.

I did get to talk to Ruby, though, and Sheila. I was standing on a stepladder, moving a display of handmade soap from a high shelf to one lower down, when Ruby came through the connecting door. The soap—palm-sized bars rich with coconut and olive oil and fragrant with lavender and patchouli—comes from Little Creek Farm in Missouri, where Sunny Gogel makes it in her kitchen. It's especially popular in our gift baskets.

"Well, what do you think?" Ruby demanded.

"I think it looks better on this shelf," I said, adding a glass jar of rose potpourri and stepping off the ladder to admire the new display. "Down here, people are more likely to pick it up and smell it." I leaned over and did just that. Sunny's soaps smell like a fresh summer morning.

"I'm not talking about your soap display," Ruby said. "I'm talking about Elaine Emery."

I put the soap down and turned around. "Two minds with a common thought. I just tried to phone Elaine a little while ago. What are *you* thinking about her?"

Ruby went over to the table where I had set out a plate of lavender cookies and my favorite brown-glazed teapot filled with cinnamon-spice tea—nice treats for customers on a chilly February afternoon.

"I hate to say it," she said, pouring a cup of tea, "but I have my doubts. About her motives, I mean."

"Doubts?" I asked. "What do you mean?"

"After you left this morning, she hung around for a little while, talking. She propositioned me."

I grinned. "Oh, yeah? She must have moved pretty fast. You hadn't even gotten to the hand-holding stage when I left."

Ruby gave me a if-looks-could-kill glance. "She wanted me to get that green folder she saw on Adcock's desk before he died. She even suggested that if you couldn't get Dolores to hand it over, I could sneak over there and filch it. She said she was willing to pay whatever I thought the job was worth." Ruby perched on the wooden stepladder, balancing her cookies on her knee. "Does that sound like responsible journalism to you, China? I suppose it's only petty larceny, but still—" She took a bite out of her cookie. "She must really want that folder. I wonder what's in it."

"Well," I said, "if you really want to know—"

So I told her what was in the folder, along with a detailed synopsis of the events of the morning: what I had found, what had happened after Amado Acosta put in an appearance, and what I thought it might mean. Ruby listened with growing attention, her eyes widening. Every now and then she would shake her head, or mutter "No kidding!" or "Would you believe *that*!" at some pertinent point.

I was nearly finished with my account when Sheila came in, elegant in a beige jacket and slacks with a cream-colored shell, gold jewelry, and beige pumps. She had gone to church with Blackie that morning (he sings bass in the First Methodist choir), and to Sunday dinner at the minister's house, and she hadn't changed yet. She had been in on this case almost since the discovery of Adcock's body. And since she knew nothing of what had happened subsequently, I went back to the beginning, to the very first conversation with Justine, and related the whole sequence of events all over again. Ruby helped, filling in the details I forgot.

The story took a little while, because there was a lot to tell and because we were interrupted by Myrtle Cowgill, who celebrated her eighty-seventh birthday last week by baking a German chocolate cake and throwing a wild party at the Pecan Springs Senior Citizens Center. Myrtle came in to replenish her supply of St. John's Wort oil, which she uses as a rub to relieve her sciatica. That transaction took a while, too, because she wanted to tell us how well her toe-nail fungus was responding to the horsetail soak she'd been using for the past two months and ask whether it was really true that peppermint oil could heal cold sores. I showed her a recent research reference to the use of peppermint as an antiviral in the treatment of herpes simplex and suggested that she might also want to try tea tree oil (*Melaleuca alternifolia*) on the fungus. Distracting, but that's the way life is. It is only in fiction that the protagonist moves with a single-minded, one-point focus, screening out everything that isn't related to the plot. Real people have to deal with the Myrtles of this world, who have sciatica and cold sores and want to tell you about them.

"Now, where were we?" Ruby asked, when Myrtle had gone.

"China was telling us about that Latin character," Sheila

said, "the one with the gold chains around his neck and the Sylvester Stallone body."

I went back to the story. When I finished, Sheila shook her head incredulously.

"You guys amaze me," she said, looking from me to Ruby and back again. "You really do. How you managed to dig up that stuff in less than forty-eight hours—" She cocked her head. "The Whiz is right. You two ought to go into the PI business. You could make big bucks. It would be exciting work, too."

"Thanks," I said, "but I've got all the exciting work I can handle right here. Where else can you find out how to soak away toenail fungus, in thrilling detail? To tell the truth, that's about enough excitement for a Sunday afternoon."

Ruby looked thoughtful. "What I want to know," she said, "is the connection between Dolores and that Acosta character. Is he her old boyfriend? A current boyfriend? What?"

"For that," I said thoughtfully, "I guess we'd need to know more about Dolores. Maybe we ought to do some digging into her background, see what kind of facts we can turn up. Like, who was she before she married Roy?"

"I thought you weren't interested in the detective business," Ruby said. "I thought you said Myrtle's toenail fungus was enough excitement for one day."

I shrugged. "Well—"

"If it's the Adcocks you're interested in," Sheila put in, "I might be able to help." She hoisted herself onto the counter and kicked off her pumps, wiggling her hose-clad toes with a look of relief. "Blackie did some checking yesterday with one or two of Adcock's colleagues in the Valley. Want to know what he found out?''

We did, so Sheila told us. And as her account went on, we listened with greater and greater attention. Until a couple of years ago, Roy Adcock's record as a Texas Ranger had been exemplary. He had been a committed lawman, a man of true grit, a believer in the Ranger mythology, and unwavering in his devotion to Truth and Justice.

But about the time he married Dolores, Adcock changed. He began to ''turn sour,'' as one of his buddies put it to Blackie. Cynical, bitter, disenchanted with the brotherhood. His work got sloppy, his attention drifted, his energy flagged. The buddy chalked up Adcock's disillusionment to the hiring of the first two women Rangers, an event that most Rangers viewed as something akin to an outbreak of bubonic plague. ''Hell,'' his friend had said disgustedly, ''*all* of us felt like jumpin' ship. We don't need no women on the force.'' Whether that was indeed behind Adcock's discontent, or something else, nobody knew. But his resignation, when it came, had not been a surprise.

If the first part of Sheila's story was interesting, the second was stunning. A little over two years ago, just three days prior to her marriage to Roy Adcock, Dolores (whose name at the time had been Dolores Francesca Dunia) was released from the Women's Unit at Gatesville State Prison, where she had served five years of a ten-year sentence for a drug-related homicide.

I shut up shop at five, cleared out the cash register, and drove home, still turning over the various bits and pieces of Sheila's story in my mind. What she had told us supported my suspicion that Roy Adcock had been mixed up in something large, lucrative, and illegal, and that his wife was an informed participant in the project.

But I was too close to the situation to be objective, and there weren't enough facts to lead to a solid conclusion. It was time to talk it over with McQuaid and get his take on the situation. After all, he was the one who had assigned me to talk to Dolores and to find out what was going on with Elaine Emery.

But McQuaid *still* wasn't there. I got home to an empty house and a hastily scrawled note on the back of an envelope, stuck under the catsup bottle on the kitchen table. I read it, then read it again.

Dear China, it began. *I'm leaving for a few days. I hope you won't mind looking after Brian. I'll check in tomorrow night to be sure he's okay—in the meantime, call my cellphone number if there's an emergency. When I get back, we have to have a talk. M.*

At the bottom, there was an arrow. I turned the envelope over. On the other side he had written: *P.S. Your mother called. She wanted to know when we're getting married. I told her she'd better ask you.*

I sat down and read the note, front and back, for the third time. McQuaid has never been known for his romantic letter-writing style, but this communication was more terse any he had ever left me. What's more, he'd never before gone away without telling me where he was headed and when he'd be back. He'd never before simply signed his initial without adding "Love" or "CYK" (Consider Yourself Kissed), or even a funny face. And the curt P.S.—I could imagine his mouth as he wrote it, set and cold, his eyes gun-steel blue.

I leaned back in the chair. Where had he gone? With whom? I could probably call him on his cell phone and demand to be let in on the secret, but to tell the truth, I didn't want to know. I sat for a moment feeling betrayed and abandoned, feeling sadder and more disconsolate than I had ever been in my life. From the tone of the note, it seemed clear that there wouldn't be much to talk about when he came back, except to decide which of us was going to move out. And Leatha could forget about white lace and promises—there wasn't going to be any wedding.

I balled my hands into fists and pressed them against my eyes, willing myself not to cry. I wanted to go to Ruby and throw myself into her arms, but she was cooking dinner for her daughters tonight, and I didn't feel like coping with curious questions from Amy and Shannon. And Sheila was with Blackie. Everybody has *somebody*, I thought self-pityingly. I was the only one who was all alone.

But I wasn't alone. Brian would be home from his Scout trip in a little while. I gathered my resources and pulled in a long, steadying breath. I wasn't going to sit around feeling sorry for myself, even if my world had suddenly tilted on its axis. I certainly didn't feel like returning my mother's call—that could wait until McQuaid and I had talked. But there was something else I could do, I thought, as my eye fell on Adcock's laptop computer, which I had left by the door.

It took a couple of minutes to find the secret combination of buttons to open the machine, the designers of which blithely assumed that if you are motivated to buy one of these things, you are smart enough to figure out how to raise the lid. I hate technological wizardry that assumes a level of competence slightly beyond a post doc in electronic engineering. After several false starts, I managed to get the damn thing set up and turned on, but that was as far as I got. I still have fond memories of an old Underwood portable that gave me carpal tunnel syndrome when I was a college freshman. I do the shop accounting on an ancient Apple IIE (older and more reliable than God). And I am minimally competent on McQuaid's IBM clone, on which I produce the store newsletter in Wordstar 5, a piece of software as archaic as Classical Latin. The laptop baffled me—until Brian came home.

"Hey, like, awesome," he exclaimed happily. "A new laptop! Where'dja get it, China?" Without waiting for an answer, he spilled his sleeping bag, his skateboard, his backpack, and a bag of cold french fries in the middle of the kitchen floor and rushed over to the table where I sat brooding over the screen, like the Hunchback of Notre Dame at the great organ.

"Jeez," he whispered, touching it with a reverent, catsup-smeared finger. "A 760-E, with a 133-megahertz Pentium processor and 16-bit stereo audio! Max cool!" Without hesitation, he went straight to the heart of the matter. "What games did it come with?"

"Games?" I asked darkly. "How should I know? I don't do Windows." I had been fiddling with the damn thing for twenty minutes, and I had not gotten beyond the initial screen. It was filled—helpfully, I am sure—with a constellation of cute, cheerful icons, all of which were Greek to me. "It isn't mine," I added, as if this fact explained my abysmal ignorance. "I borrowed it."

Brian pulled up a chair and sat down beside me. "Well, whoever you borrowed it from is rolling in bucks," he said. "Do you know how much this baby cost?"

"No," I said. "How much?"

"I saw it in a catalog for seven thousand."

"Dollars?" I asked, startled.

"Bottle caps. Of course, that was a couple of months ago. You can probably get it el cheapo today." He pushed at me. "Can I sit there?"

"Don't break it," I said automatically.

"I *won't*." He was running his fingers lovingly over the keyboard. "With this I could go anywhere in cyberspace, in a nanosecond. Who'd you borrow it from, China?"

"From a former Texas Ranger," I said, thinking that a seven-thousand-dollar piece of equipment that would fly me to the moon and back in nanoseconds was just another bit of evidence that Roy Adcock had been up to no good. "It may be a very expensive computer," I added pettishly, "but there's something wrong with it. The mouse is missing."

Brian gave me the disdainful look that computer-literate twelve-year-olds reserve for the typewriter generation. "It's right there in front of your nose," he said, pointing to a gizmo on the keyboard.

"That thing?" I scoffed. "That's not a mouse."

"Right. It's a TrackPoint Three integrated pointing device. Light-years beyond a mouse."

"Oh," I said, in a small voice. With an attempt at nonchalance, I added, "Do you think you can make it work? The computer, I mean. I'd like to know what's on it."

"We can browse File Manager," Brian said. "That'll tell us what's on the hard drive. But this little beauty's got one point oh eight gigabytes of storage. It may take a while to see what's there."

I glanced at him while he typed in a couple of commands that made the icons disappear and the screen fill with a list. Brian is only twelve, but he's already a miniature of his dad—dark hair with a cowlick that won't quit, pale blue eyes, quirky grin, sometimes so bright I marvel at him, sometimes so silly that he makes me giggle like an eight-year-old, sometimes so dense that I can only throw up my hands in despair. A regular kid, and then some. If there were games lurking on Roy Adcock's one point oh eight gigabyte hard drive, they would not escape his eagle eye.

But there were no games. "Rats," Brian muttered. "Only some old word processing program and a few data files. Not worth messing with." He reached for the power switch.

"Whoa!" I put my hand over his grubby one, which at some recent time had evidently held a chocolate bar and a grape soda, in addition to a hamburger and french fries. "Data files? What's on the data files?"

"How should I know?" He snatched his hand back. Like most pre-adolescent boys, he has an aversion to being touched by a female of the species. I have hugged him a time or two, but I have to catch him first, and he is fleet of foot. "If you want to look at the data files," he added carelessly, "just bring them up and read them." He slid off the chair. Now that he had established that there were no games, his attention span had shut down. "What's for dinner?"

"Wait!" I cried, and grabbed for him. "I can't bring the files up," I confessed. "I don't know how." I was beginning to feel (not for the first time) like a dinosaur of very little brain, mired in a decaying swamp while other, more clever creatures were out there surfing the Net, plotting their evolution into self-made lords of the universe.

He gave me a pitying look, as if I had just announced that I could not tie my shoelaces, and sat down again. "I don't know how either," he said, "but I can show you the filenames. Will that help?" With an airy confidence, he typed something and hit the Enter key. I leaned forward and peered at a long list of files. Most were abbreviated gibberish compressed into an eight-character string, but two were in plain English. *Diary* and *Notes*.

"Diary!" I exclaimed. "Let's look at Diary."

Brian shook his head. "I don't know to run the word processor," he said, and got up again. "You'll have to get Dad to help." He looked around expectantly. "Where is he? Upstairs?"

There was no point in involving Brian in our troubles. I assumed a carefully neutral voice. "Off doing research. He left a note saying he'll be gone for a few days. He'll give you a call tomorrow night, though. You can ask him then when he'll be home."

"But I'll be at Scouts tomorrow night!" he lamented.

"So? He'll remember and call later." I managed a lopsided grin and changed the subject. "When did you eat last? Not counting the french fries."

"At lunch." Brian put out his lower lip. Juvenile electronic wizard he may be, but he's still a little boy, and he was hurt. "Dad *said* he'd be here," he said. "He was going to help me with my social studies report tonight. And I wanted to tell him what I saw at the Ranger museum." He sighed. "Those Rangers, they're really cool, China. Nobody can beat a Ranger, not even the toughest, meanest, smartest outlaw. They're the best in the West. They're better than anybody who ever lived."

"I'm sorry your dad can't be here," I said truthfully. I had a thing or two of my own to tell McQuaid about Rangers, although my story didn't quite sound like his son's. I put on the grin again, made my voice light, and gave Brian an affectionate cuff on the shoulder. "Tell you what, pardner. How about if we go to the Taco Cocina for Mexican food, and you can tell *me* all about the Ranger museum. And when we come home, I'll help you with your social studies report."

His glance was skeptical. "You don't know anything about gun control. I'm supposed to write a paper on it."

Why do boy children always assume that mothers and other girl-types are totally ignorant of anything having to do with guns, cars, and space travel? "Actually, I know quite a lot about it," I said, "although I can't pretend to be totally unbiased."

He brightened a bit. "Yeah, well, Mexican food would be good." The brightness dimmed and he sighed. "I just wish Dad would stay home sometimes," he said sadly.

So did I.

CHAPTER NINE

> Thus have I lined out a Garden to our Countrey House wives, and given them Rules for common hearbes.—The skill and paines of weeding the Garden with weeding knives or fingers, I refer to themselves and their maides. . . . I advise the Mistresse either to be present herselfe, or to teach her maids to know hearbs from weeds.
>
> William Lawson
> *Countrey Housewife's Garden*, 1617

The shop is closed on Mondays, which gives me a little extra breathing space. I saw Brian off to school at seven-thirty, then sat down at the kitchen table to bring the Thyme and Seasons' cash journal up to date and get the bank deposit together. This little chore took almost an hour because I was off by $122.17, an odd amount that didn't tally with anything and proved very difficult to track down. I had just discovered with relief and a great deal of annoyance that I had double-counted a check, when the phone rang. It was Elaine Emery.

"Sorry I couldn't get back to you yesterday," she said. "What's up?"

"I've located the green folder," I said. "Are you still interested?"

"Am I interested?" she said exultantly. "Are you kidding? How quick can I get it?"

"I have to talk to Dolores Adcock," I said. "I'll try to catch her this morning." I now had several reasons for wanting to talk to Dolores. Since there wasn't anything incriminating in the folder, I didn't see why she couldn't trade it for Elaine's promise to lay off her late husband. But I wasn't sure how she'd feel about it.

"That'll work," Elaine said. "Adcock's memorial service is in Austin this afternoon, and I'm planning to go. Pecan Springs is on the way. How about if I stop and pick up the folder around one o'clock?"

I found it interesting that Elaine planned to attend Adcock's memorial service. Was she motivated by curiosity, or sympathy for the widow, or was there something else on her mind? But I only said, "Why don't we aim for lunch? If Mrs. Adcock gives her okay, I can let you have copies of the material then."

"Well—"

I could guess the cause of her hesitation. She knew I was going to pump her for information, and she didn't want to give me the chance. But it was tit for tat. She got copies of what was in the folder, and I got a shot at what she was carrying around in her head.

I primed the pump a little. "It's to your advantage to see me," I said. "For all you know, I may have other information that might be helpful to you."

That did it. "Lunch it is, then," Elaine said. "You can't begin to guess how important this is," she added fervently.

"To tell the truth," I said, "I'm beginning to be curious about your interest in the Frank Harris murder. I assume that's your target,'' I added, ''since the material in the folder concerns the Harris case exclusively.''

There was a small silence. In it, I could hear her guard coming up. ''I told you,'' she said. ''I'm writing a book.''

''I remember,'' I said, and added, quoting her, '' 'Drugs, money, sex, corruption, smuggling, you name it.' As I remember the Frank Harris case, the description fits pretty well, except for the sex. I don't recall anything particularly outstanding along that line. Or maybe you know something that didn't make the newspapers.'' Elaine probably knew plenty that the local editors hadn't seen fit to print. The controlling interests in the San Antonio media take family values to heart.

She cleared her throat again. ''Don't go spreading it around,'' she said carefully, ''but yes, I'm working on the Harris case.''

''Any special angle?''

''Well, maybe.'' She paused, debating whether to tell me or keep it to herself. Pride in her investigative talents won out over caution, and she said, ''I've uncovered a connection to Rafael Villarreal. He's a—''

No fooling. ''I know who he is,'' I said dryly.

Rafael Villarreal is a notorious Mexican drug trafficker whose name is only whispered in San Antonio, Brownsville, and El Paso—and never spoken at all south of the border, where the *policia* have learned to be circumspect. He was just beginning to come into his own the year I left the law firm, and since then I'd heard that he'd pretty much cleaned out the competition and was now Honcho Numero Uno of the border drug trade. If Elaine was planning to make the name Villarreal a household word, she should equip herself with some substantial firepower and get Sheila to teach her to use it. But she might as well double up on her life insurance, because not even an AK-47 would see her through.

Elaine laughed, high and nervous. "You can see why I don't want you to talk about it. As a matter of fact, I'm worried that the news has already leaked. I think I'm being followed."

"Why am I not surprised?" I asked. "Believe me when I say that his name will not pass my lips." I paused, thinking about the notes and clippings in the folder. "Roy Adcock was an investigator in the Harris case. Did he play any other role?"

The silence was eloquent. Finally, she said, "I don't think that has any bearing on—"

"Look, Elaine," I said patiently. "I have no intention of muscling in on your story. But I don't feel comfortable advising Dolores Adcock to turn over her husband's notes without knowing more about his connection to the case."

There was a lengthy pause while she gave this some thought. Finally she asked, "Do you represent Dolores Adcock?"

"I'm serving as her adviser in this matter," I said, my voice firm and truthful—as it should have been, for I was not telling a lie. I just wasn't telling the whole truth. "You can ask her for the folder outright, if you think she'll give it to you. Or you can work through me. What'll it be?"

She capitulated without grace. "Where are we having lunch?"

"There's a restaurant called The Magnolia Kitchen on Crockett, two blocks east of the square. A friend of mine runs it, the food is good, and we can find a private corner. Noon?"

Her "yes" lacked the enthusiasm one might like to hear from one's luncheon companion. But I thanked her politely anyway, went upstairs, and put on a tailored white blouse, tan chino skirt, and a loose beige jacket. With a business lunch on the agenda, in addition to the errands I needed to run this morning, I wasn't sure I'd have time to come home and change before the memorial service.

As I dressed, I averted my eyes from McQuaid's closet. I didn't need to look, anyway, since I'd already discovered that wherever he had gone, he wasn't planning to stay long or go to any fancy-dress events. He'd taken only the jeans he had on, an extra flannel shirt, and his gray tweed jacket. Not looking didn't keep me from thinking about him, though—wondering where he was, what he was doing, who he was doing it with. But wondering hurt, so I added a scarf to the blouse, ran a brush through my hair, and headed down the stairs and out to my car, grabbing an umbrella on the way out, on the off-chance that it might rain. I did not plan to spend any part of my day off obsessing over McQuaid—not a very workable plan, probably, but I was giving it my best shot.

The receipt from Frank Getzendaner that I'd found yesterday had been dwarfed by the discovery of Adcock's offshore bank account, but I was curious about it anyway. The missing handgun still bothered me, especially in view of the arsenal stashed in Adcock's closet. My curiosity took me to Frank's shop, which is located in a frame shanty on the alley behind Miller's Sporting Goods, south of the CTSU campus.

It's a small building, and very old, and the weathered silver-gray cypress siding is probably worth more than the structure and the land it's built on. I keep expecting to learn that some up-and-coming designer has bought the shack, dismantled it, and used the siding to create an antique look in some Dallas socialite's kitchen.

In the meantime, though, Frank Getzendaner's four cypress walls are still standing and he has a sheet-metal roof over his head. Frank is a small, loquacious man with a half-dozen cobwebby strands of white hair festooned across his shiny bald head, which he rubs from time to time like a talisman. He's old enough to remember when Pecan Springs was populated mostly by people who were born here and stayed because they wanted to. His wife, Emmaline, one of the cheeriest, most pleasantly gossipy women you'd ever hope to meet, has been the town's postmistress for over twenty years. I know Emmaline because we trade remarks about the weather at the post office every morning. I know Frank because McQuaid, who is an avid gun collector, visits him often, and sometimes I go along. Between the two of them, Emmaline and Frank Getzendaner probably know every single person in Pecan Springs.

As a gunsmith, Frank is without peer. If you want to add a poly-choke to your shotgun or a scope to your deer rifle, sporterize the World War II trophy you inherited from your grandfather or fine-tune your Glock, you take the job to Frank. He has his principles, however. He can, but won't, add a silencer, file your sear, or shorten a barrel below sixteen inches, not for any amount you might be willing to slip him. McQuaid says he's the best in the business, and McQuaid should know.

Frank's gun shop is like the man himself, small and tidy, with a pleasantly metallic odor of neat's-foot oil and cleaning solvent. There is a chest-high wooden counter just inside the door, its surface scratched and nicked with years of use. A well-lighted workbench runs the length of the back wall, backed with pegboard on which Frank hangs his tools. There's a heavy metal drill press at one end and a head-high cabinet at the other, lined with small drawers full of spare parts. You can't see under the counter from the customer side, but that's where Frank keeps the repaired guns, each one carefully tagged, in locked metal bins. (Rumor has it that he's stashed a loaded .38 there, as well, and that he feels perfectly justified in using it when the need arises.) The only two windows are high up in the walls and covered with rusty metal bars, like a jail. The front and back doors are formidable, and there's an alarm that's set to go off in the dispatcher's office at the county jail. If you want to break in some night to loot a few guns, you'll have to work pretty hard at it. But be forewarned: by the time you manage to get in, one of Pecan Springs' finest will be on hand to escort you out.

When I came in, Frank was at his workbench, disassembling a hunting rifle. He wore a blue work shirt, denim overalls, and a worn leather apron that hung down almost to his knees. He glanced up.

"Mornin', China," he said, drawling and twangy. He went back to work, speaking over his shoulder. "Yore out bright'n early fer a Monday mornin'. How's thet man o' yor'n?"

"Out of town on a business trip," I said briefly, not leaving any room for Frank to comment. "I'm cleaning up a few details for Dolores Adcock,'' I went on. ''When I was going through her husband's things, I found a receipt from your shop.''

Frank set the rifle stock aside and turned the receiver assembly in his hands. ''Read 'bout Adcock in Saturday's paper,'' he said. He ran his finger across the metal. ''A crime, thet's whut it is,'' he muttered.

''Suicide isn't a crime,'' I said. I frowned. Frank does a lot of work for Bubba's squadron of cops, and their information network relays news (men don't call it gossip, of course) even faster than the Pecan Springs grapevine. ''The last I heard, it *was* suicide. Do you know something I don't?''

''Huh?'' He looked up. ''Oh, I ain't talkin' 'bout Adcock. Just lookit here. From the rust on this-here trigger housin', somebody musta buried this piece in a hog wallow. Damn shame the way folks treat a good gun.''

I leaned my elbows on the counter. If there's anything that burns Frank, it's people who don't have the proper respect for guns—a group which in his view comprises about eighty-five percent of gun owners. Of course, he sees the basket cases. I agreed thoughtfully. Yes, that gun was certainly rusted. Yes, it was a pity that people didn't take better care of a good weapon.

There was a long silence as Frank contemplated the damage to the gun. ''Wonder whut made him do it,'' he remarked at last, half to himself.

''Bury the gun in the hog wallow?''

''Kill hisself.''

''Ah,'' I said. We were back on track. ''I don't think

anybody knows.'' I paused. ''You heard anything about the investigation?''

''Who, me?'' He put on an innocent expression. ''I'm allus th' last.'' He reached for an aerosol can of rust solvent on the shelf. ''Did hear, though, that th' Rangers come in, give the place a quick once-over, an' said it was suicide.'' He began to spray the gun, turning it as he sprayed.

''Is that right?'' I said, and waited.

He finished spraying and replaced the can on the shelf. '''Course,'' he went on thoughtfully, ''Bubba don't exactly agree.''

''He doesn't, huh?''

''Nope.'' Frank hooked a rag from the shelf and began to wipe his hands. ''Says if Adcock wanted to kill hisself quick 'n' painless, he'd of shot hisself in th' head.''

''McQuaid said something like that too,'' I remarked. ''What's your opinion?''

Frank shrugged. ''May be somethin' to it. Other hand, you gotta consider Bubba's frame o' mind, which in this case ain't any too gen'rous.''

''Meaning that he doesn't like the Rangers?''

Now that his hands were reasonably clean, Frank reached into his back pocket, pulled out a snuff can, and took two fingers' worth. ''Meanin' he's totally pissed,'' he said, stuffing the tobacco into one cheek. ''Bubba don't like nobody messin' in his territory. Don't b'lieve nobody but him can investigate worth a hill o' beans.'' He grinned, showing chipped brown teeth. '''Course, Bubba jes' may be right. Them Rangers, they ain't whut they used t'be.''

''Or maybe never were,'' I said.

''Mebbe,'' he said, and grinned. ''But you'd say thet,

wouldn't you, bein' a criminal lawyer onct upon a time? No good blood between yore kind an' Rangers."

I grinned back. "Maybe you're right." I put the receipt on the counter. "Did Adcock leave a gun here?"

Frank nodded. "When I heard he was dead, I wondered if anybody'd come and get it." He rummaged under the counter for a moment, then straightened up, a silver-plated automatic in his hands. "Brought it in fer repair last Wednesday mornin'. Broken hammer spring. Five-minute job, but I had t'git the part outta Dallas." He hefted the weapon, admiring it. "Real beauty," he mused. "Kinda glad it was under th' shelf here when Adcock decided to cash in his chips. Hate to see a good gun put to a bad use."

Living with McQuaid, whose gun collection rivals the National Guard Armory, I've come to know something about firearms. A broken part seemed a little unusual.

"How do you suppose he happened to break a hammer spring?" I asked curiously.

Frank shrugged. "Doin' some amateur gunsmithin', I reckon. The hammer lugs was filed down, prob'ly to reduce the trigger pull. If yore not careful when you put it together agin, you kin snap th' spring real easy on an old weapon like this." He turned the gun over in his hands. "Almost an antique. Bin kept good, though. Barrel's clean as a whistle. Slide and bushin' bin greased." He raised the gun and sighted down the barrel.

"Filed the lugs to reduce the trigger pull," I repeated thoughtfully. "Why would anybody want to do that?"

Frank laid the gun on the counter. "Guess he wanted it hair-trigger. A lawman onct, wadn't he? Mebbe some crook was after him an' he didn't want to waste all day squeezin'.''

I considered for a minute, thinking that Adcock's paranoia was manifesting itself in different ways. ''Would you mind keeping the gun?'' I asked finally. ''I'll tell his wife it's here, and she can pick it up.''

''Reckon that'll work,'' he said, putting the gun back in the bin. He turned to spit in a bucket, the tobacco juice plinking against the metal. He turned back, wiping his mouth with his sleeve. ''Tell her it'll come to twenty-five bucks.''

I nodded, said goodbye, and left. I like Frank, but I pity poor Emmaline, who has to wash his shirts and kiss his tobacco-stained mouth.

Doc Clarkson's office is down the street from Frank's shop, in an old house with a sloping front porch and a front door with a beveled-edged oval glass set into it. The narrow hall, walls covered in Victorian maroon flocked paper, goes straight back to the rooms where Doc sees his patients. The carpeted stairs on the right go up to Doc's private living quarters. The double doors on the left open to the reception area in the old living room, where Nellie Williams sits at a desk in front of the big bay window.

Nellie is a heavyset woman with sad eyes and a melancholy face framed by straggly curls of brown hair. If she doesn't look anything like her nieces, it's because she doesn't have any of their Cherokee blood. That comes from the other side of the family, from Laurel and Willow's mother, whom Nellie's brother met and married when he was working on an oil rig in eastern Oklahoma. If she doesn't have their cheerfulness, it's because she is by nature a tragic individual with the imagination of doom.

"Morning, China," she said, looking up from her typewriter. Her heavy chins sagged over the collar of her dark purple dress. I don't think I've ever seen Nellie wear anything brighter than forest green. "Isn't raining out there yet, I reckon?" Other people in Pecan Springs might make that remark with a degree of hopefulness. Nellie asked it with what sounded like the despairing conviction that it would *never* rain.

"No, but it might," I said, putting on a cheerful face. "The radio said there's a front coming through Waco. I've got my umbrella, just in case."

"Waco gets all the rain," Nellie said sadly. "My cousin lives up there, and I do envy her garden." She gave her brown curls a mournful shake. "Of course, they get more cold than we do, most winters. But I'd trade a few nippy days and maybe some snow for four or five more inches of rain. There's not going to be any bluebonnets this year. Not a *one*. And if we miss another year of bluebonnets, the tourist trade will totally dry up. As it is, it's down to a trickle. My friend Minnie Ruth says that if we don't get bluebonnets, she's going to close her shop."

I agreed that an April without bluebonnets could spell economic catastrophe, and added, "I've been helping Dolores Adcock clean up a few things after her husband's death. Did Willow introduce you to Dolores?"

"That Hispanic woman she works with? Yes, I met her at Wanda's when I went to buy a couple of new shade trees for the back yard. We lost two big live oaks last summer." The corners of her mouth pulled down. "Oak wilt, of course. It's been three years, coming up one side of the block and down the other. It's like losing your friends. You can't do a thing but hang a funeral wreath on a branch and watch them die. Saddest thing you can imagine. And with the trees dead and the shade gone, the air-conditioning bill has gone sky-high. We put in a couple of new trees, but it'll be years before they're big enough to shade the roof. By that time Ray and I both will be in the nursing home.'' She sighed heavily. ''Or dead.''

I remarked that oak wilt was indeed a personal and ecological disaster, and said, ''I understand that Dolores's husband was a patient here. Roy Adcock.''

Nellie's melancholy face grew even gloomier.''Well, it does come to us all, some sooner than others. I guess he decided he didn't want to wait until it came down his side of the block, so to speak. Took matters into his own hands. I can't say as I blame him. Sickness is *so* depressing, and when there's no hope—'' She raised her heavy shoulders and let them fall.

''Dolores wants to be sure that all the bills are taken care of,'' I said. ''Could you glance at her husband's account and see if there's an outstanding balance?''

Nellie pushed her long sleeves up past her pudgy wrists. ''I can tell you without looking, because I already checked. I read about the shooting in Saturday's paper, and it worried me all weekend. So when I came in this morning, I looked up his account. Paid in full.'' She looked momentarily cheerful, then darkened again. ''Of course, his passing left an empty slot in this morning's office calendar, which is too bad. Normally, somebody can't come, I call somebody else to fill in. But it being the weekend and all, there wasn't any chance. Doctor will just have to lose a whole thirty minutes."

I leaned forward. "If you don't mind my asking," I said tactfully, "what was his problem?" When she hesitated, I added, "Poor Dolores. She had no idea that he was seriously ill, you know. Perhaps if she understood the hopelessness of his situation, it would help her to deal with his death."

Nellie lowered her voice to a whisper. "It was his pancreas."

"Cancer?"

Her mouth pursed to a doleful O as she nodded. "So sad, really. Although I have to say, he never gave a hint that he was planning to end it all. Even the last visit, when he got the terrible news. Acted like he was going to be a fighter all the way. Some do, you know. Fight it, I mean." She leaned her elbows on the desk. "I don't know how they do it. If it was me, I'd be like the oak trees. I'd just wilt."

I admitted that I, too, would probably wilt under such news, remarked that Dolores would be glad to know that the account was up to date, and said goodbye. When I stepped off the front porch, the sun was shining through the gray clouds, right into Nellie's window. She closed the blinds.

The bank is on the northwest corner of the square, kitty-wampus from our hundred-year-old pink granite courthouse and directly across Pecos Street from the Sophie Briggs Historical Museum. If you come to Pecan Springs, you really must drop in at the museum and take a look around. It's not much on the outside (the building used to house Killebrew's Feed and Hardware Store, which went out of business when the last of the Killebrew brothers died), but inside, it's a different story. The Pecan Springs Historical Society bought it a couple of years ago. They stopped up the holes in the walls and swept out the bat droppings, hung country gingham curtains across the front window, and set up a gift shop in one corner. The museum itself takes up the entire back of the building. It contains the Historical Society's proudest possessions: Lila Trumm's dollhouse (a Victorian fantasy complete with tiny gingerbread trim and lady dolls drinking tea); Sophie Briggs's collection of three hundred ceramic frogs; and the pièce de résistance—a pair of scuffed cowboy boots worn by Burt Reynolds during the filming of *The Best Little Whorehouse in Texas*. The boots were donated by a former trombone player in the CTSU marching band, which was signed for the movie because its uniforms are Aggie-maroon. The Aggies—who are reputed to have had a long and agreeable liaison with the LaGrange Chicken Ranch that inspired *The Best Little Whorehouse in Texas*—were naturally asked to play themselves. On behalf of the university, however, the president's office declined. It seems that the movie's portrayal of the cordial friendship between members of the Corps and certain ladies of the night offended some of the Baptists on the board. Anyway, next time you're in Pecan Springs, drop in and see Burt Reynolds' boots, Sophie's frogs, and Lila's dollhouse. Admission is only two dollars.

Compared to the museum, the bank is quite imposing. The two-story ceiling is covered with the original pressed tin, the glass-topped oak tables with their green-shaded lamps belong to a more opulent era, and the old-fashioned tellers' cages are polished brass. But despite all this grandeur, the bank's primary historical distinction is the fact that in July of 1878 the notorious Texas outlaw Sam Bass decided not to rob it after all and headed instead for the Round Rock bank, where he was shot by four Rangers and three other lawmen who had assembled in Round Rock with that object in mind. It has always seemed like a case of overkill to me.

Bonnie Roth, one of the three tellers, waved at me as I came in carrying my deposit in its blue plastic bank bag, and I went over to her. Bonnie, a pleasant, sweet-faced woman in her late thirties, is a customer at the shop, a member of the herb guild, and an avid gardener. She tries to restrain herself during business hours, but I happen to know that she is an inveterate gossip—not out of maliciousness, but out of empathy. Bonnie carries the weight of everyone's problems on her own sturdy shoulders. If it is sometimes a terrible burden, Bonnie bears it bravely.

She ran a tape on my deposit entries, counted the money, and stamped my deposit slip.

"Did you by any chance know Roy Adcock?" I asked, taking the slip and tucking it into my bag.

Bonnie's eyes softened. "As a matter of fact, I did," she said. "I felt so *sorry* for him when I read the news in Saturday's paper. And his poor wife, out doing the shopping and all. I'm sure she was getting ready for a nice, quiet weekend, just the two of them. And then to come home and find him dead and blood all over everything." She shivered. "I know how I'd feel, if I came in the door and found Billie Lee dead in his favorite chair, China. It'd just kill me. I'd drop right down there on the floor, and they'd find the both of us, side by side in death."

"His wife has been pretty torn up," I said. "Roy was one of your customers, I understand."

"Always a smile and a kind word," Bonnie replied, sighing. She adjusted the Peter Pan lace collar on her floral print dress. "Real calm, quiet, sort of a Gary Cooper type, you know? The last person on earth you'd think would pull the trigger on himself. But people fool you all the time. They're never what they seem." She let this bit of sage philosophy hang in the air as she sorted my deposit money into her cash drawer and closed it. Then she glanced over her shoulder to see whether the next teller was listening and asked, "I keep wondering why he did it. Do you suppose he was sick or something?"

"I really don't know," I lied. "But you can imagine how terrible his wife feels. Maybe you've met Dolores—she works part-time at Wanda's. A pretty Hispanic woman, long, dark hair, very thin."

Bonnie's eyes widened and her mouth pursed. "Oh, for *pity's* sake, of *course* I know Dolores. She sold me a big pot of epazote, not a pretty plant but really useful if you suffer from you-know-what after you eat beans. Why, I had no *idea* she was Mr. Adcock's wife." She shook her head, commiserating in italics. "Oh, poor, *poor* little thing. I feel for her, I really, *really* do. I just wish I could think of *something* I could do to help her out." She thought of it and brightened. "I *know*! I'll make a batch of cookies tonight and run them over in the morning."

"That would be a nice gesture," I said, "but in the meantime, maybe you could help with something else." I reached into my purse and pulled out the safety deposit key. "I was helping Dolores clean up some of her husband's business, and I found this key among his papers. Did he have a box here?''

''As a matter of fact, he did,'' Bonnie said. ''I took him to the vault myself just last week.''

''Dolores wanted me to take a quick look in the box,'' I said. ''We haven't been able to find an inventory of the contents, and she wants to make sure there are no insurance policies she doesn't already know about.''

Bonnie hesitated. ''Gosh, I'm afraid I don't know the rules on that. Maybe I'd better check with Mr. Burkett.''

''That's a good idea,'' I said. In a state where such boxes are sealed upon the death of the owner, my request would have earned an automatic no. In Texas, however, when a representative of the estate presents a key, most banks allow a safety deposit box to be opened and inventoried in the presence of a bank official.

Bonnie nodded, locked her cash drawer, and left the cage. She was back a minute or two later, accompanied by Gordon Burkett, the bank president and its chief loan officer. Gordon is a tall, stoop-shouldered man with graying hair and gold-rimmed glasses, his face deeply lined with a lifetime of noes. (I can personally put the lie to the rumor that the man has never said yes in his entire life. In the start-up years of my business, I had occasion ask him to say yes to a loan, and I can bear witness to the painful exertion of this effort. I partially redeemed my effrontery by repaying my loan on time, for which I was now grateful. It meant that he was less likely to say no, on principle, this morning. He might even say yes if I asked him for the money for the tea room.)

We exchanged greetings and handshakes and I proffered the key, repeating the explanation I had given Bonnie, with more formality and a sprinkling of multisyllabic, legal-sounding words, in order to make it easier for him to swallow.

Mr. Burkett absorbed my request, pondered it for a moment, and answered it with a question. "You are aware, are you not, Ms. Bayles, that you may not remove anything from the deceased's box?"

"I am," I replied, and countered with, "I assume that you will make the usual inventory of the contents and have it notarized. If Mrs. Adcock wishes to remove anything from the box after she has examined the inventory and prior to probate, we will obtain the appropriate court order."

"In that case," he said, "come with me." He had managed to avoid the trauma of saying yes.

After all that fuss and bother, it was almost an anticlimax when we got to the vault, opened Adcock's box, and found that it contained nothing but a single unlabeled floppy disk.

CHAPTER TEN

> The Greeks crowned warriors and poets with wreaths of bay laurel, representing their courage and service to the state. The Romans believed that bay protected against poison, and it is said that Roman emperors wore bay wreaths not only to symbolize their nobility but to make them proof against conspiracies.
>
> Greco-Roman herbal tradition

> I have seen the wicked in great power, and spreading himself like a green bay tree.
>
> Psalms 37:35

The Magnolia Kitchen, where I was supposed to meet Elaine Emery for lunch, is across the street from Thyme and Seasons. I would probably eat there a couple of times a week even if the food wasn't good. It is, though, *very* good—at least for the moment. Who knows what's going to happen, now that the restaurant has been sold.

Until last week, The Magnolia Kitchen was owned by my friend Maggie Garrett, who is a former sister at St. Theresa's monastery, a couple of hours west of Pecan Springs. Maggie has decided to resume her vocation at St. T's, where she'll be in charge of the monastery kitchen. I'm glad for her sake, but I'm willing to bet that the sisters won't appreciate her fresh herb and mushroom omelettes as much as Ruby and I do. It remains to be seen whether The Kitchen's new owners will have anything like Maggie's culinary talent. I'm not holding my breath.

I had managed to squeeze in two other errands and was running a little late, so it was almost ten after twelve when I got to the restaurant. The tables in the dining room were filling up fast. The Kitchen has a casual country-French elegance, with red clay herb-filled pots on white tables, green-painted chairs, green floor, green ceiling, and white lattice on the walls. I glanced around and didn't see Elaine, so I gave her name to the hostess and went through the French doors.

It was a cool, bright day with a southern breeze that moved the air gently. The flagstone patio is shaded by a wisteria arbor, which was still leafless at the end of the mild winter. A couple of springs ago, Maggie and I landscaped the patio and the lot beside it with pots and beds of annual and perennial herbs—a large bay tree in an old wooden wine cask and low hedges of chives, parsley, and winter savory for the kitchen; fennel and lavender and thyme for the bees; borage and catnip and monarda for the hummingbirds. Pecan Springs' temperature doesn't drop below 10 degrees most winters, and although the bay tree has to spend a couple of months indoors, rosemary flourishes outside year-round and the climate is dry enough for sage and lavender (which often don't do well in the humid South). I hoped that the new owners would value the gardens. It would be a pity if they tore up the herbs in order to put in more parking or build a bigger kitchen.

I sat down at a table in the corner and leaned back, enjoying the sunshine on my face. There aren't many months when you can enjoy the Texas sun without courting a fierce burn. A moment later, Maggie appeared.

"China!" she exclaimed happily, and bent over to hug me. "How lovely to see you."

Maggie's graying hair is crisply razored in a boy-cut, her square-jawed face is plain, her gray eyes forthright. On the surface, she looks no different than the Maggie I have known for over two years. But since she decided to return to the monastery, I can sense a new kind of joyfulness about her that is laced with a deep, sure expectation. She's anxious to wrap up the restaurant sale and get on with the rest of her life. Some days I wish I were going with her.

Maggie sat down, a waiter brought us some herb tea and a plate of stuffed mushrooms, and we chatted about The Magnolia Kitchen's new owners—two women in their fifties from Indianapolis who came into an inheritance and decided to invest it in the restaurant business. They had driven through Pecan Springs on vacation and resolved to move here—not an unusual reaction. Pecan Springs is most people's dream of a small town.

"Lois and Barbara really want to make this place a success," Maggie said. "They may be short on experience, but they're very eager. I'm counting on you to support them."

"Maybe you'd better plan on sending Care packages to the friends you're abandoning," I said. "I'm not sure how well somebody who's 'short on experience' will do in the kitchen, no matter how eager they are."

"Have faith," Maggie said, cheerful as always. "Speaking of the kitchen, I'd better get back and see what sort of crises have developed in the last ten minutes. Would you like a bowl of corn-and-potato chowder? It has some of your very own bay in it.'' She gestured fondly toward the bay tree that stood just inside the door, in its wooden tub. ''Remember when we potted that tree together, China? It couldn't have been more than eighteen inches high, and just look at it now.''

I looked from the bay tree to my watch. It was 12:20 P.M.. ''I'm meeting someone,'' I said, ''but she's late. The chowder sounds great. I think I'll start and let her catch up.''

While the chowder was on its way, I collected my thoughts. The morning's phone conversation with Elaine had opened up something new and troubling. She claimed to have discovered a connection between the Harris case and Rafael Villarreal, which prompted a string of questions.

What kind of connection were we talking about? Did it have to do with Frank Harris, two years dead? Or was it related to the more recently deceased Ranger who had investigated the Harris murder—and who just happened to have a two-year-old offshore cache of funds, not to mention a two-year-old marriage. Did the tidy little fortune that had passed through Roy Adcock's account come out of the pockets of the *pasadores* who paid him to look the other way when they drove across the border? Or could it have been a payoff for stonewalling a murder investigation? In either of these latter two scenarios, Adcock was a crooked cop, and the proof might very well be on that anticlimactic floppy disk in the safety deposit box. Where it was going to stay, as long as I had anything to say about it. And I had the key.

And there was Amado Acosta. After I left the bank, still

pondering the mysteries that might be held by the floppy disk, my first errand was to drive by the Adcock house, where I saw Acosta's car, still parked in the drive. My second was to stop at the sheriff's office, where I asked Blackie to run a make on the black Ford and do a background check on Acosta himself. The man's continuing presence raised all sorts of intriguing questions. Acosta could be connected to the Harris case, or he might be one of the sources of Roy Adcock's secret stash. Or maybe his connection was Dolores, whom Adcock had married about the time he'd been investigating Harris's murder.

And Dolores herself—what was the story there? A homicide conviction, a prison term, and marriage to a Texas Ranger: certainly an odd combination of circumstances. What was her role in all of this? There were plenty of questions jostling one another for elbow room in my mind. Maybe Elaine could bring some order to the confusion.

But Elaine hadn't shown up by the time I finished the chowder (indeed delicious, with the sharp, unmistakable fragrance of bay), which was served with hunks of hot herb bread and a small salad of tender greens and blue-cheese dressing. I paid my check and went to a phone, but all I got was her answering machine.

I frowned, more annoyed than worried. It was entirely possible that Elaine had rethought her strategy and decided to make a stab at persuading Dolores to hand over the folder, rather than risk a grilling from me. Or something unavoidable had delayed her—a flat tire, a fender-bender, something like that. I looked at my watch. Or maybe she was simply running late and had decided to go on to Austin, planning to talk to me at the memorial service.

That's probably what happened, I decided. I'd catch her there.

There was no casket at the front of the chilly, musty-smelling chapel on Congress Avenue, south of the Colorado River. There was only a modest collection of funeral flowers, one of which bore a white ribbon with the words "Loving Husband" in glued-on gold letters. An unpracticed organist played Bach's *Sheep May Safely Graze*, out of tempo and with too many sour notes. The dozen or so mourners were respectful but did not seem unduly mournful, and I had the impression that some of them, anyway, were there because they felt obliged. I didn't recognize any of them except Dubois, the Ranger who had been at the crime scene when Ruby and I arrived to talk to Dolores. He was sitting alone at the back of the chapel, grim-faced and silent.

Dolores, black-garbed and veiled, arrived clinging to Amado's solicitous arm just as the last organ note trembled into silence. She carried a white handkerchief and used it frequently during the service, although her heavy veil hid her face and I could not be sure that she was really weeping. Acosta, patting her hand from time to time, was appropriately somber but did not seem to be taking Adcock's death much to heart.

The most moving words of the short service were not spoken by the minister, who obviously did not know Adcock and was not motivated to give his best performance. They were offered by Captain Scott, who left his white Stetson in the pew when he went to the lectern and seemed to speak out of a deep and real sense of loss for a friend and brother officer. The captain was your basic John Wayne type, a tall, lean, slow-talking man in a dark suit, cowboy boots, and a silver belt buckle the size of a mayonnaise jar lid. He gave us a history of Adcock's career as a Ranger, described several of the dangerous assignments he had worked on, and praised his courageous commitment to the Ranger ethic.

"Roy Adcock was a truly honorable man who cared for the citizens he served," he said, in firm, measured tones, his voice never wavering. "His entire career, to the day he left the service, was distinguished by courage and heroism. But Roy never rested on his well-earned laurels. He was the kind of man who just kept plugging away, day and night, doing the kind of work he could be proud of—work we can *all* be proud of. That's what we will remember him for: his respected work as a law enforcement officer, his solid achievements as a Ranger, and his strong sense of loyalty and respect for the ideals on which the Rangers were founded."

I was as straight-faced and somber as everyone else, but I couldn't help wondering, with a sharp sense of cynical amusement, what the good captain would say if he knew about the nest egg Adcock had squirreled away. Would he be so anxious to crown the deceased with honor—or would he say the words anyway, since that's what everyone expected him to say? And what about Dolores? I wondered what was going through her mind as she listened to the captain eulogize her husband's virtues as an honest, upright man.

After what Dolores had told me about Roy's poetry, I had expected Captain Scott to conclude with one of the dead man's poems. He must not have been able to find anything suitable, though, for he ended by reading a sentimental ballad by somebody named W.A. Phelson. It told the story of a noble band of Rangers standing strong against the bad guys:

> They fought grim odds and knew no fear,
> They kept their honor high and clear,
> And, facing arrows, guns, and knives,
> Gave Texas all they had—their lives.

I wasn't exactly sure what the poem had to do with Roy Adcock, who had not died in defense of Texas, or even in the defense of another Ranger, but it sounded good. Even the captain, whose voice had been firm throughout his eulogy, had to stop and clear his throat when he got to the last lines. At the back of the chapel, a man blew his nose.

The eulogy was followed by the customary prayer, and then it was over, less than thirty minutes after it began. Dolores left the chapel, escorted once more by Acosta. As she came unsteadily down the aisle, she paused and murmured something to Captain Scott. Amado, taken by surprise, put his arm around her shoulders and pulled her away. She seemed to protest, and he whispered something to her. Obediently, she broke off and went with him, stumbling a little.

I waited a decent moment, then got up and followed them out, hoping to catch her and ask if she had any objections to my sharing the contents of the green folder with Elaine. But they were just disappearing around the corner as I came out of the chapel, and when I ran around the corner after them, they were nowhere in sight. Perhaps someone had been waiting to pick them up.

Disappointed, I went back to the chapel and looked over the people who were emerging. I hoped I'd see McQuaid, but at the same time I hoped I wouldn't. If he had been there and hadn't come to sit with me . . .

I didn't want to think about what that rejection would have meant. But he didn't appear to be there, and now I wondered why. His note hadn't indicated he was leaving town—but then, it hadn't indicated much of anything else, either, only that he would be calling Brian tonight. I could ask him then where he was and when he'd be back. No, I couldn't do that, either. I wouldn't give him the satisfaction of begging bits of information from him, like a nagging wife.

I tried to stop thinking about McQuaid and looked instead for Elaine, without success. I frowned. Missing lunch was one thing, but missing the memorial service was something else, given her professed interest in it, and in Adcock. Now I felt more worried than annoyed about her absence, and I was puzzling over what it might mean when I spotted Blackie and Sheila, who had apparently come late to the service and sat in the back. With them was a strikingly pretty, dark-haired woman in her thirties, athletic-looking, discreetly dressed in a gray suit, white blouse with a narrow gray scarf, and black pumps with medium heels.

Blackie had stopped to talk to Captain Scott, and Sheila and her companion came toward me. Sheila introduced her as her friend Margaret Graham, who was, it turned out, a Texas Ranger. I nodded, remembering Sheila's mention of her at dinner on Friday night.

"Hello, China," Margaret said, and held out her hand. "It's nice to meet you." Her dark hair was softly waved, with bangs swept across her forehead, and her deep-set eyes were an odd shade of smoky lavender, fringed with long, curving lashes—eyes like the young Elizabeth Taylor. The rest of her face was pretty enough. With those eyes, she was drop-dead gorgeous.

"Margaret knows McQuaid," Sheila added, enlarging on the introduction. "They met when he started his research project. Margaret's been doing some work for him. They've gotten to be great friends."

"Oh," I said.

Margaret gave me an oddly questioning glance, but she smiled, and the corners of her full lips curled upward. "Mike is a very nice man," she said. "Smart, too. And easy to work with." Her voice was rich and throaty.

"Don't forget sexy," Sheila said with a laugh.

"Yes," Margaret said, low. She had stopped smiling. "That, too."

I swallowed. The air pressing against me seemed heavy, cold. Out on the street, tires squealed and there was the sound of angry horn-blowing, then a sudden, grating smash. A fender-bender.

Sheila put her arm around Margaret's shoulders. "Margaret's your kind of woman, China. Talk about tough—she used to be undercover with the San Antonio police. That's where she met Roy Adcock." She gave her friend a look of teasing affection. "She's been a Ranger for less than a year, and she's doing great. She doesn't take any crap from the good old boys, either. They give the other women Rangers a hard time, but not Peg. She tells 'em where to shove it, up close and personal.''

''I'm sure she does,'' I said thinly. *Margaret, Peg, Peggy.* I didn't need any more details of this woman's life. I knew who she was.

At Sheila's words, Margaret had tensed. ''Watch it, Sheila,'' she said. She glanced uneasily over her shoulder.

Sheila chuckled. ''What's the matter, kid? Afraid you'll give something away?'' She smiled at me. ''You should hear Mike rave about this woman, China. He says she's the best research assistant he's ever had—not to mention the prettiest. Better watch out, China. You've got competition.''

Sheila is a tease. All Margaret had to do was laugh and make a clever little joke to dissolve the tension. But she realized that I knew who she was, and it rattled her so much that she gave it all away—the whole story of her relationship with McQuaid—with a single guilty look. She colored, confession in her Elizabeth Taylor eyes, and spoke.

''China, maybe we could have a cup of coffee and—''

''No,'' I said. Peggy had turned my life upside down. I wasn't going to let her hand me a lame explanation and think that would make everything right.

''Excuse me?'' Sheila looked from one of us to the other, perplexed. ''Have you two met before?''

''No,'' Margaret said quickly.

''But we know something about one another,'' I said.

''Oh, sure,'' Sheila said. ''I guess I mentioned Margaret the other night. She's the one who looked into the Rangers' handling of the Odessa case. Really, if the Rangers don't have anything better to do than to waste manpower investigating the theft of a football player's high school transcript—'' She left the sentence unfinished, shaking her head disgustedly.

Blackie turned around from his conversation with Captain Scott. ''Hey, China,'' he said, ''the captain's asking about McQuaid. What happened to him? Wasn't he planning to be here this afternoon?''

I wasn't going to make any excuses for McQuaid. ''I have no idea where he is,'' I said in a chilly tone. ''He doesn't always clue me in on his schedule.''

Sheila cocked her head. ''Didn't you tell me he went to the Valley yesterday to do some sort of research?'' she asked Margaret. ''Brownsville, wasn't it?''

''I . . . I think so,'' Margaret said. ''But it was a quick trip. He planned to be back by now.'' She gave me a sidelong glance, obviously embarrassed at being cited as the authority on McQuaid's whereabouts. There were two spots of color high on her cheeks. She glanced at her watch. ''Speaking of time,'' she said, ''it's getting late. I'd better get back to the office.''

''Margaret is assigned to Austin headquarters,'' Sheila said to me. ''She's working with the new internal audit division.''

''Mmm,'' I said. Some sort of accountant, was she? ''I thought Rangers only did field work,'' I added, tacky.

Captain Scott had joined us. ''The force is changing,'' he said with a smile. ''We're bringing it up to date, taking on new responsibilities, bringing in new faces.'' He put his hand on Margaret's shoulder with a patronizing familiarity, and I saw her flinch. ''We're very proud of our female Rangers.'' He turned to Ranger Dubois, who was standing behind him. ''Isn't that right, Rick?''

Dubois nodded curtly. His square jaw was working and his eyes, a pale gray, were on Margaret. I realized something else. McQuaid was the one with the competition. Dubois' eyes were hungry.

"There are five women Rangers now." Captain Scott was warming to his subject. "After a break-in period while they get used to the various aspects of Ranger activity, we expect to see all of them in the field, working shoulder to shoulder with the men."

"Fighting grim odds and knowing no fear?" Sheila asked with a straight face. "Keeping their honor high and clear—even when they're told to make coffee?"

The captain was too much taken with Sheila's reference to the poem he had quoted during the memorial service to hear the sarcasm in her voice. And he completely overlooked her add-on remark about the coffee, which was an oblique allusion to a sexual harrassment charge that had been filed a few years before by one of the first women Rangers.

"A fine old poem, isn't it?" he asked, looking pleased. "I found it in a book by Walter Webb, one of the finest Ranger histories ever written. Roy would have been pleased to have heard it, I think. He was something of a poet himself."

"So I understood," I said. "Mrs. Adcock told me that you might be reading one of her husband's poems today."

"I'm sorry I had to disappoint Mrs. Adcock, but I'm afraid I couldn't find anything suitable," the captain said regretfully. He held out his hand. "So you're China Bayles. I'm glad to meet you. Mike has mentioned you a time or two."

"Oh, has he?" I asked with a certain archness, shaking the captain's hand.

He nodded. "I'm somewhat of an historian myself, and I'm glad to have Mike digging through the old records. Maybe his research project, whatever it is, will give us a new view of the past." He grinned affably at me. "You know, I don't think I ever heard him talk about his research topic. What exactly is he up to?"

"I don't know," I said. "We haven't had a lot of time to talk lately." I turned to Margaret. "You might ask Margaret, though. I understand she's been working with him. And doing a great job, too," I added fiercely, between my teeth. "He can't seem to get along without her." My tone made their relationship perfectly clear. And if anyone hadn't caught on, they could see the tears in my eyes.

I was immediately ashamed of making a public spectacle of a private matter. The captain raised his eyebrows knowingly, Ranger Dubois's gray eyes were like gimlets, and Sheila was staring at me, nonplussed. Blackie was the only one who didn't quite get it.

Margaret broke the silence. "I've really got to be going," she said tensely. She turned to Blackie. "I hate to pull you away, but—"

"No problem." Blackie put on his hat. "Ready, Sheil?"

"Oh, you don't want to drive all the way up to North Austin," Captain Scott said easily. He smiled at Margaret. "I'm going back to headquarters, Meg. I'll be glad to give you a lift."

Blackie looked grateful. "It would save us a couple of miles through the traffic."

Margaret hesitated as if she didn't want to go with the

captain, and I wondered, without much curiosity, whether my remark would have professional consequences for her. Then she raised her chin.

"Thanks," she said to the captain. "I'd like a lift." Ignoring me, she gave Sheila a brief hug and shook Blackie's hand.

"On the way," I heard the captain say as they started down the walk, "maybe you can tell me what you and McQuaid have been up to."

Blackie watched them go. As they got into the captain's car, he said, "I didn't quite get Margaret's reason for coming to the service this afternoon. Did she know Adcock?"

"She was on a case with him a couple of years ago," Sheila replied. The pager at Blackie's belt gave a short, metallic chirp, and he took a sideways step to answer it. "Excuse me," he said. He headed for his car, parked at the curb.

Sheila turned to me, frosty. "What the hell's wrong with you, China?" she demanded. "If I didn't know better, I'd think you were accusing Margaret of—"

"I didn't have to accuse her," I said. "It was written all over her face." I was struggling for control, without much success. My voice came up a notch. "And don't you go taking the moral high ground with me, Smart Cookie. I'm not the one who's sleeping with somebody else's man. If you want to lecture anybody, you can start with that sexy friend of yours."

Sheila stared at me. "Are you saying that Margaret and Mike—?" She stopped, her mouth curling down, and shook her head. "That's crazy, China. That's totally nuts. Mike McQuaid has been trying to get you to marry him for the last five years. *You're* the one who keeps saying no, for Pete's sake. He wouldn't—''

''Nuts, is it?'' I gave a short, harsh laugh. ''Ask Margaret how nuts it is.'' Seeing Sheila's stunned disbelief, I added, ''Go on, Sheila. You have my permission. Ask Margaret how long she and McQuaid have been lovers. She won't deny it. She can't, because it's true.''

Sheila shook her head slowly. ''Well, whatever the truth is, there's one good thing. You're jealous.''

''Who, me?'' I hooted. ''Jealous?'' I folded my arms to hide the fact that my hands were shaking, and raised my chin. I was disdainful. ''Next you'll be telling me that it doesn't matter, that he doesn't love me any less just because he has her.'' I felt my mouth tighten and I knew my face was as ugly as I felt, but I couldn't stop myself. ''As far as I am concerned,'' I grated, ''your buddy Margaret can have him. I'm *finished.*''

Sheila was open-mouthed. ''You can't be serious,'' she said. ''You wouldn't—Not over a little thing like—''

''Oh, so you *do* believe me,'' I said sarcastically. ''Well, pardon me if I don't consider it a little thing. I've never asked McQuaid to be a Boy Scout, but I do expect him to be honest and not go sleeping around behind my back.'' The tears I had been struggling against were threatening to spill over. I tried for a deep breath, but all I could manage was a shattering hiccup. ''If you'll excuse me,'' I muttered, ''I'm going to the bathroom and cry.''

''Want me to go with you?''

''Hell, *no*,'' I said, and fled.

When I got back, Sheila was still standing where I had

left her. ''You okay?'' she asked. She was obviously concerned, which was nice.

''No,'' I said. ''But I'll live.''

Her face was deeply sympathetic. ''Listen, China,'' she said, ''I'm really sorry. I had no idea—''

At that moment, Blackie came up the walk and joined us. He started to say something, then checked himself, seeing my red nose and eyes. ''What's wrong with you, China? You look like you've been crying.''

''Allergies,'' I said huskily, and blew my nose. ''I'm all stopped up.''

''Well, I've got some news that will unstop you in a hurry,'' he said grimly. ''That call just now—it was Chris, my dispatcher. She's been doing some checking on that car you asked about—and the owner.''

''And?'' I wadded up my tissue and began fishing in my bag for another.

''And it's registered to a man named Amado Dunia.''

''Dunia?'' I asked, startled.

Sheila's eyes widened. ''As in Dolores Francesca Dunia Adcock?''

''Yeah,'' he said. ''Interesting, huh?''

I stared at Blackie. What *was* the relationship between Dolores and Amado Dunia? Brother and sister? I remembered the sexual tension between them and discarded that possibility. Cousin, maybe, or former husband? That was it—maybe they had once been married, before she married Adcock!

Blackie was continuing. ''When Chris put a trace on Acosta, she drew a blank. When she sorted through the Dunias, though, she found one who matched the description of the man you gave me—the man who was here this afternoon. He has a prison record."

"You're talking about that good-looking guy who sat with Mrs. Adcock?" Sheila asked. "He kept his arm around her all during the service, as if he was afraid she was going to fall apart."

"Or run away," Blackie said.

I gave him a thoughtful look. That idea had not occurred to me. "What was Dunia in prison for?"

"Possession. He and Dolores Dunia, as she was called then, were fingered by a snitch and popped in the same bust. She got ten years and served five. He got five and walked in two and a half."

"Not what you'd call parity," Sheila said.

"Maybe she took the fall for him," I said, thinking about Dolores, yielding herself compliantly to the curve of Dunia's body. Things were beginning to seem a little clearer. I paused. "Any word from the Travis coroner?"

Blackie shrugged, grinning. "Hey. It's only Monday. What do you want, a miracle?" His grin disappeared. "Something's going on here, China, and Dolores Adcock and that sleazy friend of hers are in it up to their eyebrows. Roy wasn't the suicide type. He had ideals. He cared about honor. He wouldn't dirty his name that way."

"You don't have all the facts," I said, thinking that I ought to tell him what I'd found. But I was suddenly too weary and too depressed to cope with it. Tomorrow, I'd stop in at the sheriff's office, tell Blackie what I had uncovered, and hand the whole mess over to him, including the contents of the green folder, the gun receipt, the key to Adcock's safety deposit box, and Doc Clarkson's phone number.

Blackie gets paid to deal with the dark side of humanity. Let him root around in this dirty, corrupt mess, looking for the truth.

"You're right," Blackie said, his eyes slitted, "I don't have the facts. But I aim to *get* them. Those two had something to do with Roy's death. I'll wring the truth out of them, whatever it is."

"China should go with you, Blackie," Sheila put in urgently. "Dolores is more likely to talk if China's there. And you'd better go right now. For all we know, she and Dunia may be planning to leave town tonight."

I shook my head wearily. "You two go," I said. "I'm going home." I looked at Blackie. "I'll stop in tomorrow." I said. "There are a few things you need to know."

"Wait, China," Sheila said. She put her hand on my arm. "Don't you want to find out what happened to Adcock? Don't you want to see justice done?"

"Justice?" There was a sour taste in my mouth, a dark hole deep inside. "Even if you can prove that Dolores shot her husband, her lawyer will bargain it down to manslaughter. She'll get a felony two and be out on parole in a couple of years. Is that your idea of justice?"

"Hey." Blackie raised his eyebrows. "I thought you were the hotshot criminal lawyer who was committed to the American judicial system."

"That was me in a former life," I said. I hitched my bag strap up over my shoulder. "Now I've got a garden and plenty of nice *clean* dirt."

Chapter Eleven

> Calamint, being inwardly taken or outwardly applied, it cureth them that are bitten of Serpents: being burned or strewed it drives serpents away.
>
> John Gerard, *The Herball*, 1597

The porch light went on and Ruby opened the door dressed in an old red leotard, her hair tied up with a red scarf. Over the leotard she was wearing a black T-shirt with a hand-painted green frog and the declaration: ''Princess, fed up with Princes, seeks FROG.'' From inside the house I could hear the sound of flute and harp playing a haunting melody in a minor, mystical key, and smell the musky fragrance of burning incense.

''Well, hi, China,'' Ruby said. She seemed pleased but a little taken aback at my turning up on her front porch. Since McQuaid and I moved in together I rarely come over at night anymore. ''What are you doing out and about on such a chilly evening?''

The gray clouds that had sulked around doing absolutely nothing most of the afternoon had finally decided to bring us rain, slicking the streets and dropping the temperature into the forties. Good for bluebonnets, subsequent tourists, and the local economy, soggy and cold for people caught out in it. The raw damp matched my gloomy mood.

"I'm seeking a frog," I said. "It's the right night for it, but I haven't been having any luck."

"A good frog is hard to find," Ruby agreed, playing along with my weak attempt at humor. "They hang out in slimy ponds." She opened the door wider. "Want to come in, or are you just going to stand out there and make bad jokes all evening?"

"I can't stay long," I said. "I have to pick Brian up from Scouts at eight, over at the Methodist Church." It was just seven. I hesitated in the doorway. "Am I interrupting your meditation or something?"

"No, you're not interrupting. I've been doing a tarot spread, but I'm finished." She pulled me through the door. "Come in, for heaven's sake, It's *cold* out there!"

I took off my jacket and drippy fur-lined boots and left them beside the door, then padded in my socks into Ruby's living room. When Jo Gilbert lived here, the long, narrow room was crowded with antique furniture and Victorian bric-a-brac and hung with heavy red draperies. Now, it has the airy, open look of a gallery, with glossy wood floors, light walls and rough-weave curtains, several large plants in baskets and clay pots, and Ruby's eclectic, ever-changing collection of women's art. An Amish quilt hangs on one wall and a painting of an Indian woman on another, a couple of stone goddesses sit in the corners, and a half-dozen ceramic frogs are gathered companionably on the coffee table. Ruby is into frogs these days. Frogs and fairies and angels. Her fairies—carved and painted figures that she's collected from all over—live on the kitchen windowsill, overlooking the garden. She says she's hoping that with a little encouragement they'll take over the kitchen chores.

''Sit,'' Ruby commanded, pointing to an overstuffed chair beside the fireplace, where a bright, warm fire was blazing. ''I'll get you a little something to warm you up.''

Obediently, I sat, and since there was a plump footstool in front of the chair, I put my feet up and felt the flames warming my woolly socks. On a red rug before the fire lay a deck of round Motherpeace tarot cards and Ruby's journal, along with several flickering votive candles in glass cups. Only one lamp was burning, and the room was pleasantly dusky and sweet-smelling. I sank back into the chair, letting the scent and the celestial melodies of flute and harp wash through me like a fragrant ocean wave. I began to feel looser, a little less wired. Ruby has a theory that certain kinds of music and scents resonate compatibly with the human body, complementing each other to soothe or energize or make us more receptive or whatever—an idea that probably can't be (or won't be) proven scientifically, but certainly *feels* right. My head sank back and I was half-dozing when Ruby came in with a tray.

''You look like you've had a hard day,'' she said, putting the tray on the coffee table. ''Did you go to Roy Adcock's memorial service?'' She poured a glass of cold milk from a stoneware jug.

''Uh-huh.'' I took the glass with some surprise. ''We're having milk? Are we making up our calcium deficiency? Supporting the dairy industry? Or will somebody be around to photograph our mustaches?''

''Funny,'' Ruby said, and handed me a plate of cookies. ''Be careful,'' she warned as I took one. ''They bite back.''

''Oh, yeah?'' The cookie was small, I was hungry, and I popped it, fast. It was nutty, sweet, and hot.

Hot as in *caliente.*

As in cayenne.

''Wow!'' I gasped, and went for the milk. ''Those are incendiary,'' I said, when my mouth was cool enough to get the words out. ''What the devil is in them?''

Ruby grinned. ''I thought that would warm you up a little. I'm calling them Hot Lips Cookie Crisps. Did I put in enough habenero powder?''

''They're soul-searing,'' I said. ''Cookie monsters. My palate may never recover.'' My eyes were watering and my lips tingled. In a moment, the hot pepper high would set in—the state of mild euphoria that is caused by the capsaisin in peppers, a chemical that fires off a complicated chain of biochemical responses culminating in the release of endorphins in the brain. A totally legal, socially acceptable trip.

I took another cookie. ''I'll have to get your recipe for McQuaid,'' I said. ''He loves to cook with peppers, but I don't think he's ever used them in cookies.''

I stopped, remembering. McQuaid and I might not be sharing a kitchen much longer.

Ruby took several cookies and a glass of milk and sat down on the round rug, crossing her legs and tucking the soles of her bare feet against her inner thighs. Ruby is amazingly supple, the result of years of pretzeling herself into weird yoga postures. I envy her, but I don't have the discipline it takes to get where she is.

''So how was the memorial service?'' she asked, taking cautious bites around the edges of her hot-pepper cookie, like a wary squirrel. "Who was there? Did that Acosta character show?"

"His real name is Dunia," I said. "Blackie ran a make on his car and found out that Acosta is an assumed name."

"Dunia?" Ruby frowned. "Wasn't that the name Dolores was using when she got out of prison?"

I took a sip of milk to quench my burning tongue. "Excuse me, Ruby, but I don't want to talk about it. The more I learn, the uglier and more sordid it gets. I'm not going to have anything more to do with it."

"Does that mean we're off the case?" Ruby asked, disappointed. "We're abandoning the mystery?"

"Ruby," I said firmly, "we were never *on* the case. And as a matter of fact, there *is* no mystery—at least, not one with a plot that you and I would enjoy. A Ranger goes bad and starts taking from the Mexican drug lords. Then he finds out that he has pancreatic cancer—"

Ruby leaned forward. "Really?" Her green eyes were alight. "Cancer? How do you know *that*?"

"Doc Clarkson's receptionist told me." I went on. "So Adcock learns that he's terminal and decides to cash in his chips. Then his widow's sexy Latin ex shows up, she takes him up on his offer of a rerun, and they return to their former lives. See? No big deal. No mystery. And definitely *no* case."

"But—"

"Look, Ruby. I left criminal law and moved to Pecan Springs because I was sick of crooks and hoodlums. I wanted to live a clean, calm, quiet life. If you're dying for cops and robbers, go to the library and check out one of Patricia Cornwell's thrillers. She'll give you all the serial-killer psychos you can ever hope to want.'' I reached for another cookie. ''But I'm out. Life is short. It doesn't have to be ugly, too.''

There was a silence while the fire crackled and popped. After a while, Ruby said, ''Well, if you didn't come to talk about murder, drugs, and the underworld, why are you here? You'll forgive me if I point out that you and I haven't spent an evening together for quite a few months now.''

There was another silence while I stared into my milk. ''My frog turned into a prince,'' I said finally.

Ruby gave me an oblique glance. ''They do that sometimes,'' she said. ''They can't always help it, though. It's hormones. Testosterone. What's he done?''

''He's found himself a princess with an open door policy.''

Ruby's red-gold eyebrows shot up under her frizzy hair. ''McQuaid? You're making that up. He's Mr. Clean!'' She gave me a narrow-eyed, scrutinizing look. ''You *are* making it up, aren't you?''

''People aren't always what they seem,'' I said. Witness Roy Adcock, whose captain praised him as a hero, the pride of the Rangers. Ditto Adcock's widow and Amado Dunia, neither of whom were what they pretended to be. And ditto McQuaid.

''I don't believe it,'' Ruby said flatly.

''He told me, Ruby,'' I said. ''I asked him straight out if he was having an affair, and he didn't deny it.'' And then I related the whole story, from beginning to end, including meeting Margaret and making a total fool of myself at the memorial service that afternoon. ''I can't believe I did that,'' I said disgustedly. ''I acted like a blithering idiot. Margaret was cool and dignified. I was a jealous, raging shrew."

"That's in the hormones, too," Ruby said. "Try burdock and dandelion root. They're good for PMS."

"I can't blame this on PMS."

"Well," Ruby remarked philosophically, "I imagine McQuaid feels as bad as you do. Maybe worse. After all, he has to deal with the guilt." She picked up the tarot cards and began turning them, fingering them. Ruby has several decks, but the round Motherpeace, which was designed by two women, especially for women, is her favorite.

"Guilt? Well, maybe." I stared at the dying fire. "When you get right down to it, though, it's not entirely his fault. Until the last month or so, I was opposed to getting married. I enjoyed living with him, but I wanted to keep my independence, live my own life." I sighed heavily. "Maybe Margaret doesn't care about her independence. Maybe she wants to quit working and get married and have his babies. He's always wanted more children." I was feeling very mixed up, ashamed of myself and sorry for myself at the same time.

"She doesn't sound like that kind of person to me," Ruby remarked. "I mean, police work isn't the easiest job for women. She's probably pretty tough."

"Put the accent on *pretty*," I said bleakly. "And young."

"How young?"

"In her early thirties, I'd guess. She's only been a Ranger for a year or so. Before that, she worked undercover for the San Antonio police. I suppose that's how she got to know Adcock. Maybe they worked on the Harris case together."

Absently, Ruby separated the cards into two stacks and

began to shuffle them. "Speaking of the Harris case—" She hesitated. "I know you don't want to talk about it, but I'm curious. What did you find out from Elaine? Weren't you going to see her today?"

"I was. We made a lunch date, but she didn't show up. She didn't come to the memorial service, either. I wonder—"

I frowned. I'd been so busy stewing over Margaret and McQuaid that I had totally forgotten about Elaine. What *had* happened to her? She had definitely intended to come to the memorial service, and she had really wanted the information in the green folder. Surely she wouldn't have blown it off without calling me.

"Well?" Ruby asked, looking up. "So what happened to Elaine? Did you call her?"

I shook my head. "I don't want to talk about Elaine, Ruby. I want to talk about Margaret and McQuaid. I need to make a decision."

There was a pause. A card fell out of the deck, facedown on the rug. "I know McQuaid wants to get married, but are you sure he wants more children?" Ruby asked. "Brian's twelve. There'd be quite a few years between him and the baby." She moved the card in front of her, still facedown. She didn't pick it up.

"I've never actually asked how McQuaid feels about children," I said. "I wasn't ready to talk about marriage, so what was the point? But he's young, and he loves kids. He's a natural dad. And I'm forty-five," I added glumly.

"So? Liz Johnson just had a baby, and she's forty-six."

"Yes, but it wasn't the first, and Liz doesn't have a business to run. What would I do with a baby? Tote it around in a backpack while I work? It's too much. Damn it, Ruby, I'm forty-*five*.''

Forty-five, with a wide gray streak in my hair, the beginnings of wrinkles at the corners of my eyes, and a few extra pounds that I haven't been able to bicycle off. McQuaid was thirty-eight, and if Margaret wanted to, she could pass for twenty-five—not to mention that she was gorgeous. All of a sudden, I felt despairing. I could feel the tears filling my eyes, spilling over.

''You should see her, Ruby,'' I said hopelessly. ''She's young, she's beautiful, she's smart. There's no way I can compete with her.''

''Stop crying,'' Ruby said. She fanned out the cards in front of her. ''Or at least cry for the right reasons. Do you *want* children?''

''I don't know,'' I said, wiping my eyes. ''I don't think so. But I *do* want McQuaid.'' And suddenly it was true, and the clear, strong truth of it blazed through me like a blowtorch, burning everything else away. ''I love him, Ruby. I don't want to lose him.''

''Well, hallelujah!'' Ruby said softly, laying another card facedown.

''I beg your pardon?''

She looked up. ''It's about time you woke up and realized where your heart is. Believe me, there are plenty of women in this world who'd like to trade places with you. McQuaid is a good-looking guy with a sharp mind and a sexy bod. I've often wondered why the hell he puts up with you.''

I stared at her. ''Have I been that bad?''

She gave a little shrug. ''Not bad, exactly. Just self-absorbed.''

"I've only been doing what women ought to do in a world that's organized by and for men," I said stiffly. "Look out for themselves first."

"That's true in the business world," Ruby said. "That's where everybody has to compete for jobs and money and power. At home, everybody has to give a little." She met my eyes, direct, challenging. "McQuaid puts you first," she said quietly. "Most times, you put yourself first."

"Like when?"

"Like when he got a job offer in a big city and decided to stay here, because you wouldn't move."

"But I've lived in big cities," I said. "I don't want to do that anymore."

Ruby gave me a patient look. "I'm not saying you should. I'm just pointing out that you chose the way you wanted to live, and McQuaid chose you. That's all."

"I guess, when you put it that way—"

"Is there another way to put it?"

I was silent for a minute or two. Finally I said, in a small voice, "I've been a real jerk, haven't I?"

"Well, not a *jerk*, exactly." Ruby was comforting. "More like a dumbbell. But you're coming around. There's hope."

"I'm not so sure. You should see her, Ruby."

She slitted her green eyes. "You're sure you're not overreacting? Maybe you're just jealous."

"Oh, I'm jealous, all right. Next to her I feel like I'm ready for retirement. But I'm not *just* jealous." I glanced at my watch. "What should I do, Ruby? McQuaid's due to call in a little while."

Ruby put down a third card, also facedown. "Why don't you ask the cards?"

I should explain that the tarot is Ruby's thing, not mine. I took a class from her once, and she told us that the cards are symbols. They tap a part of us that our everyday conscious minds would just as soon not connect with, an unconscious part that we're afraid of and want to keep repressed. When we choose a card, it tells us something about that deep-down dark stuff inside us. Ruby's explanation had been intriguing, and I respected her right to believe whatever she wants. But I wasn't convinced.

"The cards? I don't think so," I said. "You know how I feel about that hocus-pocus stuff."

"I know," Ruby said regretfully. "Your right brain is badly underdeveloped. You know how to use rational, linear logic, and you're very smart, but you don't use your intuition. You don't trust your heart." She paused. "Anyway, there's no hocus-pocus to the cards. The images are only mirrors that help us look inside ourselves. Microscopes that help us see something we might not otherwise see."

"Yeah, sure." I laughed briefly. "Something we imagine. Something we make up."

"What's wrong with that? Maybe what we imagine has more truth than what we know. What do you have to lose, China? You're facing some tough questions. I can't answer them, and you can't either. The cards might shed some light on your problem."

"I doubt it," I muttered. "Anyway, I don't believe in that stuff."

"Doubt is fine too," Ruby said with a little shrug. "But

something can be possible, even *true*, whether you believe it or not.''

She was right, but I didn't want to say so. I swung my feet off the footstool and put my hands on the chair arms, ready to hoist myself up. ''I don't have time for a card reading,'' I said. ''Scouts will be over in twenty minutes. I have to get Brian.''

Ruby didn't move. ''The cards are right here.'' She pointed to the three that were lying facedown on the rug in front of her. ''Don't you want to know what they are?''

''Hey,'' I objected. ''*I* didn't pick those. You can't just choose any old card out of the deck at random and claim that they're going to mean something to *me*.''

''These are the cards that emerged from the deck while you were telling me how you feel. They're your cards, just as if you reached into the deck and picked them out.''

I was resigned. Whether I believed this stuff or not, whether it would do me any good or not, there was no way I was going to get out of it. I heaved a mighty sigh. ''All right, all right. These are the cards that have volunteered to give me advice. So what do they have to say?'' I glanced at my watch. ''Tell them to make it fast.''

Ruby picked up the first card, turned it faceup, and studied it for a moment. ''It's the Seven of Swords,'' she said, handing it to me. On the round card was a primitive colored drawing, like a child's drawing, of a fox lurking outside a pen. Inside, crowded into one corner, was a flock of frightened chickens, huddled together. Stuck into the fence were seven sharp knives.

''What's it supposed to mean?'' I asked.

Ruby regarded the card. ''The fox is a predator,'' she said

slowly. "He might represent stealth, trickery, deceit. The chickens can represent—"

"Victims," I said. "They're about to be a midnight snack. Fast food for foxes."

"They might represent suspicion, fear, apprehension." She handed me the card. "See how they're all crowded together in the corner, as if they're waiting for something to happen?"

Suspicion, fear, apprehension. The words described the way I'd been feeling about McQuaid, ever since I overheard that phone call. And now that I really looked at the card, it was clear what was going to happen. The fence wasn't very high. The fox was going to take it in one leap, and those chickens would be history.

I put the card down. "How is this supposed to connect with me? Am I the fox, or the chickens?"

"What do you think?"

"The chickens," I said. "Cornered."

Ruby smiled a little. "Maybe the card wasn't meant for you. Sometimes, when you're deeply connected to someone, you get a card that's meant for that person. Maybe the card refers to McQuaid."

I laughed shortly. "Well, I can guess which one *he* is. He's the fox, which definitely makes me a chicken. I don't like this card, Ruby. What's the next one?"

Ruby turned the next card over and held it up. It showed a woman kneading bread dough, tension in the lines of her body, an anxious expression on her face. "The Five of Discs," she said. "People usually get this card when they're worried about something."

"No kidding," I said. "The chickens are worried, the

woman with the bread is worried, *I'm* worried. No big news here. What I want to know is what I'm supposed to do about it."

"You might try doing what this image suggests," Ruby said. "When you knead bread, you turn the dough around, move it up and down, fold it over and over, every which way. It takes muscle and energy and time and the right conditions for dough to become bread. You have to be patient."

Ruby could have her symbols. I needed an operator's manual. "But what am I supposed to *do* while I'm being patient?" I pointed. "That's the last card. What does it say?"

Ruby frowned. "Not so fast. These images have a lot of different meanings. You have to think about them for a while before you can grasp what they—"

"I don't have a while," I said. "I have to pick Brian up in ten minutes. Come on, Ruby. Turn the card over. I want to know what's going to happen to those chickens."

Ruby turned it over. She didn't say anything, just stared at it, her expression unreadable.

"What's wrong?" I asked. "What is it?"

Ruby held the card up against her so I couldn't see it. "Before we talk about this, China, I have to warn you not to jump to conclusions. This card doesn't mean what it seems. It means change, transformation. It doesn't necessarily mean—"

"For Pete's sake, Ruby, will you show me the damn thing?" I demanded. I reached over and plucked the card out of her fingers, holding it to the last, flickering light of the fire. Involuntarily, I pulled in my breath. The card was black. It pictured a large snake encircling a skeleton. My right brain might not be optimally functional, but it didn't take a hell of a lot of imagination to interpret this card. It was the Thirteenth Trump.

Death.

Ruby took the card away from me. "Remember what I said, China. You can't interpret these symbols too literally. And you have to pay attention to details. Look closely at that snake and you'll see that it's shedding its skin."

"Oh," I said dryly. "So that what it's doing. Funny thing, though. I thought skeletons usually symbolized death."

Ruby paid no attention. "It could mean something else entirely. It could mean that a new identity is emerging. You or someone close to you is undergoing a radical change, taking on a different personality. Or it could mean that a disguise is coming off and the real self is being revealed."

"Yeah. McQuaid. He's showing his true self."

"Sure, it looks threatening," Ruby went on, as if I hadn't spoken. "Change is like that. But you don't need to be afraid of change, because it's natural, the way a snake shedding its skin is natural. Maybe the symbol points to something like renewal or an ego death or the end of a dream or—"

"Bullshit," I said, and got up out of the chair. "You accuse me of being skeptical about tarot cards and astrology and stuff like that—well, now you see why. I came over here for advice, and all I get is a bunch of symbolic mumbo-jumbo that doesn't make a lick of sense. Chickens cowering in the corner, women making bread, a snake shedding its skin." I shook my head. "For crying out loud, Ruby, you can find symbols anywhere you look. They can mean anything you like. It's *facts* that count.''

The phone rang, and Ruby got to her feet, reaching for the phone on the table beside the sofa. ''Whoever it is, I'll ask them to call back. We haven't finished talking about this card. I don't want you to go away frightened.''

''I am not going away frightened,'' I said. ''I'm just going away. Thanks for the cookies and milk.''

Frightened? Ridiculous, I thought, heading for the hall. Why should I be frightened by a flimsy piece of cardboard with a skeleton on it? Ruby could waste her time playing fortuneteller, but I had better things to do.

I had shrugged into my jacket and was pulling on my boots when Ruby appeared at the door. Her face was a white mask, her hair, back-lighted, a coppery halo.

''It's Justine,'' she said. She was holding the phone. Her voice was high-pitched, tinny. ''For you.''

I had yanked my boot on crooked. I unzipped it, slipped it off, and stamped my foot into it. ''What does she want?'' I asked, trying to pull the zipper up. ''Did she hear from Elaine?''

A thought suddenly struck me. Elaine had said that she was being followed, but I'd had so much on my mind that I hadn't thought about what that might mean. Maybe whoever was following her had caught up with her. Maybe Elaine hadn't shown up today because she was in trouble. Maybe—

''Just *take* it, China,'' Ruby said urgently, thrusting the phone at me.

I took it and cradled it under my chin while I wrestled with the zipper on my boot. ''What's up, Justine?''

''Get down here. On the double.''

''Here where?'' I asked, and spotted the problem. My sock was caught in the boot zipper.

''San Antonio. Good Samaritan Hospital. It's an emergency.''

''Emergency?'' I forgot about the zipper. ''Who? Elaine?'' Then I remembered about Brian. ''I can't drive to San Antonio tonight, Justine. I have to pick up Brian and get him home and—''

''Ruby can pick Brian up,'' Justine barked. ''You get in that car and start driving, *now*! I'll meet you there. And hurry, damn it.''

''But why—'' I stopped. ''Is it Elaine? Did Villarreal's boys catch up with her?''

''Elaine, hell!'' Justine shouted, totally losing it. ''Didn't Ruby tell you? For God's sake, China, McQuaid's been shot. If you don't get your ass in gear and fly it down here, you might not see him alive!''

Chapter Twelve

More in the garden grows
Than the gardener knows
Folk saying

I don't remember anything about the next few minutes, except shouting to Ruby as I rushed out the door that she had to pick up Brian at the First Methodist Annex and take him home and stay with him and invent some plausible excuse that a twelve-year-old would buy for his father not calling and my not picking him up. He'd have to live with Ruby's lie until I got home to tell him the truth, whatever it was.

I don't remember much about the trip to San Antonio, either, except driving through a terrifying cloudburst on I-35 south of New Braunfels, where the freeway funnels down to a single slick, lane hedged with plastic barrels that popped up out of the dark like fat orange funhouse lollipops. The headlights illuminated nothing but these barrels and the quicksilver streaks of slanting rain and the rocket-flashes of lightning. The windshield wipers, *slish-slosh, slish-clickety-slosh,* barely swept the torrents of water from the windshield, which I had to swipe with my sleeve because the defroster couldn't keep up. It was like driving under Niagara, piloting a submarine, flying a Cessna through the eye-wall of a hurricane, chaos and tumult all around me.

Even in daylight, in good weather, it's a bitch to navigate the freeway spaghetti that loops around San Antonio. At night, in a pouring rain, it's an ordeal, a ghastly initiation rite into some unholy fraternity of truckers and bus drivers. I managed, though, except for a heart-stopping near-collision with a burly Pizza Hut van as I turned off the exit ramp. I braked at the last instant, the force smashing my face into the steering wheel. I banged my nose and split my chin and bit my lip, hard. It hurt like bloody hell and I couldn't sue the Pizza Hut guy because it was my damn fault—I wasn't paying attention.

The gash in my chin wasn't life-threatening, but my nose was bleeding and blood was dripping down the front of my jacket. I made it down Nueces to Rio Grande, made a right turn and then another into the parking lot of Good Samaritan Hospital. I jumped out of the car and tripped over the curb and fell on my face in the muddy median strip. I scrambled to my feet and started to run through the slamming rain, toward a red neon sign, Emergency Room Ambulance Entrance. Somewhere close I heard a shrill, pulsing siren. I was running through a nightmare, lifting my legs, pumping as hard as I could but in slow motion, barely moving but driven forward by a lashing fear and the reverberating echo of Justine's words: *McQuaid's been shot been shot been shot been. . . .*

Justine herself was standing inside the automatic doors that slid open as slowly as if the mechanism were primed with molasses, finally opening just wide enough for me to lurch through. The waiting room was frigid, the walls glossy white, the white tile floors a frozen lake. The room was soundless, the people motionless.

"What the hell took you so long?" Justine demanded.

"How is he?" I gasped, pawing wet hair out of my eyes with muddy hands. "Where is he? Is he—"

My teeth closed on the word and I couldn't say it. I was shaking violently. I was going to throw up.

The siren shrieked to a stop outside the door. Inside, the frozen room erupted into a volcano of slams, shouts, cries, yells. Justine grabbed my arm and pulled me away from the door as the ER trauma team—three or four techs in blue scrubs and running shoes—swarmed toward it, pushing an empty gurney.

"How is he?" I shouted again at Justine. Outside, a door slammed, then another, while the strobe flashed, painting Justine's face alternately red and blue. The siren burped and quit. People yelled instructions. An EMS attendant chanted information as the trauma team bundled the victim out of the ambulance and onto the waiting gurney. "White male, age twenty-three, drive-by shooting victim. Bullet wounds to right shoulder and lower right abdomen. Shoulder, front entry, rear exit. Abdomen, entry, no exit. Blood pressure, 60 over 40—" The strobe went off and the bright white room seemed suddenly dark.

"They've taken him to OR," Justine said loudly, over the noise. "Elaine's up there, waiting for us." She was wearing her orange sweatshirt inside out and backwards, the label in front: XL (46-48). Her eyes were owl-like and scared behind her glasses. She put her hand on my arm, squinting at my chin, at the blood on my coat.

"What the hell happened to you? Did you get mugged?

Your face is a disaster. Your nose is dripping blood. Is it broken?''

The trauma team barreled through the door again, pushing the gurney, now loaded with the shooting victim, an oxygen mask over his face, an IV unit swinging over him. They hurtled out through a double door straight ahead. A fat woman in tight black pants and a gold lamé blouse with flapping sleeves, her moon of a face streaked with blood and tears, ran behind, arms outstretched, weeping. ''Joe!'' she cried. ''Joey, baby, my little boy!'' She disappeared through the door after the gurney.

I wrenched myself away from Justine's restraining arm. ''He's in the OR? Where? Where's that? Let's go!''

Others in the waiting room looked up from their *People* magazines and *Sports Illustrated*, turning in their hard plastic chairs to gawk first at the bat-winged fat woman, then at me, their mouths flapping open, silent spectators at a circus. A nurse in a starched white uniform was bearing down on us, her expression frozen into a hard glare. A snow maiden. An ice queen.

I clutched The Whiz's arm. ''Come *on*, Justine! I have to see him! I have to I have to I—''

''Okay, okay.'' Justine grasped my shoulder and shook it. ''Calm down, slow down, get hold of yourself.'' She nodded to the approaching nurse. ''Hysteria,'' she said with clinical authority. ''Where's the coffee?''

The nurse pointed to another door. ''Follow the yellow line. But you'd better skip the coffee and get her admitted. She needs an ice pack on that nose, it's a gusher.''

I put my sleeve against my nose to stem the tide. ''Forget it,'' I said, my voice muffled. ''I want to see McQuaid.''

The nurse pulled my arm down and peered closer. ''Well, if he's the one who slugged you, I hope you slugged him back. You're going to have a hell of a scar on that chin if you don't get reconstructive surgery.'' She gave up on me and bore hard left to confiscate a cigarette from a skinny, shrunken black man hunched under a No Smoking sign.

The Whiz pulled me toward the door and pushed me through, steering me along a yellow line that ran down the middle of the hall. Dazed, I stopped wondering where we were going and why and hung on to her hand. Med techs strode purposefully past, masks with plastic eye-shields hanging loose on their chests, stethoscopes carelessly flung over their shoulders. One wore a large button that admonished, ''You have a life. Go home!'' Metal-railed beds filled the curtained cubicles on either side of the open hallway, and people filled the beds. A man was screaming, heavy gutteral screams, *help me help me help*, and a young doctor pushed into the cubicle. ''Waddya think this is, the Civil War?'' he roared to a nurse. ''Knock the poor sonofabitch out!''

The Whiz spotted a stack of wound dressings that looked like Pampers, swiped one off the top, and thrust it at me. ''Hold this on your nose,'' she commanded. ''You're dripping like a stuck hog. Somebody's gonna have to mop up after you.''

We followed the yellow line as it turned a corner, through a door and out of the ER, then turned again into a gloomy cave of a cafeteria, deserted except for a gathering of empty tables and chairs, a drift of newspapers, a choir of vending machines humming to themselves along one side of the room.

"Sit," The Whiz said, and pushed me into a chair. She went to the ice machine and brought back a cup of cubes. I wrapped them in the Pamper and held them against my nose while she went to the coffee machine, then came back. "I forgot my purse. You got a buck on you?"

For some reason, this struck me as funny, and I giggled. But the giggling made my mouth hurt, and I stopped abruptly. Still holding the Pamper to my nose, I put my fingers to my lower lip. It was as big as a pigeon egg, and throbbing.

"Damn," I muttered. I touched my lip again, and my muddy fingers came away wet and red. "I'm bleeding."

"No kidding." Justine was rummaging through the purse that had slid from my shoulder onto the floor. "You're a fucking mess. You're gonna need a whole new chin. Who mugged you?"

"Pizza Hut," I said unintelligibly, exploring the inside of my lower lip with my tongue. I shuddered. My mouth felt like raw liver. I could taste blood.

"I don't do casualty work," Justine replied, feeding a handful of coins into the coffee machine, which returned liquid tar, hot enough to melt holes in the plastic cup she set in front of me.

"Cream and sugar," I mumbled numbly. I was shivering.

"This is not Starbucks," Justine said. She forced the cup into my right hand and headed for the machine again. "Don't think. Drink."

Five minutes and two dollars' worth of coffee later, I was beginning to feel human. It was a mixed blessing, because although I wasn't shivering so hard, my mouth hurt more.

My nose was still bleeding, and it hurt too. I hoped to hell it wasn't broken. But I said no to Justine's suggestion that we detour through the ladies' room to do something cosmetic to my face. We put fresh ice cubes in my blood-soaked Pamper, and took the elevator to the third floor.

After an eternity, the doors slid apart in front of a nurses' station. A security guard was leaning against the desk, talking to two deputy sheriffs. He blinked at the bloody wad I was holding to my nose, then recognized Justine and nodded. Behind the station was a pair of doors with a sign: OR Suite A. To the right of the station was a small waiting area, with blue upholstered furniture, dark blue tile, muted lighting, a TV set high on the wall tuned to CNN. An anxious huddle of people clustered in the corner by the window. A old man was asleep on a sofa, head back, mouth open, snoring.

Elaine Emery was slumped in a chair next to a pile of coats, her legs stretched out in front of her. She stood up when she saw me, her eyes widening. "Who hit *you*?"

"A steering wheel," I said, past my fat lip. "How's McQuaid?"

Justine was glancing around. "Where'd she go?"

"The phone," Elaine said. She looked at me. "He's in the OR, China. They're still trying to stabilize him."

My throat closed when I saw that her gray slacks were heavily bloodstained. "What did the doctors say? What happened?"

Her eyes slid away and my heart dropped into my stomach. "How bad?" I managed.

"Pretty bad," she said. "He's got a bullet in his neck. He was unconscious when they took him in there, and he couldn't move. He was having trouble breathing.''

Her words fell on me like lead. My knees folded and I sat down to keep from falling down. I dropped the Pamper and the ice cubes went all over the floor.

''More coffee,'' Justine muttered, looking around frantically. She scuttled off.

Elaine sat down next to me. Her face was pale, her rain-damp hair straggled loosely around her ears, and her nylon jacket was smeared with mud and blood. We were a fine pair. But the blood on me was mine. The blood on her was his. I couldn't remember seeing McQuaid's blood before, except for the time he gashed his thumb in the workshop and bled all over the kitchen floor. I reached out and touched it.

''How long has he been in there?'' I whispered.

She looked over my shoulder to the clock on the wall. ''Forty, maybe fifty minutes. Long enough for the cops to come and go.'' I realized that the deputy sheriffs at the nurses' station must have been part of the police investigation. I turned to look for them, but they were gone. ''Somebody ought to be coming out before too long,'' she added.

As she spoke, the double doors opened. A weary, defeated-looking gray-haired man in scrubs stepped through. He pulled his mask down and looked at us, failure drawn in the lines of his face. My heart plummeted. Then he looked past us to the group in the corner. He went to them and spoke briefly. Someone, a woman, let out a loud cry and began to sob.

I swallowed past the hurt. *Please, God*, I said, to someone I haven't believed in since I was six, *Not him, please, not him.* The sobbing grew louder. Someone else joined in. The old man on the sofa kept on snoring. On the television, a smiling, gray-haired man with shiny teeth was peddling life insurance.

"What happened?" I asked Elaine. "When? Where? How did *you* get involved?"

"At a roadside picnic stop," she said evenly. "A pair of men in a car drove up with automatic weapons and fired on us. I rolled under the truck. They were coming back to finish the job when McQuaid's backup opened fire with a shotgun. They got away."

A picnic stop? Automatic weapons? A classic drive-by hit. "But what was McQuaid doing there?" I demanded. "Why were *you* there?"

She wasn't looking at me. "I was there because I was promised certain information. I don't know why McQuaid was there. I wasn't expecting him." She raised her glance and her eyes met mine. "I didn't know he was connected to you until—"

The Whiz skidded up. "Coffee," she announced triumphantly, and thrust a cup at me. "Had to go a mile to get it, but it's hot." She pulled a chair forward and sat down across from me, close enough for our knees to touch. She threw a questioning look at Elaine.

"I'm filling her in," Elaine said.

The Whiz nodded, lawyer-like. "Now's a good time. When he comes out, there'll be other things to think about."

I put the cup on the table next to me, not letting Elaine's eyes get away. "Where did this shooting happen?" I asked. "When?"

"Thirty, forty miles west of here on U.S. 90, the other

side of Hondo. About seven-thirty. It was pretty dark.''

''Who got there first?''

''He was already there when I drove in. He was sitting in an old blue truck. I parked behind him and got out. He got out too.''

The Blue Beast. Site of many memories, most of them pleasant. Picnics, camping trips, drive-in movies, the fireworks. Tears threatened, and I sucked in my breath. I could cry later. Now, I needed to stay cool, get to the bottom of this.

''Seems like an out-of-the-way place,'' I said tightly. ''How did you happen to choose that particular spot?''

Elaine hesitated. ''I really don't think I—''

Justine leaned forward. ''I don't believe Elaine needs to get to that level of detail with you, Hot Shot. If you want to question her, perhaps I should—''

''Fuck off, Justine,'' I said, holding Elaine's eyes. ''How did you happen to be on U.S. 90 west of Hondo, Elaine?''

Elaine's lips compressed.

''*How*?'' I roared, coming out of my chair. ''Did you set him up?''

The old man quit snoring with a loud gurgle. The sobbing in the corner stopped. Out of the corner of my eye, I saw the security guard straighten up, watching us.

''Set him up?'' Elaine asked, as if she hadn't heard me right. She got to her feet. ''Are you suggesting that—''

Not to be outdone, Justine stood up too. ''Don't be ridiculous, Hot Shot. My client doesn't have to put up with such baseless, unfounded accusa—''

''I'm not your client,'' Elaine said tautly. ''I didn't ask you here, Justine. You volunteered.''

I turned to The Whiz. "Why the hell *are* you here?"

"Because I'm your friend," The Whiz said with dignity, "and I thought you might need me." She pulled herself up to her full height, still half a head shorter than me. "Now. Sit down, both of you, and we'll talk this thing over in a rational, civilized manner."

Still standing, I fixed my eyes on Elaine. "Well, did you?" I demanded. Not that I expected the truth, of course.

Elaine scowled. "Set him up? Of course not." She sat down, and Justine and I followed. "Look. It's a very simple story. I was leaving my apartment this morning, not long after you and I talked, when the phone rang. Somebody—a man, Hispanic, maybe, I couldn't identify his voice—told me that if I wanted information about . . . if I wanted certain information, I should go to the Highway 90 Motor Hotel in Hondo and wait until I was contacted." She picked up her purse and began to fish for something. She pulled out cigarettes and a lighter, still talking, then realized where she was and put them back. "So I drove to Hondo and checked into this crummy little motel room with cockroaches as big as armadillos in the bathroom. I sat around all day, doing nothing. About seven, the phone rang. A man—the same man who called that morning, I think—told me to drive to the picnic pull-off ten miles west of town. I did."

I waited. When she didn't say anything more, I said, "Is that all?" I didn't think so. Journalists are closed-mouthed on principle. A journalist who is a party to a drive-by shooting has even more incentive to keep her information to herself.

She nodded, emphatic. "That's it. That's all. That's how it happened, I swear."

''Can you corroborate your statement?''

''Oh, come on, now, China,'' Justine began, but Elaine cut her off.

''You can check the motel records. I got there about ten A.M. Around two I phoned the desk and asked them if anybody in town did takeout at that hour. The owner's wife brought me a tuna fish sandwich with dill pickles and a glass of milk.''

''Did you make any other phone calls?''

Elaine looked uncomfortable. ''I don't see what relevance—''

''Through the desk? Or did you use a credit card?''

Her lips set tight. She didn't answer.

''We can check that out,'' I said. ''Your calls can be traced, you know.'' I switched subjects. ''The information you thought you were going to get. Did it have to do with Rafael Villarreal?''

Justine started to speak but Elaine silenced her with a quick head shake. ''I really don't want to get into that part of it, China. You have to trust me when I say that the story I'm working on simply has no bearing on what happened tonight.''

''Look, Elaine,'' I said flatly, ''I don't want to scoop you or screw you out of a book deal. I am trying to find out who set McQuaid up. I want to know why he was with you at that picnic—''

''He wasn't with Elaine.'' The woman spoke defiantly, from behind me. ''He was with *me*.''

My heart began to knock against my ribs. For a few seconds, I couldn't move. Then I forced myself to stand and turn slowly, knowing who I would see.

Margaret.

Chapter Thirteen

By a rose petal I discover
If false or true be my fine lover.
English folk saying

We stared at one another. She was wearing navy slacks and a matching turtleneck. Her dark hair was skinned back away from her face, emphasizing the finely sculptured cheek bones, the full mouth. She was wearing his blood, too, quantities of it smeared across the front of her muddy slacks, her dirty sweater, caked on both sleeves where she must have cradled him in her arms.

The Whiz stood. ''Well, it's about time, Margaret,'' she said with a false cheeriness. ''I wondered where you were.''

''I was on the phone to Headquarters,'' Margaret said. ''When Mike gets out of the OR, we need security. They're sending someone.'' She glanced back at me. Her eyebrows went up, and she shook her head. ''Boy oh boy, you are a mess,'' she said. ''What does the other guy look like?''

''*I'm* a mess?'' I stared at her, feeling the crazy laughter welling in my throat. ''You look like you've been mud wrestling in a slaughterhouse.''

''Ladies, ladies,'' Justine said equably. ''We're all on edge. Let's not make matters worse.'' She pushed me back into my chair and pulled out a chair for Margaret. There we were, the four of us, close enough to do one another's nails.

I looked at Margaret, at the blood all over her. *She* had been with him when he was shot? "Would somebody please please *please*," I said passionately, "tell me what is going on?"

Margaret leaned forward. "Somebody—a woman, he didn't recognize the voice—got Mike on his cell phone today around three. She instructed him to drive to Hondo and check into the—"

"Let me guess," I interrupted. I glanced at Elaine. "The Highway 90 Motor Hotel. Very convenient, Elaine."

"Wait a minute," Elaine said, flushing. "I don't like your tone. I've already told you—"

"Did you call him from the motel?" I asked savagely. "Because if you did, there'll be a record of it."

Margaret's head turned. She gave me an appraising look.

There was a silence as Elaine's glance slid away, evasive. "Actually, I did call your friend this afternoon," she said apprehensively. "But not to—" She interrupted herself, gnawing on her lower lip. "I . . . had some information. I thought he might . . ." She looked at me. There was a little bead of sweat along her upper lip. "You don't believe me, do you? You think I was the one who got him to Hondo."

"I think it's entirely possible. How do you happen to know McQuaid?"

For a minute, I didn't think she was going to answer. Finally, she said, "A couple of weeks ago I got a tip that Mike McQuaid was working on the Harris case for the DPS, and that he was onto something important. I thought it might be something I could use."

Margaret's head zipped around. Her smoky lavender eyes fastened on Elaine. "The Harris case?"

I turned to Margaret. "McQuaid was working for the DPS?" I asked, surprised. "Is that true?" As far as I knew, McQuaid hadn't done any formal investigative work since he left the Houston Police Department.

Margaret nodded reluctantly.

"Since when?"

"Since the first of the year."

Ah, that sabbatical. So it wasn't a grant that was paying McQuaid's salary, it was the Department of Public Safety. No wonder he didn't want to talk about his so-called research. He was doing *police work.*

Margaret's eyes went to Elaine. "It wasn't true that he was working on the Harris case, though. That was only peripheral."

"What *was* he working on?" I asked.

"You'll have to ask him." She bit her lip and blinked the tears away.

I turned to Elaine. "Who told you he was working on the Harris case?"

"Hot Shot." The Whiz was reproachful. "You know that a journalist's sources are protected."

"Hot Shot?" Margaret asked.

"Old law-school nickname," The Whiz said.

Elaine shifted in her chair. "Honestly, China. You've got to believe me. I had no idea McQuaid was on his way to Hondo."

If I had a dime for every *honestly, you've got to believe me* that my clients handed me, I could buy greater metropolitan Houston. "What time did you call him?"

She swallowed. "Three-fifteen, or thereabouts."

"True?" I glanced at Margaret, who seemed to be clued into what had been going on with McQuaid all day—for weeks, probably, maybe months. "Were there two calls? One from Elaine, one from somebody else?"

"I don't know," Margaret said slowly.

She had to know as well as I did that journalists sometimes help to create the news they report, and that chances were better than fifty-fifty that that Elaine was no passive observer. In fact, I was willing to bet next month's cash receipts that Elaine knew who was behind this job, although she might not have expected it to turn out the way it did.

Margaret turned to me. "Mike didn't mention any other calls. It's possible that she had something more to do with it than she's letting on."

The Whiz gave Elaine a querying look. "If you have any information that would straighten this out," she said, "we'd better hear it."

Elaine was beginning to see her problem. "You guys have got this all wrong." She squirmed in her chair. "I just called him, that's all. I had no idea that he—"

I cut her off with a gesture. She wasn't ready to talk yet, and I wanted to hear from Margaret. "What about you, Margaret?" I asked. "What was your part in this?"

The old man on the sofa was snoring again. Outside, I could hear the urgent wail of another emergency vehicle. Margaret gave me a long, cool look. "I was Mike's backup."

I blinked. "Backup?"

"She was the one with the shotgun," The Whiz offered helpfully.

Elaine took this opportunity to cast herself in the role of potential victim. "If it hadn't been for Margaret, they would have finished McQuaid off," she said eagerly. "And killed me, too."

"Maybe not," Margaret said. Narrow-eyed, she studied Elaine. "Maybe you were there to be sure McQuaid got out of the truck, so he'd be a better target. And if it hadn't been for you, I would have had a clean shot at the attackers." Her voice rose angrily. "I saw the whole damn thing coming. I had that Ford in my sights. If you hadn't blocked my shot, I'd have blasted them off the road before they shot him." She dropped her head into her hands. "He counted on me," she said, her voice muffled. "I let him down. If I'd gotten that shot off before they opened fire—"

"But it wasn't *my* fault," Elaine cried. "You're not thinking straight, Margaret. How could I have blocked your shot when I didn't even know you were there?"

"You're the one who isn't thinking straight," I interrupted angrily. "Nobody in her right mind would have gone out there alone, after dark, unless she—"

Justine cleared her throat. "I think," she said, "that it would be a good idea to start over again, a little more calmly. To take it from the top, as it were. Who wants to go first?"

Margaret and Elaine traded scowls. It was clear that Margaret had begun to suspect Elaine, and that Elaine wouldn't or couldn't tell us anything that would clear her.

Justine leaned forward with a little smile, putting on her mediating face. "Come now, ladies, don't be shy. Margaret, why don't you begin? Tell us what you and McQuaid were working on together and why—"

"Excuse me," a woman's voice said behind me. "I'm Dr. Kerr. I'm looking for Mrs. McQuaid. I've been working on her husband."

Justine spoke. "There is no Mrs.—"

I scrambled to my feet and whirled around. "I'm Mrs. McQuaid," I said. My heart was in my throat, and I had to choke out the words. "How is he, Doctor?"

She stripped the surgical cap off her hair, and its abundance, honey-brown, tumbled around her shoulders. "I think he's going to make it," she said wearily, and pulled out a chair. "If we're lucky."

He was going to make it! I was flooded with grateful relief. "Thank you, *thank you*," I breathed. Then her other words caught up to me, and I was suddenly, deeply afraid. "If we're . . . lucky?"

She nodded. She looked very tired—face drawn, heavy circles under her eyes, shoulders sagging. "I'll tell you straight, Mrs. McQuaid. This is a very bad thing. Spinal cord injuries are unpredictable, and this one . . ." She shook her head, her eyes dark. "There's a massive contusion and major soft-tissue trauma, all of which makes it very difficult to determine the extent of the neural damage. The bullet—probably a ricochet, or he'd be dead by now—is putting a great deal of pressure on the spinal cord."

Fear squeezed the air out of my lungs. I had to suck in my breath, hard, as if I were pulling it in through a closed valve. "You didn't . . . take it out?"

She shook her head. "Not yet. His condition is critical, and I don't want to risk surgery unless it's absolutely necessary. I've called in another specialist, and we'll see what he says. I would prefer not to do anything until your husband regains consciousness and we can evaluate his progress and determine the motor function loss. Most gunshot wounds are sterile, so infection isn't a major concern.''

''Motor function loss?'' Margaret asked. Her face was white, her voice thready.

Dr. Kerr glanced at her. ''We can't be sure, but he appears to be paralyzed from the neck down.''

Paralyzed? She kept on speaking, but there was a roaring in my ears that blotted out her voice. I focused dizzily on her lips, trying to separate her words from the *no no no* shrieking inside my head.

''From my experience with wounds of this kind, I expect some recovery of function—some,'' she added, her eyes on me, ''although it will likely not be as complete as we would like. But it's too early for a prognosis. Right now, we're concentrating on getting him stabilized.'' Her face softened and she reached for my hand. ''I'm sorry I can't be more encouraging, Mrs. McQuaid. He's alive, and that's something. But he's still in trouble.''

''I want to see him,'' I said, forcing the words past numb lips, past the fear that closed my throat.

''He's unconscious, but—Yes, of course you can see him.'' She hoisted herself wearily out of the chair. ''He's in ICU, down the hall to the left, through the doors. He's on a ventilator, so even if he were conscious, he couldn't talk to you.''

I stood, and Margaret stood too. ''I'm going with you,'' she said.

Dr. Kerr shook her head. ''I'm sorry,'' she said. ''Only his wife—''

Margaret looked at me, her eyes full of mute pleading.

I swallowed. I could shut this woman out, keep her away from him, and nobody, not even McQuaid, would blame me for that. McQuaid. The recollection of his ample smile, his deep, generous laugh, filled me. If the situation were reversed, if I were the one in ICU and he were here, choosing—

"I want her to go with me, Doctor," I said thinly. "She's my . . . my sister."

Dr. Kerr put one hand on my shoulder and the other under my chin, tipping my face to the light. "You look like you could use some attention yourself," she said. "You need to get some stitches in that chin. And you're going to have a beautiful pair of black eyes."

"It's nothing, really," I said. "An argument with a pizza truck." How could I worry about my face when his *life* was in danger?

"It's something, really," Dr. Kerr insisted gently. "What do you want him to see when he wakes up? A wife with a bloody chin and a couple of shiners? Go with her," she said to Margaret. "And keep her away from pizza trucks."

We tried to smile, but none of us managed it. Margaret and I walked away together, down the hall. Just as we reached the ICU suite, she put her hand on my arm.

"We're forgetting something," she said. "Don't you think you ought to call Mike's folks? They'll be terribly upset if they're not notified about this. And if you call them now, you won't have to tell them how he . . . looks, or anything. Just tell them to come."

I gulped. The McQuaids live on a farm near Seguin, less than an hour away. "Yes, of course," I said, reluctantly grateful for her reminder of something I should have thought of myself. ''I wonder where the phones are.''

She pointed, and I went. It was the most difficult call I have ever made. When I hung up, my hands were shaking and McQuaid's parents were on their way.

Margaret and I spent three-quarters of an hour in ICU, I on one side of the bed, she on the other, McQuaid lying between us, unconscious, his neck fixed in a plastic sleeve that immobilized his head, a plastic mask over his nose and mouth. The ventilator was breathing for him and mechanical monitors of various sorts were observing and recording heartbeat, brain waves, oxygen level—the critical data generated by even a minimally functioning human body. The dials and digital readouts told me the most important thing, that his heart was still beating, his brain still functioning, his lungs still filling with air. But they couldn't tell me when he would be laughing and walking and holding me again. Or if.

We had been there a long while, silent, when Margaret spoke. ''Maybe it's too personal, and you won't tell me,'' she said, not looking at me. Her eyes were devouring him. ''I want to know whether you call him McQuaid when you're . . . making love.''

''Yes,'' I said, thinking how young she sounded, and how old I felt.

She touched his hand, lying motionless on the bed. ''Why do you do that? It's so impersonal, as if you don't . . . love him.''

''We met in court,'' I said. ''His cop friends called him McQuaid, so I did, too. It felt natural then. It still does. 'Mike' wouldn't sound right. Not to me.''

She raised her eyes and our glance met across the bed. She was standing straight and tall, her slender waist cinched by the belt of her bloodstained slacks. Looking at her, I felt thick and heavy.

"Friends," she said. "Is that what you are?" The question was hopeful, its implication clear.

I sighed. "Yes, we're friends. Friends first, and I hope always. But we're lovers, too." I looked down at him, remembering how it felt to have his arms around me, his mouth on mine, the length of his body against me. Remembering nights of shared passion—powerful, tender, unforgettable—and days of shared pleasures. Friends and lovers. Lovers and friends.

The hopefulness had reached her eyes, giving her a kind of innocence. She took his hand and held it. "You can be friends and lovers and still not be in love. Romantically, I mean."

Romance. It's a word that ignites jealousy, fires wars, fans feuds. Spark without substance, it burns itself out. It isn't the kind of fire that warms your heart and your life, day in, day out.

"Romantically," I said. "Is that the way you love him?"

"You make it sound . . ." She frowned. "What's wrong with romance?"

If she didn't already know, she wouldn't believe me when I told her. "Nothing," I lied. "It's just that romance comes and goes. Once it's gone, there's nothing left. Friendship lasts."

I touched his forehead. His eyes were closed, the dark, heavy lashes lying against his pale cheeks. The oxygen mask was taped to his face, pulling the skin. He hadn't shaved this morning, and his dark beard was showing.

"Are you friends?" I asked.

Her grip on his hand tightened. "It's hard to talk about my feelings for him . . . to you."

"I know," I said. I managed a wry grin. "I hate you too, Margaret."

"You?" She was taken by surprise. "Why should you hate me? You *have* him! He sleeps with you, every night!"

"He'd laugh if he heard you equate sex and ownership," I remarked mildly. "Anyway," I added, "he sleeps with you, too. More often than I know, I expect."

There was a long pause, while the oscilloscope beeped reassuringly and McQuaid's chest rose and fell. "He *slept* with me," she said finally. "Past tense. As in over and done with." Her voice was low and hard, as if she were steeling herself against sadness.

"Ah," I said. I felt glad for myself and sorry for her, both at once. I was a hundred years younger, a thousand pounds lighter, and I wanted to shout with happiness. But all I said was, "Thank you for telling me."

She darted a glance at me. "You didn't know? He didn't tell you?"

"We haven't had much time to talk since I found out about you," I said. "That was on Friday night. I overheard part of your conversation." Friday night, Valentine's Day. And this was only Monday. I felt as if I had lived decades since then.

The silence lengthened. "If he hasn't told you, I suppose I should," she said. "I seduced him." She spoke deliberately, as if she had wrung all the hopes and dreams out of what happened and was left with only the facts. "Mike isn't to blame. Not the first time, not the other times.''

I chuckled dryly. ''I imagine he did his part.'' I looked down at him, imagining him kissing her, touching her breasts. ''You're a very attractive woman.''

''All I mean to say is that the relationship was more my idea than his.'' She spoke earnestly, as if she wanted to convince me of the truth of what she was saying. ''It started early last month. You were gone for a couple of weeks. We went out after work and—'' A smile played around her mouth as she remembered. ''Well, I suppose you can guess how it happened.'' She gave me a sideways look, checking to see how I was handling it.

I didn't give her a lot of help. ''Yes. I can guess.''

She squared her shoulders. ''After you came back, it wasn't the same anymore. Finally he said we shouldn't be lovers again. He said . . . he was hoping you would marry him.''

She spoke the last sentence with a kind of determination, as if she were forcing herself to speak a truth she didn't want to accept. Her eyes locked with mine, and her voice was low, vibrating.

''I told him I still wanted him. And I'm telling *you*, China Bayles. This man is a good man. He's straight and he's true. If you don't marry him pretty quick, I'm going after him again. And I'll keep after him until he's mine. Do you hear?''

I reached across McQuaid's body, took her free hand, squeezed it and dropped it. ''I hear,'' I said. ''But I've already decided. If he asks, I'm going to say yes. If he doesn't, I'll ask him. So don't get your hopes up, Margaret. One way or another, you're out of luck.''

I leaned over and kissed his forehead lightly. Yes, I would ask him, the moment he woke up. I disregarded the cold fear congealing in the pit of my stomach and concentrated on that moment, on my asking, on his agreeing. We could have the ceremony here or wherever—that didn't matter. What mattered, what was suddenly urgent, was that we do it, and do it quickly.

Margaret and I stood there a few moments more, each of us thinking our private thoughts, both of us watching McQuaid's almost imperceptible breathing, listening to the mechanical sounds of medical miracles at work. And then Margaret kissed him too, and we left.

Chapter Fourteen

> The leaves, flowers, and seedes [of St. John's Wort] stamped and put into a glass with oile olive, and set in the hot sunne for certaine weekes together and then strained from those herbes, and the like quantitie of new put in, and sunned in like manner, doth make an oile of the colour of blood, which is a most pretious remedy for deep wounds.
>
> John Gerard, *The Herball*, 1597

We met the nurse as we came through the doors into the main hall. "I was just coming to get you, Mrs. McQuaid. Your mother's here and she's anxious—"

"Mrs. McQuaid!" Leatha exclaimed. She had darted around the corner just in time to hear the nurse. She raised her hands with a despairing cry. "You and Mike got married and didn't *tell* me?"

I diminished Leatha's apprehension by a few words of reassurance (no, we hadn't gotten married without her) and answered her worried questions. It turned out that she had called our house and spoken with Ruby, who told her, more or less, what had happened. Leatha had jumped in the car and driven from Kerrville, leaving in such a hurry that she hadn't fluffed her bouffant hairdo or replaced the foundation, blusher, eyeshadow, and lipstick that she'd already taken off.

It was the first time in many years that I had seen my mother without her makeup, or as anything less than impeccably groomed, exquisitely elegant, polished, ageless. She looked old and vulnerable, and I was suddenly moved by the naked network of fine lines around her mouth and eyes and her short, stubby eyelashes, like the broken teeth of a comb. Even her straggling hair, two weeks past a touchup, looked authentic, and she was wearing a pair of coffee-stained purple sweats with a three-cornered rip above one knee. Watching her weep, seeing her blow her red nose and wipe her streaming eyes, I was amazed, and for some idiotic reason, I thought of the Velveteen Rabbit. Was my mother—whom I thought of as a man-made woman, a seventy-year-old plastic Barbie—becoming real at last?

And when she put her arms around me and we cried together for the first time since my father's funeral, I had to ask the same question of myself. Like my mother, but in different ways, I had escaped. I'd focused my attention on the herb shop, my gardens, the domestic coziness of life with McQuaid and Brian, and closed my eyes to ugliness: crime and criminals, the underworld of drugs and guns and violence. But I couldn't escape the stark, ugly reality of what had happened tonight. It was in my life, and I had to face it.

While this was going on, Margaret was talking quietly to the uniformed San Antonio police officer who had just got off the elevator. The two of them went in the direction of ICU; then Justine came up to tell me that she had to leave, promising to call every couple of hours to check on Mc-

Quaid's condition. Elaine, pointedly looking at her watch, wanted to leave too, but I managed to delay her departure.

At this point, Mother and Dad McQuaid arrived, and there were more tears and explanations. McQuaid's mother, a short, round woman with a soft and ample bosom, enveloped me in a weeping embrace, while his father (tall and strong-featured, like McQuaid) rubbed our shoulders and kept muttering helplessly, "What the devil was Mike *doin'* out there?"

The third time he asked the question, he added, half-uncertainly, "Was he doin' somethin' he shouldn't a been doin'? Somethin' wrong?"

Margaret had just returned alone from the direction of ICU, where she must have left the police officer standing guard over McQuaid. She sprang hotly to his defense.

"Doing something wrong?" she repeated. "Absolutely not! This isn't for publication, but your son was on an undercover assignment for the Texas Rangers. I was with him."

At Margaret's revelation, which she must have thought would make them proud, Mother McQuaid burst into a deluge of fresh tears.

"Damn," Dad McQuaid said disgustedly. "Mike said he was done playing cops and robbers. Said he was gonna be a university professor the rest of his life. Gonna be respectable." He peered contentiously at Margaret. "And who the dickens are *you*?"

Margaret couldn't have known it, but she had stumbled into the quicksand of a long-time family squabble. The McQuaids had never wanted their son to be a cop, and when he left Houston Homicide, they were the two happiest people in the state of Texas.

"I can finally sleep nights," his mother had said with tearful relief, and his father had added, "Glad you're gonna be a teacher, son. Cops don't get no respect."

With some reluctance, I introduced Margaret, who looked as if she wished she'd kept her mouth shut.

Dad McQuaid eyed her suspiciously. "You said you was out there with Mike when he got shot up?"

"Yes, sir," Margaret muttered. "I was his backup."

The subject of women in law enforcement is another of Dad McQuaid's hot-button topics, and Margaret was in for it. "Well, if you was his backup," he demanded, "how come you didn't blow them bastards off the face of the earth? Did you just stand around with your hands danglin' on the ends of your arms while they used Mike for target practice?"

"If it hadn't been for Margaret," I intervened, "he might be dead right now. She got one shot at the car, but there was a civilian in the way and she couldn't risk another."

Dad McQuaid ignored me. "Some backup you are," he growled. "If the good Lord wanted women to be cops, he woulda—"

"Come on, Dad," Mother McQuaid said tearfully, tugging at his arm. "We're wasting time. Let's go see him."

The two of them hurried off down the hall, while I settled Leatha, still red-eyed and tearful, in a chair near the nurses' station.

"I would appreciate it if you would wait here and keep an eye on things," I said. "Margaret and Elaine and I have to talk." Elaine gave me a sharp glance and started to object, but Margaret silenced her with a darted look, sharp as a knife. ''We'll be in the cafeteria,'' I added to Leatha. ''Come and get me if there's any change. Okay?''

Leatha blew her nose. ''Okay,'' she said. She looked at Elaine and Margaret. ''What are you going to—''

''Somebody did this to McQuaid,'' I said grimly. ''Between us, maybe we can figure out who.''

The cafeteria was still deserted, but somebody had turned on the lights. The fluorescents washed the room with the bleak, chill light that always reminds me of the Houston morgue, and I shivered. We furnished ourselves with coffee from the vending machine and took the cups to the nearest table.

''I don't want to go over it again,'' Elaine said as we sat down under a No Smoking sign. ''I've told you everything I know, and I'm exhausted.'' She opened her shoulder bag and took out her cigarette pack and lighter. ''When I finish this cigarette, I'm outta here.''

''No, you're not,'' Margaret said evenly. ''You're not going anywhere until we get to the bottom of this.'' At Elaine's hostile glance, her voice roughened. ''I'm officially in charge of this investigation, Elaine, and what I say goes. You don't like it, I can arrange to conduct the questioning downtown. You got that?''

I had momentarily forgotten that Margaret was a Ranger, and I was a little surprised at her declaration that she was in charge. Not that I had any objections, though. If anybody was motivated to get to the bottom of tonight's attack, she was.

Elaine arched both eyebrows. ''So what happened to the

police who were here earlier? I thought it was their investigation.''

''This is a Ranger matter,'' Margaret said. ''I've talked to Headquarters. I've been assigned to find out what happened and who was responsible, and that's exactly what I mean to do. Understood?''

Elaine took her time lighting her cigarette. ''You're not exactly a disinterested party, are you?'' She tapped her nails on the table, tendrils of blue smoke curling from her nostrils. ''Oh, well, let's get it over with. I don't want to spend all night here.''

Margaret turned to me. Her mouth had its usual mild, pleasant look, but her eyes had lost their warmth and sexiness. They were steely and cold, the eyes of men you see in cop films. This was a serious woman. ''When I came back from arranging security for Mike, I overheard you ask Elaine whether her presence in Hondo had anything to do with Rafael Villarreal. How'd you make that connection, China?''

''Elaine told me over the phone this morning that she had opened a lead to Villarreal through the story she was working on.''

Margaret turned to Elaine. ''That would be the Harris murder, I take it.''

''That's right,'' Elaine said. She flicked her cigarette ash into her nearly empty cup. ''You know, Margaret, if you and Adcock had done a more professional job of investigating, I wouldn't have any story.''

Margaret flinched as if Elaine had stuck her with an ice pick. Elaine went on, pressing her advantage, not giving Margaret time to recover.

"I wonder why you didn't wrap it up. Who were you covering for?" She paused, and her voice became sharper. "Because my story isn't just about drug smuggling, you know. It's about payoffs. Crooked cops. People like that kind of story better, actually. It confirms what they already know, way down in their gut. There are no more heroes."

Questioning somebody is like playing tennis. You have to keep the ball moving, control the net and the baselines, make your opponent play your game. Fail to return, and you've lost a point. Lose a couple of points, and you've lost the set. Margaret was still chasing Elaine's backhand. I stepped in.

"So you were lying when you told me you'd make Adcock look like a hero," I said.

She gave me a look I couldn't read. "Not necessarily. I wanted the information in that green folder I saw on Adcock's desk, and I was willing to do whatever it took to get it. I'm still willing."

Recovering, Margaret leaned forward. "The phone call that sent you to the motel. Did the caller mention Villarreal?"

Elaine gave a scornful laugh. "Are you kidding? It's not a name people throw around just for the hell of it. The caller said that if I wanted information about my story, I should go to Hondo and wait. So I went. I wasn't about to miss out on an opportunity like that." She glanced at me. "I figured I could connect with you later, China."

"Could you identify the voice if you heard it again?"

"I doubt it. As I said, he was Hispanic. His accent was pretty pronounced, but other than that—" She shook her head.

I leaned forward. "Your call to McQuaid. You said you had information for him. What did you want to tell him?"

She didn't seem anxious to answer. After a moment, she said, evasively, "It was about the Harris case."

"How did you know he was working on that case?" Margaret asked.

"He told me," Elaine replied. I thought she looked relieved at the shift in questioning. "A couple of weeks ago, he called and said he'd heard I was looking into the matter and asked if we could talk. We set up a date at a coffee shop in San Antonio, and he told me he was part of a hush-hush official inquiry. He said he'd keep me informed of developments on his end if I'd let him in on what I'd dug up so far."

"You do deals with cops?" Margaret asked wryly.

"I do deals with whoever is willing to tell me what I need to know." Elaine's eyes glinted. "Anyway, Mike seemed more trustworthy than your average law enforcement type. And he's cute. So I agreed."

"What kind of information did you give him?"

Elaine lifted her chin. "Nothing worth writing home about. I told him I was digging into some of Roy Adcock's other cases—"

"Which other cases?" Margaret interrupted.

"—but I didn't tell him what I'd found. I was saving that until he came up with something worth trading for." Elaine picked up her purse and stood. "I need to go to the john."

"Well, now you've got something worth trading for," Margaret said. "Tell us what you know about Adcock, and we'll let you go."

Elaine's face became pained. "Excuse me," she said,

''but unless you want me to pee my pants—''

''One second,'' Margaret said, and reached for Elaine's purse. She opened it, took out a small, short-barreled .357 Magnum, and slipped it into her own bag. ''You can show me your concealed-carry permit when you get back.''

Elaine rolled her eyes. ''Ooh, Officer, you are *so* rough and tough,'' she said, and walked off.

''Shit,'' Margaret said eloquently.

I put my elbows on the table. ''I don't know what Elaine has dug up about Roy Adcock, and I don't know how much you and McQuaid know about the guy. But here's what I've learned in the last couple of days.''

Quickly and compactly, I outlined my discoveries: the offshore bank account, the phony ID, the laptop, the safe deposit box with the computer disk. By now, the picture was clear and unambiguous and depressingly familar. Adcock had been on the take.

Margaret had dropped the tough-cop mask and I could see the exhaustion and disillusionment underneath. ''It's a sad business, isn't it?'' she said. ''A good man goes bad, and everything else feels rotten.'' She turned her empty coffee cup in her fingers. ''But maybe I shouldn't say Adcock was a good man. He just *looked* good, on the outside.'' Her voice grew bitter. ''Damn it, China, we worked on that case for months together, and I never suspected a thing. That's the worst of it, you know. I liked him, I trusted him, and he fooled me.''

What I had said might have been news to her, but it had come as no surprise. ''So you already knew that Adcock was on the take?''

''Yes. We got onto him a couple of weeks ago, through

an informant who tipped us that Roy had a connection to Villarreal.''

''We. You and McQuaid?''

She nodded. Her shoulders were slumped and she wore a weary, defeated look. ''But we didn't have any concrete evidence—nothing like what you've uncovered—and we weren't sure what the connection was. Personally, I thought it was Dolores.'' She eyed me. ''You know about her record?''

''Blackie told me. She was part of the Villarreal gang, I take it. She and Dunia, the guy who was at the memorial service with her. He's her ex-husband?''

''Uh-uh. Ex-brother-in-law. She was married to Raymondo Dunia. All three of them—Dolores, Raymondo, Amado—were small-time *pasadores* bringing in marijuana and cocaine. Twelve years ago, they were involved in a drug-related robbery in Brownsville. Raymondo was shot to death. Amado got five and did half of it. Dolores got ten and served five. The day after she walked, she and Roy Adcock took out a marriage license. It was the week before Frank Harris dropped out of sight.''

''Did you have reason to think that Dolores Adcock had something to do with Harris's disappearance?''

''During the investigation, I dug up a witness who claimed he saw her with Harris. When I questioned her about it, she denied it—her word against his. The witness vamoosed. Last I heard, he was dealing in Tijuana.''

The implications fanned out like a poker hand. ''You're suggesting that Adcock called in some chips?''

Her voice was corrosive. ''I told you, Adcock conned me.

I thought we were working together. I thought he was straight.''

''If his new wife was involved in the case, why didn't Adcock's superior pull him off?''

''Captain Scott?'' Margaret shrugged. ''Why would he? The witness could have been mistaken, or lying. And even if he was telling the truth, it didn't necessarily follow that Dolores had anything to do with Harris's disappearance. Scott wouldn't have taken Adcock off the case for something that insubstantial. You heard the poem about the dead Rangers he read at the memorial service. He really believes that chickenshit stuff about keeping your honor high and clear.''

''The brotherhood has a habit of conveniently looking the other way,'' I murmured.

''That's what it's all about.'' Margaret straightened her shoulders. ''Anyway, when we got this tip about Adcock a couple of weeks ago, I thought first of Dolores, not Roy.'' Her lips tightened. ''But when Adcock killed himself, both McQuaid and I began to think he might be the connection. The offshore account you uncovered clinches it.''

''The suicide's definite, then?''

''The report was in the office this afternoon, when Scott and I got back. Which tidies it up, of course. Now the Rangers won't have to wash their dirty linen in court. And Adcock *was* their dirty linen, you know, even though he'd already resigned. If the media had gotten a glimmer of his activities, they'd have been onto him like a duck on a June bug.''

''Elaine was onto him.''

''Yeah,'' she agreed. ''That could have been part of it.

He didn't want the publicity. His father was a Ranger, you know.''

`` 'Keeping their honor high and clear,' '' I said, ``even when their hands are filthy.'' I paused. ``And of course, there was the cancer.''

Margaret glanced up, startled. ``Cancer?''

``Pancreas. Doc Clarkson told him he was terminal.''

``No foolin'.'' She whistled, half-grinning. ``You *do* get around, Hot Shot. So I guess he thought that his bullet would put an end to a messy business, in more ways than one.''

``And keep Dolores out of it.'' I frowned, remembering that Dolores had seemed surprised by my discovery of the Cayman Island account. If she was involved in this thing, why hadn't she known about the money? Had her husband kept the information from her in an effort to protect her? That would fit the picture that was emerging in my mind.

``Maybe Adcock hoped to keep her clean,'' Margaret said. Her jaw was working. ``But it ain't gonna happen. Not after tonight.''

``Why? What do you mean?''

``Because Dunia is the registered owner of the black Ford that opened up on Mike. I got enough of the plate to phone in an APB. I am personally going to see that he's charged with attempted murder. If Dolores was in that car, she'll be charged too.''

``Dunia!'' I stared at her, my anger icing down into a cold, rock-hard fury as I thought of McQuaid, lying motionless with a bullet nosing his spinal cord, and swarthy, swaggering Dunia on the other end of the gun. ``What was his motive?''

''McQuaid was digging pretty deep. I'm guessing that somebody in Villarreal's network—it could even have been Dunia himself—got wind of his investigation and clued Adcock in.''

Dunia. Dunia. The name suddenly jarred loose something that had been half-buried in my memory since early that morning.

''Elaine was with Adcock on Friday afternoon, an hour or so before he killed himself,'' I said. ''During their conversation, he got a phone call that upset him. She doesn't know who called, but she caught a name, something like Dude or Dugan. Maybe it was Dunia.''

''Oh, yeah?''

''Yeah,'' I said, putting it all together. ''Dunia tipped Adcock off that McQuaid was onto him. Adcock decided that the cards were stacked against him, and he cashed out. He probably figured that once he was gone, McQuaid would lay off.''

Margaret tapped her forefinger against her pursed lips, thinking. ''But Dunia took a more proactive approach. Dunia *and* Dolores—both of them, together.''

''How do you know that?''

''There were two people in that car tonight, Hot Shot.''

The anger became colder, more intense. ''You said you put out an APB?''

''On the Ford, on Dunia, *and* on Mrs. Adcock.'' Margaret's mouth was taut, her eyes smoldering. ''They're not going to get away. We'll find them. And when we do—'' She didn't have to finish her sentence. Her face said it all.

There was one more thing I needed to know before Elaine

got back. ''McQuaid's undercover work—what can you tell me about it?''

''Some time ago, a federal investigation into Villarreal's activities turned up some indications that one or more Rangers were compromised, although the feds couldn't or wouldn't name names or come up with any substantiating evidence. The new director of DPS—Phil Gordon—decided it was time to take a close look into the Ranger organization. But he had a manpower problem. He felt he couldn't turn the investigation over to any of his boys.''

I chuckled. ''The fox standing guard over the chickens.''

''Right. They've all done something, somewhere, sometime, that they'd just as soon nobody know about. Narrowed an investigation too soon, or planted evidence, or covered up for somebody who did. Even the ones who are clean and straight carry a hell of a chip. You step on their turf and they'll eat your lunch.''

''So the big brass figured it was time to bring in a woman, huh?'' I said dryly. ''A new broom.'' It's a funny thing. Good old girls usually seem more trustworthy than good old boys, and they sweep clean. So where are they when the medals are being handed out?

Margaret's grin came and went. ''Yeah, well. I don't have any turf to protect. I've been a street cop, I'm an experienced undercover investigator, and I wear a Ranger badge. But I'll never belong to the club. I'll always be an outsider.''

I thought about that. ''And McQuaid is an outsider too.''

She nodded. ''The director assigned me to Internal Audit, where I'd have a legitimate excuse to work with computer records—man-hour reports, expense accounts, travel logs, interview notes, stuff like that. The Rangers used to be almost totally independent. A law unto themselves. Now, they have to account for what they do. Gordon, the new director, thought that a computer search of their reports might turn up evidence of extralegal activities.''

''Big Brother is watching you,'' I said. I shook my head, tch-tching. ''What do you think your Ranger buddies would do if they found out what you're up to?''

Tar and feather her, likely, or worse. I remembered the stories that had circulated about the woman who had challenged the Rangers on sexual harassment charges a couple of years before. The brotherhood had made their new sister's life a pretty sorry mess. Suddenly I thought of Ranger Dubois and his hungry-eyed glance at Margaret, at the memorial service. How much did he know about what she was doing? Maybe it wasn't sexual hunger I'd seen, but a different kind of eagerness, an appetite for reprisal. If I were Margaret, I'd watch my back.

Margaret gave a brittle laugh. ''You asked about Mike. His cover story was that he was doing research for a book about the Rangers—an updating of the myth.''

''*The Texas Rangers in the Twentieth Century*?'' I asked, with a wry chuckle.

''Exactly. I would feed him information about questionable activities, he would interview the officers involved, and we would compare notes.'' She gave me a sidewise look. ''We spent a lot of time combing reports, searching for discrepencies. He even had me looking through phone logs. He didn't tell me what he was looking for or who he suspected, though. He operated on a need-to-know basis.''

''Why didn't he—'' I cleared my throat. ''Why didn't he tell *me* what he was doing?'' Maybe that was the part that hurt most. Didn't he trust me to keep my mouth shut? Did he enjoy keeping secrets from me? Or did it have something to do with Margaret?

She hesitated. "For one thing, he might not have thought you were interested. He said you were pretty tied up with your business. And I suppose he was operating under the need-to-know rule with you, too."

I considered that. Need-to-know is not a frivolous standard. Pillowtalk has been the undoing of legions of politicians, ministers, kings, and cops, some of whom paid dearly for their indiscretions. What's more, I had been up to my eyebrows with Thyme and Seasons since well before the holiday rush. In fact, I hadn't thought about anything else but the shop ever since McQuaid and I moved in together last summer. And maybe his affair with Margaret had made him edgy, made him decide to keep the whole thing to himself.

But somewhere, something had gone wrong. Somebody had figured out what he was doing and blown the whistle. Someone from inside Villarreal's gang? or someone else? I thought for a minute. Who knew that McQuaid was working undercover? The DPS director, Margaret, Elaine. *Elaine.* Elaine knew!

I looked up at the clock. She had been gone almost five minutes. I stood up.

"Elaine's taking a hell of a long time in the john," I said tersely. "Maybe we'd better have a look."

Margaret jumped up and we both walked swiftly to the restroom. The door was ajar, the light was off, and the place was empty.

"Damn," Margaret said.

"You'd better put out an APB for her too," I said grimly. "She knew what McQuaid was up to. She could have set him up. Or she could have let it slip and somebody else picked up on it."

Margaret slammed her fist into her hand. "I was an idiot to let her go into that restroom alone."

"Just goes to show," I said, following Margaret as she headed for the pay phone. "You can't always trust the good old girls, either."

A few minutes later, Margaret put down the phone and turned to me. "Done?" I asked.

"Done," she said. She grinned bleakly. "And there's news, China. A DPS trooper spotted Dunia's Ford in a parking lot in Castroville, about twenty miles west of here. When he opened the door, Dunia fell out." There was a dark, unruly satisfaction in her face, in those Liz Taylor eyes. "I must have got a better shot than I thought. The bastard's dead."

I tasted a fierce exultation. The man who had shot McQuaid was dead. But there was another thread hanging loose. No, more than one.

"What about Dolores?"

She shook her head. "No sign of her—yet. But we'll get her, and that will wrap this whole thing up."

I stood for a moment, picturing Dunia's tumble out of the car, seeing his grinning face, crude and arrogant, twisted in death. The exultation began to seep away, and in its place there was a desperate weariness that made my head feel thick and soupy.

"Think again, Margaret. Dunia pulled the trigger, but he wasn't the brains behind the hit. Not Dolores, either.

They're just puppets. A couple of two-bit *pasadores* with no stake in this thing.''

Margaret stared at me. ''So?'' she said finally.

''So somebody else set McQuaid up. Somebody with more to lose.''

Margaret made a sour face. ''I could've gone all night without hearing that. Who do you think? Villarreal?''

I shook my head. My face hurt, my lip felt fat, and I was bone-tired. ''I've done my part. You get paid for being a detective. When you figure it out, let me know.'' I looked at my watch. We had been down here for more than a half hour. ''Come on. It's time to check on McQuaid. And I need to call Ruby and see how Brian is doing.''

Brian. He was asleep by now, curled in his bed with the assorted lizards and frogs and snakes he smuggles under the blankets. Somehow, I don't know how, he manages to maintain harmony between the species and avoid being bitten. I smiled crookedly, wondering what Ruby would do when she went to tuck him in and encountered Ivan the Tarantula toasting his soft underbelly on the lampshade, or turned back the blanket and found a complacent Uhura curled in a scaly knot against Brian's pajama-clad stomach.

I stopped smiling, remembering with a jolt Ruby's tarot card, the snake shedding its skin, the skeleton, death. *Somebody is due for a radical change*, Ruby had said. And sometime early tomorrow, before Brian went off to school, I would have to tell him that there'd been an unexpected change in plans, that something had come up, that—

That what?

That his dad might not be able to hug him again, or throw

him a spiraling forward pass, or teach him how to water ski? That his father might never walk again?

No. A twelve-year-old can take in only so much anguish, can stand the loss of only one dream or two at a time. I would keep these bitter eventualities to myself. I would tell Brian only that his father was in the hospital. That he had been shot working on a dangerous case, against desperate criminals. That his dad was a hero. And that where heroes were concerned, things always turned out okay.

I sighed, the weariness settling into an exhausted sadness. It's easy to believe in the invincibility of heroes when Superman is one of your favorite TV characters.

It's not so easy when you've watched John Wayne and Steve McQueen die of lung cancer and you've seen what happened to Christopher Reeve.

Chapter Fifteen

> He who sees fennel and gathers it not, is not a man but a devil.
>
> Welsh Mydvai, 13th century

Hospitals are eerily silent in the hours after midnight, the nurses like restless ghosts patrolling dimly-lit hallways, the buckets and mops of cleaning crews standing sentinel at corridor crossroads. Outside McQuaid's room, a stern-faced policeman stood at attention—legs apart, arms folded, bulky gun on one hip, hefty nightstick on the other—keeping watch.

"Just a precaution," I heard Margaret tell Mother McQuaid, when she inquired nervously why her son needed police protection.

A precaution, yes. But the cop outside the door was also an ominous reminder that even though the man who'd shot McQuaid was dead, there was somebody out there who had a vested interest in his continuing silence, and that Margaret, no more than I, believed that the man she had killed was the only one who had to be brought to justice.

Inside the room, McQuaid lay frighteningly still, his face gray under streaks of dark beard, his skin waxy, his breathing as mechanically regular as the machine that pumped the air into him. Margaret and I stationed ourselves in chairs on either side of the bed. Leatha hauled Mother and Dad McQuaid off for something to eat. I picked up the phone on the wall beside McQuaid's bed and dialed the house.

Ruby answered on the second ring, her voice tight, tense, wary. "Bayles and McQuaid."

"You're hired," I said. "But next time, try a little more warmth."

"China! Thank God. How is he?"

"He is not chasing nurses. We won't know how he is until he wakes up and the experts start doing damage assessment." I paused, sensing that all was not well. "What's the matter, Ruby?"

"Dolores is here. She's scared to death. What do you want me to do with her?"

"Dolores is there?" I exclaimed.

Margaret's chin had dropped to her chest as she caught a couple of winks. Now her head came up like a shot, her eyes wide open and alert. She grabbed the arms of the chair and hoisted herself half out of it. "Dolores? Where?"

"Margaret says to tie her wrists and lock her in the bathroom."

"Margaret? You mean, McQuaid's girlfriend?" Ruby's voice got squeaky. "She's there, *with* you?"

"Right," I said. "We're getting to know one another better."

"You're punchy," Ruby said. "You need a drink. Anyway, Dolores just got *out* of the bathroom. Her face is a mess, and her wrists are worse. Rope burn or something. He trussed her up tight."

"Excuse me?"

"Actually, I don't know how she managed to get loose. And she cut her knee pretty badly climbing out of the bathroom window. I've cleaned her up, but I think she's going to need some stitches in that knee."

"Look," I said, "let's take this from the top, okay? Who tied Dolores up? When? Why?"

Ruby told the story straight through in an admirable left-brain narrative, with only one or two right-brain digressions. After I left on Sunday morning, Dunia confiscated Dolores's car keys, unplugged the phone, and told her that the two of them were going back to Mexico right after the memorial service. But on Monday morning, he plugged the phone back in and made a couple of calls, and the plans changed. Immediately after the memorial service, he took her back to her house. Some other man met them there. The two men wanted her to go with them—a job for Villarreal, they said. But she refused, saying she wasn't going to have anything more to do with the drug world. That's when Amado grabbed her, tied her up and gagged her, and put her in the bathtub. Then he locked the bathroom door and left with the other man. It took her hours to free herself, break the window, and crawl out. She tumbled headfirst onto the grass in front of a startled Minerva, who had taken Andromeda out to go potty before bedtime. At Dolores's hysterical request, Minerva had brought her to our house, where Ruby had taken her in, washed her up, and was trying to figure out what to do next.

"Hang on a minute," I said when Ruby had finished, and relayed the gist of the story to Margaret.

Margaret went straight to the heart of the matter. ''So Dolores wasn't involved with the shooting.''

''Sounds that way,'' I said, and went back to Ruby. ''Later, you can tell me why an adult woman with working vocal cords would allow a man to tie her up and lock her in the bathroom. But for now, why don't you just fix her a good stiff drink and bed her down in my room?''

''Because she's afraid,'' Ruby said thinly. ''She wants protection, and by God, so do I. Listen, China. This woman has *information*. She knows about Villarreal, and you know who *he* is. She also knows about—'' She broke off. ''I don't want to tell you over the phone. Can you come home?''

I looked at McQuaid, still and white as a corpse. ''No,'' I said. ''What exactly are you afraid of?''

''Of somebody tracking her here and shooting her to keep her from talking. Shooting me and Brian, too, while they're at it.'' She stopped and took a deep, shuddery breath. ''I keep remembering the Seven of Swords,'' she said in a low voice. ''If you want to know the truth, I feel like one of those chickens, waiting for the fox. I'm scared.''

''If she's afraid,'' Margaret said, ''tell her to call Sheila. And Blackie.''

''Good idea,'' I said. ''Call Sheila, Ruby, and ask her to come out and sleep over. Tell her to alert Blackie to beef up the patrol on the county road. I'll bet you didn't bring your gun.''

''Of course I didn't bring my gun! For heaven's sake, China, I'm just a *baby sitter*!''

''Don't let Brian hear you say that. He thinks he's too old for baby sitters. McQuaid's handgun is in the nightstand on his side of the bed. Maybe you'll feel better if you put it in your pocket.''

''He must have it with him,'' Ruby said. ''I looked. It's not there.''

''Then get his .30-.30 out of the hall closet. It's locked, but the key is in the flowerpot on top of the refrigerator. And tell Sheila to bring the appropriate firepower. When she gets there, lock the doors, turn out the lights, and take turns standing watch.''

''I feel better already,'' Ruby said. ''Give me your number and I'll call you back when Sheila gets here.'' She paused. ''McQuaid *is* going to be all right, isn't he?''

''I don't know, Ruby,'' I said wearily. ''I honestly don't know.''

For the next few hours, I told time by people's movements, and by the telephone. Every fifteen minutes an ICU nurse would come in, check the monitors, adjust the IV that was stuck into the back of McQuaid's left hand, and leave. Every thirty minutes or so, Ruby would phone to let me know that she and Sheila were still alive and well. Every hour, Margaret would call her dispatcher to see whether Elaine had been picked up. Once, she answered the phone and spoke briefly to Captain Scott, who was calling to check on McQuaid's condition. Measured by these small events, and by the robotic inhalations and exhalations of the ventilator, the time passed ponderously, like water dripping from an icy faucet, one glacial moment at a time.

Around three in the morning, I took a break. Except for our apprehensive little party, the waiting room had emptied out. I wadded my mud-stained jacket into a makeshift pillow, begged a blanket from a sympathetic nurse, and claimed the sofa for a nap. I was exhausted, but I slept only intermittently and woke after an hour, feeling sour and gritty and longing for clean clothes and a bath. It was nearly four and Margaret took my spot on the sofa while the McQuaids and I watched over McQuaid, whose condition was unchanged. Leatha went out in search of decent coffee and came back after a while with several quart-sized containers, a dozen doughnuts, and the news that she had rented two rooms in a motel a block away. She rounded up Mother and Dad McQuaid and, over their protests, forced them to go with her and get some sleep.

The three of them gone, Margaret woke and we carried Leatha's provisions to McQuaid's room, where we sat drinking coffee and wolfing doughnuts and listening to the hiss of the ventilator. By this time, Margaret's face and voice were as familiar as my own. I felt as if we had spent years, decades, centuries, facing each other across McQuaid's silent body. I couldn't remember when I hadn't known her. We might have been sisters.

"I can't stop thinking about what happened," I said, and reached for another doughnut. "I've gone over it in my mind so often, I'm groggy. Or maybe I'm just tired. I feel like I'm drunk." I looked with distaste at my doughnut. "High on fat and refined sugar."

"Me too," Margaret said, her face slack and weary, her eyes half-closed. She was slumped down in the chair, her feet crossed on the bed. I could see mud on the soles of her bloodstained black loafers. "The damn thing is like a B-movie on an endless loop. I can't turn it off." She was silent for a moment. "But at least I nailed Dunia," she said. "The sonofabitch might've been just a triggerman, but knowing that I took him out satisfies my soul. Now, if I could only figure out who master-minded the hit—'' Her eyes came open. They were like cold stones. She raised one finger and aimed it at me, an imaginary gun. ''Blam. Blow the bastard away.''

''How you talk,'' I said mildly, thinking that McQuaid had not made a bad choice of backup. I paused. ''If you ask me, it had to be somebody who—''

The door opened and I turned around. A plump, gray-haired nurse with a prim mouth and a name badge that identified her as Miss Pendergast stood in the doorway, frowning. Her glance fell on Margaret's offending shoes.

''Off the bed,'' she commanded briskly. ''We can't have muddy footprints on our sheets.'' Her eyes went to the open box of doughnuts sitting on McQuaid's bed and she raised her chin in the air. ''Do you ladies know how much polysaturated fat there is in those doughnuts?''

''Enough to plug our arteries for a week,'' Margaret replied cheerily. She swung her feet onto the floor and held up the box. ''Take one, if you like, Miss Pendergrasp. Hell, take two.''

''Take the whole box,'' I said, with a generous wave of my hand. ''McQuaid won't like it if we get fat while we're waiting for him to get well.''

''I never eat sugar, thank you,'' Miss Pendergast said, her face severe. She came around the bed, checked the ventilator, and looked down at McQuaid, making little clucking noises with her tongue. ''Such a good-looking man—it's too bad. A drug shootout, I heard.''

''I don't think you could call it a shootout,'' I said. ''It was more like an ambush.''

She shook her head, reflecting. "Nurses aren't supposed to make moral judgments, of course, but I always feel sad when I see a man completely lose his moral compass and allow his life to be totally destroyed by drugs and violence."

"I really don't think—" I began.

"The hospital doesn't like me interjecting a religious note into patient care," she said, reaching into a pocket and taking out a small New Testament. She handed it to me. "But I want you to know that I'll add Mr. McQuaid to my prayer list. Not just to get well, but to be morally and spiritually healed." Her eyes were misting over. "And to find the Lord, who forgives all our trespasses, even as we forgive those who trespass against us."

"Hey." Margaret was on her feet. "You've got the wrong idea about—"

"Which of you is his wife?" Miss Pendergast asked, looking from Margaret to me. "I'll pray for you, too, at this hour of special need."

"I am," I said loyally. I stroked McQuaid's motionless left hand, avoiding the IV needle that was punched into a vein.

Margaret stretched her lips into a smile. "And I'm his lover." She raised McQuaid's other hand to her lips and gave it a loud, passionate kiss. "Actually, that woman's lying, Miss Puckergasp. They're not married. She's his lover too."

"Or three or four," I acknowledged thoughtfully. "We've sort of lost track, he has so many."

Margaret looked at me, cocking her head to one side. "It looks like we can stop worrying about his moral compass, though," she added. "If he's paralyzed from the neck down, he won't be able to indulge quite so—''she sketched a delicate shrug—''indiscriminately.''

''Pity the loss to womankind,'' I remarked. I looked at the nurse. ''But I understand that paraplegics can have an active sex life, under certain circumstances. Perhaps you know something about that, Miss Pendergast. If you do, my friend and I would appreciate a few handy tips.''

''That's a super idea, Hot Shot,'' Margaret said enthusiastically. ''Miss Prickergasm is a nurse. I'll bet she's an expert at physical manipulation.'' She raised the sheet and peered under it with interest. ''Maybe she could take a few minutes right now to give us a hands-on clinical demonstration of—''

Miss Pendergast gave a small, offended ''Ooh!'' Clutching her clipboard to her starched bosom, she backed rapidly out of the room. When the door had closed behind her, Margaret and I stopped struggling against the laughter and let it come in hysterical whooping gasps. I don't know about Margaret, but laughing made me feel almost human again.

After a long while, Margaret wiped her eyes. ''Thank God she left,'' she breathed. ''One more minute, and I'd have been rolling on the floor. She would have sent for a man with a straight jacket.'' She looked toward the door. ''In fact, she may yet. *Two* straight jackets, one for each of us. A preacher, too, to cleanse our souls.''

''Or an exorcist.'' I looked down at McQuaid, and blinked away tears. ''I wish he could have heard that little exchange,'' I muttered. ''He would have loved it. He hates pompous hypocrites.''

''Yeah. He would probably have grabbed her and ripped open that starched white uniform of hers—just to see if there was a real person in there.'' Margaret tweaked one of his motionless toes under the sheet. ''Wouldn't you, buddy?''

For a moment, an inexpressible sadness crossed her face. Then she sat back in the chair and put her feet on the bed again. ''Now, where were we when we were so rudely interrupted?'' she asked, reaching for another doughnut.

''Figuring out who sicced Dunia on McQuaid,'' I said.

''It was Villarreal,'' Margaret said. ''It's got to be,'' she added, at my quizzical look. ''It was your standard druggie drive-by.'' She glanced at McQuaid. ''Wouldn't you agree, Mike?'' She raised his hand and waved it. ''He agrees.''

''You're both wrong, then. You're forgetting something, Margaret. There's somebody else involved in this besides Villarreal's drug gang.''

''Somebody else?'' Margaret's lips thinned. ''Yeah, you're right. *Elaine* is involved in this.'' She sat straighter. ''Who was the last person to see Adcock alive? Elaine. Who was on the scene when Mike got blasted? Elaine.'' She looked at her watch. ''It's time I checked with the dispatcher again. Maybe she's been picked up.''

''I didn't mean Elaine,'' I said, ''although I think she knows more than she's told us—a lot more, actually. She's keeping a tight lid on it for her book. No. I meant somebody on *your* side.''

Margaret stared at me, her forehead puckering. ''My side?''

''Think about it, Margaret.'' I leaned forward and put my elbows on the bed. ''The feds come onto the scene, thrash around, and turn up a couple of compromised Rangers—they think. Unfortunately, they have no names and no hard evidence. The new DPS director figures that he'd better clean house and brings you and McQuaid in to do his dirty work. Meanwhile, Adcock—one of the corrupt cops the feds sniffed out—has been contacted by a crime writer who is making it her business to shake the skeletons out of the Rangers' closet. In fact, Adcock is talking to her about the Harris case, one of her principal areas of interest, when their conversation is interrupted by a phone call from somebody he knows pretty well. According to Elaine, whatever is said unsettles Adcock so thoroughly that he terminates the interview. Shortly thereafter, he shoots himself."

"According to Elaine," Margaret said skeptically. "Who may or may not be telling the truth."

"Agreed," I said. "But suppose she is. Suppose that this person, whose name Elaine recollects as Du-something, has bad news for Adcock. Suppose he's found out that the investigators are getting close and may be about to blow the whistle."

"Dunia," Margaret said. "We already figured that out."

"Wait," I said, "you're jumping to conclusions. You and I both know that Rafael Villarreal is a veteran of the trade. He's carrying the scars of dozens of attempts on his life, and he's survived any number of efforts to muscle him out of the business. To him, you and McQuaid are just a couple of flies in the ointment. There's nothing you could dig up that would even make him nervous. But you might scare the shit out of somebody else, and that person might carry enough weight in Villarreal's organization to persuade them to assign some low-level manpower to take McQuaid out."

"Somebody else? You mean, somebody *inside* the Rangers?"

"Yeah. Just for the sake of argument, let's suppose that

Villarreal merely provided the hit man, and somebody else called down the hit. The same somebody who found out about your investigation and phoned Roy Adcock to alert him. Is there somebody Adcock knew whose name sounds like—'' I paused, trying to remember exactly. ''Like Dude or Duke or Dugan—something like that. That's the name Elaine thought she heard in that phone conversation.''

Margaret thought for a minute. ''Well, there was a Ranger named Dukas who worked in the North Texas district until a couple of years ago. But he died of a heart attack six months ago. And there's Howard Dunnigan, who works in the San Antonio area. He was disciplined last year for planting a gun on an informant.'' She paused. ''I'm sure there are others, but those are the only two I can come up with off the top of my head. You know, Dunnigan isn't out of the question. He's a bad actor, been in trouble off and on. But maybe if I sat down at the computer and ran the name file I could—''

''What about nicknames?''

''Nicknames?''

''Like Dude or Duke—those were the ones Elaine mentioned.''

Margaret stared at me. She had thought of it, and the realization rattled her. She opened her mouth a couple of times and closed it without saying anything. Then, at last, she shook her head and said, ''Nah. No way.''

''Who?''

''Uh-uh. It couldn't be.'' There was a long silence as she pondered. Then she raised her head, warily. ''Duke, you said?''

''Right. You've got a candidate in mind?''

"Yes, but—" She picked up McQuaid's hand and turned it over, touched the palm with her finger. "Would you believe it, Mike?" she muttered. "But maybe you would. Damn it, maybe you were onto the bloody devil all along, and you didn't tell me. Maybe you figured it would be dangerous for me to know."

"Believe *what*?" I demanded. "Onto *who*?" But when she told me, it was my turn to shake my head. "Maybe we'd better go back to the beginning," I said.

We did. Ten minutes later, we had worked through the whole scenario from start to finish, testing Margaret's guess against my assumptions and what we knew of the facts, filling in with speculation where the facts were scarce. Given the limited evidence—all we had was a name and a couple of odd bits and pieces of information—we couldn't be sure of our conclusion. And what was worse, there wasn't a damn thing we could do about it. Unless we could dig up some hard evidence.

"So what do we do now?" Margaret asked. She touched McQuaid's cheek. "Come on, Mike, wake up and help us out," she said fervently. "You know the skunk we're after. Tell us how to trap him."

The phone rang and both of us jumped. I reached for it. It was Justine.

"How is he?" she asked. "How are you?"

"For him, no change," I said. I sighed. "For us, it's been a hard night."

"I'm afraid I'm about to make it harder. I heard from Elaine a short while ago."

"That would do it," I said. "Did she tell you that she's AWOL?"

"No," The Whiz said, "but I'm hardly surprised. Elaine runs with scissors. Do you want to know where she is?"

I looked at Margaret. "It's Justine. Do we want to know where Elaine is?"

"You bet your ass we do," Margaret said. "She's in this every bit as deep as—"

"Yes," I said into the mouthpiece. "We do."

"She came to my house a little while ago to tell me that her apartment had been rifled during the night. She asked me to keep a briefcase of papers for her. She said she was was on her way to Driftwood."

"Where?" I asked, startled. "Why?"

"To Driftwood. It's a little town north of San Antonio about seventy miles and west of—"

"Oh, yeah. I know where it is," I said. "But why?"

"Hey." Margaret leaned forward. "Where did she say she was going?"

"She refused to give me a reason," Justine said judiciously, "although I inferred that her visit to that microscopic wart of a community has to do either with the assault on McQuaid or with the ransacking of her apartment. Or both. She has a gun."

"A gun?" I said, surprised. "But Margaret took it away from her."

"Obviously she has a spare," Justine said.

Margaret stood, her face dark. "She's going to shoot somebody," she said grimly. "Where was she going, China? Who's she after? She must have proof, or she wouldn't—"

"Wait a minute, Margaret," I said. "Why are you telling us all this, Justine?"

Justine hesitated. "Because it is not clear to me that Elaine herself is above suspicion in the attack on McQuaid," she said finally. "Because Margaret is a law enforcement officer, and I am an officer of the court. And because you are my friend."

"Thank you," I said.

"You're welcome. For the record, I should add that I am not Elaine's attorney, nor did I invite her to confide in me this morning, nor promise to keep her confidences confidential."

"I see," I said.

"Finally," Justine said, "she told me that if I did not hear from her by nine A.M., I should presume that she had met with some untoward accident and notify the proper authority. I deem Margaret to be the proper authority."

I looked at the clock on the wall over McQuaid's bed. "It's only six-thirty."

"By my clock," Justine said equably, "it is now nine."

"You always were a couple of hours ahead of everybody else. So what's Margaret supposed to do? Go to Driftwood and look for her?"

"Driftwood!" Margaret exclaimed. "Elaine's gone to Driftwood?" She started for the door. "That's it, Hot Shot. That's the evidence we need. She's in cahoots with him!"

"I would be glad to go," Justine said, "but regrettably, I must appear at an important trial this morning. Driftwood is only an hour's drive, but I am not confident of making the round trip in time for the opening of court."

"I don't think that will be necessary," I said. "Margaret is itching to clear up this business herself." She was standing by the door, jiggling anxiously from one foot to the other. ''Do you know where you're going, Margaret, or do you need an address?''

''I don't need an address,'' Margaret said. ''*He* lives in Driftwood—just outside it, anyway. Come on, China. We're wasting time!''

''Me?'' I asked. ''We?''

''You don't think I'd tackle this alone, do you? And there's no time to explain this mess to anybody at Headquarters. They'd think I was crazy. Come on!''

''Rats,'' I said.

''Pardon?'' Justine asked.

''Margaret says I'm going with her.''

''Very good,'' Justine said. She paused. ''You may confront a certain amount of danger. Be careful.''

''I'm too old for this,'' I said. I hung up and bent over McQuaid. ''Margaret is going after the person who set you up,'' I said. ''She wants me to go with her.''

He didn't move.

I smoothed the dark, unruly hair back, refusing to think about what the doctor had said. ''I love you,'' I whispered, and kissed his forehead. ''I'll get back as soon as I can.''

''Hurry up and get well, Mike,'' Margaret called from the doorway. ''China and I are dying to climb in the sack with you. And here's Miss Pumpernickel,'' she added cheerily. ''She'll give you a hand.''

We left the room as Miss Pendergast swept in, clipboard under her arm and chin in the air, pretending she hadn't heard the last remark.

Chapter Sixteen

> The Yewe tree is found planted both in the corners of Orchards, and against the windowes of Houses, to be both a shadow and an ornament . . . but ancient Writers have ever reckoned it to be dangerous at the least, if not deadly.
>
> John Parkinson
> *A Garden of Pleasant Flowers*, 1629

The February morning was drizzly and foggy, and the traffic around the northwestern rim of San Antonio moved like blackjack molasses on a cold plate. To complicate matters, an eighteen-wheeler loaded with pigs had tipped over on 281 just past the airport exit. The cops hadn't arrived to divert traffic yet, and there was a good deal of swerving and cursing as northbound cars tried to avoid a herd of southbound swine. A few weren't making it—281 was becoming a sausage grinder.

Once out of the city, we made good time on the four-lane highway, a legacy of the seventies and eighties, when the governor and the legislature conspired to pour the bulk of the state's oil profits into concrete, rather than education. What the kids missed out on, though, helped to speed us on our way across the prairie and through the rolling hills, dark green with cedar and live oak and dotted with grazing cattle, horses, and goats. My little Datsun is getting cranky in her old age, but once she's up and rolling, she's fleet of foot. In spite of the pig jam in San Antonio and the slow-moving tractor-wagon rig that led us at a funereal pace through Blanco, it was only 7:50 A.M. when Margaret directed me to stop behind a patch of scrubby cedars on a well-maintained gravel lane a mile outside Driftwood. The sky was gray and there was no sign of the sun, but it was light enough to be able to see clearly.

"I guess we've come to the right place," I said, turning off the ignition. I pointed to a blue sports car parked on the other side of the road. "That's Elaine's car."

"And that's his mailbox," Margaret said, through clenched teeth.

It was your standard black mailbox, with gold letters on the side. Underneath the address, 215 Sportsman's Club Road, was the name: J.W. Scott.

"Captain Scott," I said quietly. "John Wayne Scott. The Duke."

Margaret had pulled her gun out of her purse and was checking to see if it was loaded. "He even looks like the Big Man, don't you think?"

"As a matter of fact, he does," I said. "I thought about that at the memorial service yesterday afternoon." Yesterday, before McQuaid was shot. A thousand years ago.

"Duke is an old nickname," Margaret said. She shoved the gun into the waistband of her slacks, then pulled out a pair of handcuffs and put them into her jacket pocket. "Dates back to his Academy days."

"That's when Adcock knew him," I said, warily watching these preparations for battle. ''Dolores told me they'd been friends for a long time.'' I glanced up. There was a steel-gray Lexus in the drive, very sophisticated, very expensive, and a white Bronco parked beside it. ''Duke is married, I take it.''

Margaret was diving into her purse again. ''Nope. He drives both vehicles himself. He dumped his wife three or four years ago. She got the house in West Lake Hills, and he built this.''

I was surprised. ''Just for himself?''

''Yeah. Disgustingly posh, isn't it? Wait until you see the hot tub.'' She pulled out Elaine's .357, opened the cylinder, and spun it. ''That hot tub should have tipped me off,'' she added. ''Your average Ranger doesn't pull down anything like the kind of money it took to build this place. But I figured he'd inherited it.''

The house was a large, two-story custom-designed log affair with wraparound porches, a wide flagstone walk, and carefully planned native landscaping. It was the kind of house McQuaid once said he wanted but figured he'd never be able to afford. I didn't want to think about that. I didn't want to think about any of it. I just wanted this two-gun Texas Ranger to do whatever she had come to do, so we could get the hell out.

''Come on,'' Margaret said.

I glanced down at her blood-stained slacks, at my muddy jeans and the disreputable jacket I'd used for a pillow. Neither of us would win a prize for Driftwood's Best-Dressed Tourist. ''We don't exactly look like the Welcome Wagon. The neighbors see us, they'll call the cops.''

''No neighbors,'' Margaret said, hefting the .357 with a

slight smile. "This is a dead-end road, and there are no other houses." She eyed me. "Can you hit what you aim at?"

"What with?"

Her laugh was ugly. "Don't be dense. Can you shoot?"

"More or less, I guess." I frowned. "But I've promised myself I would never again—"

"Forget it." She thrust the gun into my hand. "I hope you won't have to use this. But just in case—"

"Hey," I said. "Didn't you hear me, Margaret? I don't like guns. I don't like what they do to people. I don't—"

"I don't like guns, either," Margaret said. She pulled her jacket around to cover the pistol in her waistband. "But they're good discipline. This is serious shit, China. Elaine is armed. And Scott has already tried to kill McQuaid."

"Don't remind me," I said thinly.

"Well, then, stop giving me a hard time." She opened the car door. "Consider yourself deputized."

I shoved Elaine's .357 into my jacket pocket, reminding myself that carrying the damn thing didn't mean that I had to use it. We got out of the car, closing the doors quietly.

"We'll go around the back," Margaret said in a low voice. "There's a patio, and plenty of cover. Follow me."

"Yes, ma'am, Officer," I said.

She gave me a grin, ducked under a redbud tree, its bare branches covered with tiny purple flowers, and set off around the house. I trailed her at a fast saunter, trying to look as if I didn't have a care in the world, hoping an observer might mistake us for casual visitors in search of unseasonable bluebonnets. The morning air held a wintry chill, and the grass was wet and slippery.

The lot sloped steeply down and away from the road,

burying itself in a dense woodland that was laced with the pale pink of Mexican plum and the rich purple of redbud. Once behind the house, we stayed under the cedars, taking cover and scanning the area. There was no sign of Elaine, although I hardly expected to see her hanging around in the back yard.

Margaret nudged me. "Let's do a visual check on the windows on both floors," she said, "starting with the lighted rooms. Look for movement inside, or any signs of forced entry. Broken shrubbery, smashed glass, open window, etcetera."

Lights were on in about half the first-floor rooms. I began to scan the windows. "She apparently knows him. Wouldn't she just show up at the front door and knock? Then he'd let her in and they'd go somewhere to talk. To the kitchen maybe, or his office, and—" I stopped. "There's a shape moving behind the curtains in the window to the right of those French doors," I said. From this distance, and behind some shaggy Japanese yew, it was just a shape. I couldn't tell whether it was a man or a woman.

"And see that pane of glass in the left-hand door, just above the handle?" Margaret said. "It's smashed. Breaking and entering, on top of obstruction of justice," she added with grim satisfaction. "Boy, am I gonna nail her ass."

"That's wonderful," I said. I hunkered down, the gun a dead weight in my pocket. "The two of you have fun. I'll wait here."

"What you are going to do, Deputy Bayles, is position yourself under that window, where you can cover me when I come through the room door."

"What happens then?" I asked nervously. Cops and robbers stuff is all well and good on television and in mystery novels, but I could think of at least three or four things I'd rather be doing this morning than riding shotgun for a Junior G-person.

Margaret had her gun in her hand. "We'll know what happens when it happens. Stop fussing and come on. And don't use your gun unless you have to." She set off at a fast clip for the patio and the double doors.

"Yeah, right." I muttered, and went after her. In a moment, I was crouched behind the yew under the window, peering in over the shoulder-high sill with Elaine's revolver in my right hand. The sheer, light-colored curtains were not quite closed, and the window—no screen, no storm window—was raised about six inches. Through a gap in the curtains, I could see into the room, which was obviously an office, the opposite wall lined floor to ceiling with bookshelves, interrupted by a closed door in the middle of the wall. I could also see the person who, from across the yard, had been only a shadowy bulk.

That person was Elaine. She was bent over a desk that sat three or four feet in front of the window, facing out into the room. She had taken the time to skin her blond hair back under a black scarf and change into black jeans, black boots, and a black turtleneck—ideal breaking and entering attire. Her back to the window and to me, she was pulling out drawers and methodically going through them. On the top of the desk was a pair of black wool gloves which she had probably discarded because they were too clumsy, and a small gun, lying within easy reach. There was no sign of Captain John Wayne Scott.

I pulled my head down, flattened myself against the log

wall, and glanced toward the patio. Margaret had already disappeared through the French doors. It would take her a couple of minutes to get to the room. I waited, listening to the sounds of Elaine opening what sounded like a file cabinet drawer and rustling through the papers in it. She was certainly making no effort to cover the noise. Why? Was Scott a sound sleeper? Or had he already left the house? But both of his vehicles were in the drive. Why wasn't she worried that he'd step out of the bathroom or kitchen or wherever he was and discover her rifling his desk?

I was considering the perplexing question of Scott's whereabouts when I heard another noise, much louder. A smashing thud. The sound of a heavy object, a vase maybe, toppling onto the floor. Not in the office, but somewhere else in the house. Had Margaret, or Scott, knocked something over? I raised my head cautiously and looked through the window.

Elaine had heard the noise too. She slammed the drawer, grabbed her gun, and was around the desk in a flash, against the bookshelves on the opposite side of the room, gun poised, ready to shoot. She was waiting for the door to open. When it did, she was going to kill whoever stepped through. Margaret, Scott, whoever.

There was a bitter, metallic taste in my mouth. I lifted the .357 up to the sill and rested it there. The door moved slightly, as if someone on the other side had pushed it, testing Elaine's intentions.

Elaine seemed to hear something I couldn't. She raised her head and straightened her arm, her finger on the trigger. It was time for me to do something.

I ducked down. "Drop that gun!" I thundered. "We've got you covered!"

Elaine spun toward the window and squeezed off a quick shot. It *whanggg*ed through the glass six inches over my head. If I'd been standing up, I'd be dead.

I raised my head in time to see the door crash open and Margaret storm through, whirl to her right and smash her gun down on Elaine's outstretched forearm before she could squeeze off another shot.

Elaine shrieked and flailed with her left arm, catching Margaret in the eye. Margaret stepped back, then forward again and socked Elaine hard in the stomach. Elaine bent over, clutching herself. Margaret shoved her gun into one pocket, pulled her cuffs out of the other and stuck them between her teeth. Swiftly, she grabbed Elaine by one shoulder, forced her into a straight chair, and cuffed her wrists behind the back. Then she patted her down, top to toe.

I put my hands on the sill. "Good job, Margaret," I said admiringly.

Elaine's head came up. "China?" She turned her head, staring up at Margaret, whom she seemed to see for the first time. "Margaret?"

"Present and accounted for," I said. I raised the window as high as I could and climbed through, scraping my knee, painfully, on the sill. I glanced at Margaret. There was a gash above her eye. It was beginning to bleed.

Margaret glared at Elaine. "Sit there and keep your mouth shut until I tell you to talk." She turned, her attention riveted to something on the floor in front of the desk. "Take a look at this, Hot Shot."

I limped around the front of the desk, and what I saw

made me suck in my breath. A man in a maroon bathrobe lay facedown on the blood-soaked carpet. I couldn't see his face, but it was a good guess that he was Captain John Wayne Scott, late of the Texas Rangers.

Elaine was glowering at both of us. "That stupid Justine. I should've known she couldn't keep her mouth shut."

"You haven't exactly been the soul of discretion," I said.

Margaret measured out a half-smile. "Moronic is more like it. If I were intending to kill somebody, I sure as hell wouldn't blab it to an officer of the court. She might think it was her obligation to—"

"Kill somebody!" Elaine exclaimed. "Is that what she said?" She motioned with her head toward the dead man on the floor. "Listen, you guys. If Justine told you I came here to do *that*, she's lying!"

Margaret took a pencil off the desk and poked it through the trigger guard of Elaine's gun. She scooped up the gun and dropped it on the desk. "You're under arrest."

"No!" Elaine cried. "You can't believe I—"

"Youhavetherighttoremainsilent," Margaret said, and rattled off the rest of the Miranda warning without taking a breath. I've seen this done by experts, and I'd have to put Margaret at the top of the class.

Elaine's jaw was working. "I don't believe this," she muttered.

"Better believe it," I counseled. I looked down at the body. "He's *very* dead."

Elaine turned to me. "You're a lawyer, China. I need a lawyer. Tell me what to do! Tell her I didn't—"

"Excuse me, but you'll have to find another attorney," I said. "I have a conflict of interest in this matter."

Elaine thought for a minute and switched tactics. "I don't need a lawyer, anyway," she said, toughening up. "I didn't kill Scott, which would be immediately apparent if either of you would take the trouble to look at him."

I glanced at Margaret and raised an eyebrow inquiringly.

Margaret pulled a used tissue out of her pocket and swiped at the bleeding cut over her eye. "Roll him over, Hot Shot."

I bent over the Duke, grasped his left elbow, and heaved. The maroon bathrobe fell open. He wasn't wearing anything underneath it. His belly was bloody. He looked like he'd been stitched across the gut—six or eight holes, evenly spaced, in a straight line. I suppressed a shudder.

Elaine watched without flinching. "Check my gun," she said. "I fired one shot, just now. That's all. There are five cartridges left." She spaced the words out emphatically. "I did not shoot him."

"You could have reloaded," Margaret replied, folding her arms across her chest and leaning against the desk.

I arranged the captain's bathrobe so that he was decent. Still dead, but decent. I stood up and gestured at the gun on the desk. "That little mouse gun didn't cause this kind of damage, Margaret. This took an automatic weapon."

"Scott was a law enforcement officer," Margaret said calmly. "I'm sure there are a half-dozen guns around here. We'll find the one that killed him."

"Well, if you do," Elaine muttered, "you won't find *my* prints on it."

"Because you used those gloves," Margaret said, nodding toward the wool gloves on the desk.

"Hey," Elaine said desperately, "I didn't kill the guy.

He was dead when I got here. All I did was go through the desk.'' She made a motion with her head. ''If you're looking for evidence to tie him to Villarreal, that's where you'll find it.''

''Later,'' Margaret said. Using the business end of her pencil so as not to disturb possible prints, she punched a number into the phone. When the brief conversation was over, she turned around. ''The crime scene team is on its way.''

''I can tell you why he's dead.'' Elaine's voice rose. ''Isn't that worth *something*?''

Margaret's mouth was set.''You've been Mirandized. If you're going to talk, I intend to listen and take notes. That's the only guarantee you're going to get. Got it?''

Elaine got it. She closed her eyes briefly, then opened them again and began to talk, without any further coaching. Her story, told without elaboration in her terse crime reporter's style, didn't take long and it wasn't pretty, but it had the ring of truth.

Captain John Wayne Scott had been selling protection to Villarreal for four or five years. From his vantage point in Texas law enforcement, Scott's part of the operation was so easy it wasn't funny. He would get word of a particular drug shipment through the Personals section of the Austin *American Statesman.* He then arranged for the shipment's safe conduct by moving local personnel somewhere else, or by creating a small diversion to keep his men busy. If questions were asked or an inquiry launched, he was in a perfect position to thwart the investigation. In other words, he was your basic corrupt cop.

But Duke's game was a risky one. Frank Harris, who had

been deeply involved with the Villarreal gang, learned about the protection racket, and threatened to expose it. Whether Scott himself killed Harris, or whether Villareal did it, Elaine didn't know, or at least professed ignorance. But it was during the Harris murder investigation that Ranger Roy Adcock got wind of his boss's illegal activities.

"That was where it got dicey," Elaine said. "Adcock was as straight as they come, and he and Scott went back to Academy days together. When Adcock uncovered his old friend's corruption, he was appalled. He did what a man of high principles would do. He confronted Scott with the truth."

"High principles?" I interrupted, startled. "We're thinking of the same Roy Adcock?"

"Adcock was a victim," Elaine said, and Margaret sighed a small sigh. Elaine glanced at her and went on. Adcock was trapped between his loyalty to an old friend and colleague and his responsibility as a law enforcement officer. Here, though, Elaine's understanding became a little murky. It was not clear to her whether Scott capitalized on Adcock's loyalty and persuaded him to drop the leads he'd been investigating, or whether Scott blackmailed Adcock into it—there was the interesting business of Adcock's new wife, who was, after all, on parole and could be trundled back to prison with very little effort. Elaine thought it was entirely possible that Scott could implicate Dolores in Harris's murder. It was also likely, she thought, that it was at this point that Scott decided he had to get rid of Adcock. So he had framed his old friend—again, Elaine was unclear about the details, but claimed she could tell Margaret where to look for the proof. During an investigation in Laredo, another

Ranger turned up evidence that pointed to Adcock's complicity in a money-laundering scheme—planted, according to Elaine, by Scott. Generously, Scott offered his friend a choice: early retirement, or a grand jury. Adcock saw the handwriting on the wall, although he apparently never knew who wrote it. He quit.

Confused by what had happened and distraught over his career disgrace, Adcock took his wife, moved to Corpus Christi and then to Pecan Springs, looking for a place to begin a new life. But fate dealt him a second double-cross, and he was diagnosed with some sort of terminal illness.

''Pancreatic cancer,'' I said.

''He wouldn't tell me what it was,'' Elaine said. ''But his illness was one of the reasons he agreed to talk to me.'' When Elaine tracked him down and approached him with questions about the Harris case, he had been about to tell her what he knew—if his old friend the Duke hadn't interrupted with a phone call.

''Do you know what Scott said to Adcock that would lead him to kill himself?'' I asked.

Elaine shook her head. ''What I know for certain is that Scott was crooked,'' she said. ''He found out that I was onto him, and he arranged for somebody in Villarreal's organization to kill me. And take McQuaid out at the same time.''

Margaret's breath hissed out. ''*Scott* did?''

''How do you know?'' I asked.

Elaine chuckled without mirth. ''I'm a journalist, remember? It's my business to know.'' Margaret made a threatening move, and Elaine added hastily, ''I've got sources within Villarreal's gang. I did some checking after I walked out of the Good Samaritan restroom late last night. As I said, Scott arranged a setup for me. Yesterday afternoon, he discovered that McQuaid was onto him. So he made a phone call and got McQuaid included in the ambush.'' She glanced at Margaret. ''If it hadn't been for you, they would have taken out both of us.''

''Yesterday afternoon?'' Margaret's voice was hollow.

''Wait a minute,'' I said. ''How and when did Scott find out that McQuaid knew about him? He didn't give any sign of it at the memorial service.'' I turned to Margaret. ''Did he say anything on the way back to Headquarters?''

I saw my answer in the anguish on her face.

He had learned it from us. From Margaret and me, at the end of the memorial service. I had blurted out that Margaret was working with McQuaid, and on the way back to Headquarters, Scott had gotten just enough from her to confirm his suspicions. He had already arranged Elaine's ambush for the early evening. It took only one phone call to add another victim.

Elaine was looking at us. ''Do you believe me now? I didn't set McQuaid up. And I didn't kill Scott. I swear I didn't.''

I swallowed, still trying to cope with my new knowledge. ''Who . . . who did?''

''When Margaret shotgunned Dunia, Villarreal's people thought she was acting for Scott, that he had arranged a double-cross. They killed him in retaliation for Dunia's death—and because he was now a hundred percent liability. Somebody close to Villarreal was beginning to suspect that Scott might find it profitable to trade what he knew about the drug transport routes for immunity from corruption charges.''

Margaret broke in. ''So that's what brought you here, Elaine. You knew he'd be dead by dawn, and you wanted to see what you could find before the body was discovered.''

Elaine shook her head. ''When I saw that my apartment had been ransacked—somebody looking for my research materials, I guess—I cashed in a past-due bill. My informant let it slip. About their being after him—Scott, I mean. I thought I could warn him.''

''You'll excuse my skepticism,'' I said. ''You could have warned him with a phone call. What were you after?''

''Yeah, right,'' Margaret said. ''You put yourself in danger by coming here. You were after something, Elaine. Spill it.''

''What is this?'' Elaine asked. ''Cagney and Lacey?'' She looked from one of us to the other, then gave it up with a sigh. ''I was after proof,'' she said. ''I knew there had to be some kind of documentation of Scott's criminal activities. I wanted to find it before the Rangers did.''

''Oh, yeah?'' Margaret said softly. ''Why?''

''Surely you can figure that one out.'' Elaine's voice became acid. ''If I got to it first, I knew it would be put to good use. If they got to it first, it would never come to light. The Rangers are on shaky ground with the legislature already—Scott's moonlighting could finish them off.''

There was a silence. ''Well?'' Margaret inquired finally.

''Did you find it?'' I asked.

''See for yourself,'' Elaine said. ''I told you. It's on the desk.''

I turned to look. What Elaine had found was a stack of statements from the Bank of Cayman Island and a current Texas driver's license. It bore a photo of Captain Scott and the name John Wainwright.

Chapter Seventeen

Over the ages, herbs and flowers have taken on various kinds of symbolic meanings. By the late 19th century, these meanings were recorded in 150 different floral dictionaries. Nightshade signified truth, for instance, while savory suggested that the truth has a bitter taste. Marigold ambiguously represented both friendship and pain, while borage and thyme stood for courage. Hawthorne signified hope, while petunia, more emphatically, advised "Do not despair."

China's Garden Newsletter

That was Tuesday morning. Tuesday afternoon, McQuaid began to wake up.

It took quite a while for him to figure out where he was and who was with him. When he did, he shut his eyes again.

"Oh, God," he said.

"It's okay." Margaret was cheery. "We've decided to be friends. We haven't figured out which one of us gets you, though," she added, taking his left hand.

"Hey," I objected, "you're playing dirty, Margaret. I *told* you. You're out of luck. I'm going to ask him to marry me."

He opened one eye and squinted at me. The words came

out with an effort, in a half-whisper. "Did Peggy give you those shiners?"

"A close encounter with a pizza truck," I said. "No fatalities."

He opened the other eye, slowly, and looked at Margaret, who was sporting a stitched-up gash above her eyebrow. "How'd you get that cut?"

"I had a run-in with an intruder," she said. "Nothing serious."

He peered down at his own unmoving length, stretched out under the sheet, the IV on one side, the bank of monitors on the other. "Jeez," he said. "What the hell's been going on?"

"It's a long story," we said, at the same time. We told it in collaboration, Margaret taking some parts, I others, filling in as many of the details as we could and making an entertaining suspense thriller out it.

"I don't believe it," McQuaid muttered. "You two did all *that*, while I—" He broke off. There was a silence. "I can't move," he said despairingly. "I can't feel anything."

"The doctors are looking into that," I said, as reassuringly as I could. "You've got a bullet in your neck."

"Against your spinal cord," Margaret added. "It's temporary, though. You don't get to keep it."

"The doctor says she'll be giving you a first-class going-over now that you're awake," I said. "We'll know more after that."

"She?"

"Aren't you the lucky one," Margaret marveled. "Women falling all over themselves to make you well and happy. Even Miss Prickerpoodle."

"Is she the one with the clipboard?" McQuaid asked. He twisted his mouth. "I thought she was a dream."

"I doubt that it was a wet dream," Margaret said. She leaned over and kissed his cheek. "I'm laying the case on our dear DPS director late this afternoon. Any messages?"

"Tell him to make sure my hospital insurance is good," McQuaid said. "This must be costing a bundle." He followed her with his eyes as she left the room; then his glance came to me. "You all right, China?" he asked softly.

I pulled the chair forward, sat down, and rested my forehead on his arm. "Not yet," I said, in a muffled voice.

"I'm sorry." His voice was full of a deep sadness. "I owe you an apology for what's happened since the first of the year. I haven't been straight with you. I should have told you what I was doing with the DPS. I shouldn't have let myself get involved with Peggy."

I raised my head, willing myself to meet his eyes. "She's pretty . . . nifty. I see why you . . . why it happened. Some of the responsibility is mine, too."

"I just mean—" His voice faded, his eyes shut.

"There'll be a time to talk about that later. But it's over, behind us. It's time to look ahead. I want us to get married, McQuaid."

He didn't answer for a minute. Then he said, very quietly, "I've been asking you to marry me for four years. Why all of a sudden do you want to do it now?"

"Because I . . . love you."

"Because you're sorry for me? Because you think I need you?" He sighed. "There's an irony here somewhere, China, but I'll be damned if I can figure it out. Let's let it ride for a while."

And that was all the answer I was going to get.

• • •

Three Sundays later, Ruby came over. She had brought a plate of Hot Lips Cookie Crisps, and I put the kettle on for tea. But we had no sooner sat down at the kitchen table when Sheila, a bag of Maria's hot *sopaipillas* in her hand, knocked at the kitchen door. Margaret was with her. *Sopaipillas* call for hot chocolate, and it was a cool, gray morning, so I turned off the kettle and poured milk in a saucepan to heat.

"How is he?" was Margaret's first question, after she was introduced to Ruby, whom she had never met. Ruby knew all about her, though, having heard the story of McQuaid's fling from me.

"Anxious to leave the hospital," I said, glancing at the clock. "The ambulance is scheduled for two." He was moving to the Colonial Manor Care and Rehabilitation Center in Pecan Springs, for Phase One of what promised to be a lengthy recovery. I adjusted the burner under the pan of milk and got out the spicy chocolate mix I'd made up a couple of days ago for Brian and his friends.

"A big day, huh?" Sheila said, dumping the sugar-covered *sopaipillas* onto the plate with Ruby's cookies. "The whole clan is gathering, I suppose."

I nodded. "Mom and Dad McQuaid, and Leatha, and Brian. And me, of course. Everybody's bringing a gag gift, and Leatha made a big banner. We're billing it as Mike's Marvelous Moving Day." I spoke with the lightness you use to mask the painful dark underneath. The dark of not knowing, the dark of anger and of fear. The dark you hide from your small boy, and from your mother. And even from your friends.

"The Colonial Manor isn't a bad place," Ruby said, with uncharacteristic restraint.

Sheila coughed.

"Look," I said, "we're putting him at the Manor because it has a top-ranked physical therapy unit. One of the best in the state, believe it or not. As for the nursing home itself—" I made a face and busied myself with the chocolate. "We're hoping he'll only be there a few months. And he'll have a private room, where he can have a phone, a fax, and his computer. We're getting it rigged so he can manipulate it with a mouth stick. Of course, he'd be happier with a secretary." I laughed a little. "He says it's a hell of a way to spend a sabbatical, but—" I let the sentence drop. His sabbatical would be over at the end of the spring semester. This wouldn't.

"What's the latest word?" Sheila didn't ask whether he was going to walk again, or even move again. That was the question I read in everyone's eyes, although almost nobody came right out and asked it. People can be polite when it comes to disabilities. Or maybe they're scared. A moment's inattention behind the steering wheel, a fall from a ladder, a drive-by bullet—if it can happen to one of us, it can happen to any of us. Life is full of deathly risks.

"They say they don't know." I couldn't hide a small sigh of just plain weariness. I had temporarily shelved most of my ambitious projects—the gardens, the tearoom—in order to spend time with McQuaid and with Brian. But even though Laurel and Ruby were carrying the shop between them, there was still a lot to do. I was tired most of the time.

" 'Uncertain prognosis' is the phrase the doctors like to use," I added. "But we'll know more after he starts therapy and we see how he responds. He's got a good attitude. In fact, he keeps the rest of us going.'' Somewhere at the back of my heart I heard his wry laugh, saw his face creased with that familiar smile, his eyes alight with the small pleasures of our visits, our trifling gifts, our hugs. Words like bravery and courage were coming easier to me these days.

Ruby pushed me into a chair. ''Sit down and let me make that chocolate,'' she commanded. ''You look beat.''

Margaret squeezed my hand and let it go. ''How's Brian doing?''

''He's been great,'' I said. The first few days had been rough, but kids are resilient. They know, better than adults, that life is unpredictable, that you can't control what happens to you. ''He found a color photo of Christopher Reeve walking with braces and crutches, and we got it blown up into a poster. Yesterday, we went to the Colonial Manor and he taped it on the wall across from his dad's bed. Last night, he made a batch of broccoli muffins. That's his gag gift for today. It's a family joke,'' I added, at their puzzled looks. ''Superman eats broccoli.''

'' 'Hope is the thing with feathers that perches in the soul,' '' Ruby said from the stove, where she was stirring the chocolate.

''What?'' Sheila asked. She ate the last of a *sopaipilla*, snowing sugar all over her tunic.

'' 'And sings the tune without the words,' '' I said, '' 'and never stops at all.' ''

''Emily Dickinson,'' Ruby said to Sheila.

Margaret reached for a cookie. ''I filed the last report on the case this week,'' she said. ''Everything is on Gordon's desk now. It's going to be interesting to see how he uses it.''

''Watch those cookies,'' Ruby cautioned, over her shoulder. ''They're pretty spicy.''

''Did you turn up anything new?'' I asked. ''If you did, McQuaid will want to know. He's taking a personal interest.''

''Who can blame him?'' Sheila asked with a little laugh. ''What happened to him was pretty personal.''

''I finally got a hard copy of the text on the computer disk in Adcock's safety deposit box,'' Margaret said. She popped the cookie into her mouth. ''It turned out to be Adcock's journal—more like a memoir, actually. *My Life as a Texas Ranger*, that sort of thing. It was interesting, actually, all two hundred pages of it. He wrote about his early days with the Rangers, when they had much more freedom than they do now. He wrote about Dolores, too. He really loved her, you know. He—Oh, wow!''

Her eyes opened wide and filled with sudden tears. She jumped up and dashed to the sink, turned on the faucet and held her mouth under it, making gargling noises.

''Dear God!'' she cried, when she could get her breath. ''Somebody laced those cookies with—''

''Habanero powder,'' Ruby said penitently. ''I'm really sorry, Margaret. I tried to warn you. A little bit goes a long way.''

I got up and took a carton of milk out of the refrigerator and poured a glass. ''No more Hot Lips for you,'' I said, handing it to Margaret.

''Is that what they're called?'' She shuddered and sipped her milk. ''I'm blistering!''

"The fire will fade," Ruby said. "When it does, you might try another—but not all at once. Chiles kind of grow on you."

"I doubt it," Margaret said in a strangled voice. There was a moment's silence, then Sheila prompted her, "You were saying something about Adcock and Dolores?"

"He really loved her," she said, running her tongue experimentally around her lips, "but in a protective sort of way. He hoped that by marrying her, he could keep her away from guys like the Dunia brothers, who would use her for their own ends. He said, and I quote, 'She's a lovely victim, and there are some men who can't keep their hands off women like her'. I'm sure that wasn't for publication, but it's there, in the notes."

"It's in her, too, though," Ruby said, and I nodded, remembering the way Dolores had curled herself against Amado. "Do you think she's going to grow out of that style of relating?" she added. Ruby had gotten to know Dolores much better during the uncomfortable evening she and Dolores and Sheila had spent barricaded in our house against a threat that never materialized.

"There's hope," I said, "if she can figure out a way to make it on her own. Adcock's insurance company paid off early this week, and she left yesterday for Chimayo." Chimayo is a small, dusty town north of Santa Fe, where a friend of mine, an herb grower named Karen, has been looking for a working partner. I hoped the two women would get along. Dolores's knowledge of plants (gained during the time she spent working in the prison gardens) and Karen's business skills could make for a potent partnership.

"It's too bad you couldn't get her into the Federal Witness Protection Program, Meg," Sheila said.

Margaret nodded. "She knows enough about the Villarreal group to put her in danger, but her information isn't current enough to qualify her for protection. But at least she's got a new identity." She regarded the cookies thoughtfully. "Now that the burning has died down, I think I might try another one of those. They're good, actually."

"You put together a nice clean set of papers for Dolores," I said. Margaret had done a competent job assembling the documents. Driver's license, birth certificate, passport, all in the name of Juanita Maria Escobar. If Villarreal's boys wanted to track Dolores down, they'd have to work at it. From now on, Juanita Escobar's past was going to be her own private business. What she did with her future was up to her.

"Does everybody want chocolate?" Ruby asked, and at our nods, began pouring it into four mugs.

Margaret reached for another cookie. "Yeah. Dolores's papers were about the same quality as the licenses Scott had made up. Oh, by the way," she added, "we turned up the forger who created those licenses for him. He's down in San Antonio."

"Somebody known to the police, I suppose," I said. To anyone who is considering buying forged documents off the street, my advice is, don't. The cops often have a cozy relationship with forgers, allowing them to continue practicing their illegal profession as long as the police get a cut, or the right information now and then. If you buy a set of papers today, the cops could know about it tomorrow.

"You bet," Margaret said. She nibbled carefully around

the cookie, avoiding touching her lips to it. "Scott had the first license made before he opened the offshore account. In fact, he constructed a whole new identity for himself, birth certificate, college transcripts, marriage certificate, all under the name John Wainwright, with the post office box as an address. It was easy to do, for a man in his position. He was obviously planning a grand getaway."

"But China said there was only ten thousand dollars left in the Cayman Island account," Ruby objected. "That might take him on a cheap vacation, but not for very long."

"That was just one of his bank accounts," Margaret explained. "The one he planted among Adcock's papers when he came to the house the Saturday evening after Adcock's suicide—ostensibly to look for material for the memorial service. So far, we've tracked down three others, with a little over a half-million total."

Sheila whistled. "Lucrative business the man was in."

"Yeah," Ruby said, "and I'll bet he didn't pay any taxes on it." She handed out the steaming mugs of chocolate.

I reached for a cookie. "You said Scott got the first phony license before he opened the account. He got the second fairly recently?"

"About three months ago," Margaret replied, "when he decided he was going to use Adcock as a fall guy. Scott was apparently getting nervous. He'd bought Adcock's silence, he thought, with the threat to send Dolores back to jail, and he'd pushed Adcock off the force. But he wasn't out of the way—at least, not far enough out of the way. Adcock didn't know as much as Scott thought he did, but he was at least a potential threat. And there was Elaine, who was asking very probing questions among her sources in the

Villarreal gang, several of whom knew what Scott was up to. When Elaine showed up to talk to Adcock, which Scott learned when he made that that final, fatal phone call, it was the last straw.''

''And there was McQuaid, of course,'' I said, ''who had enough on Scott to hang him.'' McQuaid had put it together after a weekend of undercover work in San Antonio and the Rio Grande Valley. In fact, he was on his way back to Austin to make a report to the DPS director, Phil Gordon, when he got the cell phone call that sidetracked him to Hondo and the picnic spot on Highway 90.

Margaret made a face. ''Right. But Scott only guessed about McQuaid. He didn't know for sure until I gave him away.'' She shook her head sadly. ''I'll never forgive myself for being so damn stupid. The Duke had me completely fooled.''

''Don't blame yourself.'' I put my hand on her arm. ''If I hadn't started babbling about you and McQuaid working together, it would never have come up. It was my jealousy talking.''

Ruby pulled out a chair and sat down. ''Have you made any progress toward finding Scott's killer?''

''Not much,'' Margaret said. ''Ballistics matched the bullet the doctors took out of Mike's neck to the bullets that killed Scott. They were shot from the same gun. But Dunia was dead by the time Scott was taken out, and we have no idea whose finger was on the trigger.''

''And what about Elaine?'' Ruby asked. ''What's going to happen to her and her book project?''

''What do you think?'' Margaret asked cynically. ''She's made a trade, of course. The charges against her were dropped in return for what she knew about Scott's activities. Someday soon, you'll probably see the book in the bookstores."

"And then Elaine will need a new identity," Ruby said.

"Probably not," I said. "McQuaid says she's very good at covering herself."

"Speaking of McQuaid," Sheila said, "is he still holding out? When's the wedding?" She glanced from me to Margaret. "You two are all right on this, aren't you? I mean, it's okay to talk about it in front of both of you?"

Margaret pushed her face into a pout. "Are you kidding? Of course I'm not okay. My heart is permanently broken."

"Serves you right, too," I said. "Messing around with another woman's man."

"If you really wanted him," Margaret retorted, "you should have said yes when you had the chance."

"You're right," I agreed. "I should have." I turned back to Sheila. "Yes, he's still holding out. But I have hope. When this thing is over—"

A silence fell around the table. None of us could know when it would be over, or how it would end. All we could do was shrug our shoulders, and hold hands, and hope.

But that's all we can do anyway, isn't it?

References and Resources

For centuries, herbs have been known to hold many mysteries, culinary, medicinal, agricultural, ornamental, and even religious. In my opinion, they are the most rewarding plants in the garden. The following books and writers will help you explore some of the fascinating mysteries of herbs.

Maggie has her own secret recipe for the corn and potato chowder she serves to China in Chapter 10, but there's a great one on page 73 of *Herbs in the Kitchen*, by Carolyn Dille and Susan Belsinger. If you want to make some hot herb bread to serve with it (as Maggie does), try the Herb Spiral Bread on page 124 of Lucinda Hutson's *The Herb Garden Cookbook.* Lucinda is an Austin, TX resident whose book is full of original herbal recipes, including a section on Mexican herbs. (That's where you might look for information on epazote, the useful herb mentioned by Bonnie, the teller at the Pecan Springs Bank.)
Here is Ruby's recipe for the Hot Lips Cookie Crisps she serves to China in Chapter 11 and again at the end of the book. But beware! This scorcher will certainly light your fire.

Ruby Wilcox's Hot Lips Cookie Crisps

1 cup soft shortening
2 cups brown sugar
2 eggs

1 tsp vanilla
1½ cup finely chopped cashews
1½ cups whole wheat flour
1½ cups unbleached flour
½ tsp soda
1 tsp baking powder
½ tsp habanero powder

Preheat oven to 325 F. Cream butter and sugar. Add the vanilla and eggs and mix well. Mix the dry ingredients together with the nuts, and stir into the creamed mixture. Chill. Roll out like a log, about 2" in diameter, slice and bake until golden.

The Tarot deck that Ruby uses in Chapter 11 is the Motherpeace deck, designed by Vickie Noble. Noble has written an accompanying book called *Motherpeace: A Way to the Goddess through Myth, Art, and Tarot*. In it, you'll find an intriguing discussion of the way the tarot works, pictures of the cards that Ruby turned up for China, and an extensive discussion of their possible symbolic meanings.

For most of the history of humankind, herbs have been valued chiefly for their medicinal uses. If you're interested in using herbs in this way (like Myrtle Cowgill, in Chapter 8) you'll need to consult the experts. I like David Hoffman's *The Herbal Handbook: A User's Guide to Medical Herbalism* and his *The Holistic Herbal*. For a gentle, healing approach designed to fit the seasons of women's lives, try Susun Weed's three fine books: *Healing Wise*, *Wise Woman Herbal for The Childbearing Year*, and *Menopausal Years: The Wise Woman Way*. You may also want to subscribe to

Herbs for Health, a magazine published by Interweave Press (also the publishers of *The Herb Companion*). It is full of reliable, up-to-date scientific information, offered in a very readable format.

In Chapter 8, there is a mention of Sunny Gogel's soap, which I particularly like: her brochure may be obtained by writing to her at P.O. Box 1664, Nixa, MO 65714-9998. If you would like to try making your own soap, read *The Natural Soap Book*, by Susan Miller Cavitch, or *Soap: Making it, Enjoying It*, by Ann Bramson.

If you've envied China her work, you can read all about the mysteries of the herb business in two books: *Herbs for Sale: Growing and Marketing Herbs, Herbal Products, and Herbal Know-How*, by Lee Sturdivant, and *Growing Your Herb Business*, by Bertha Reppert, who founded The Rosemary House more than 25 years ago. Both of these writers interviewed people who, like China Bayles, have been there and done that. They will give you more ideas than you know what to do with.

In Chapter 17, China stirs up some South of the Border Hot Chocolate Mix, using a recipe she contributed to a book called *Herb Mixtures & Spicy Blends*, edited by Deborah Balmuth. Here's how you can make it. Just blend together ½ cup sugar, 1 tblsp. flour, ¼ cup cocoa, 1 tsp ground cinnamon, ¾ tsp ground cloves, ⅛ tsp ground allspice, and ¼ tsp salt. Store in a closed container until ready to use. To make the hot chocolate, add ¾ cup mix to 2 cups water and simmer for 4 minutes. Stir in 6 cups milk and reheat. Add 1 tsp vanilla and a dollop of whipped cream, and serve.

Several of the chapter headnotes in this book contain references to *China's Garden*. This unique 16-page newsletter is published four times a year by China Bayles and her friends, and is overflowing with herbal fun, folly, and information. A sample copy is $3, a year's subscription is $12. Write to *China's Garden*, PO Drawer M, Bertam, TX 78605.